AMERICA
THE BEAUTIFUL

A NOVEL

Moon Unit Zappa

Scribner Paperback Fiction
Published by Simon & Schuster
New York   London   Toronto   Sydney   Singapore

SCRIBNER PAPERBACK FICTION
Simon & Schuster, Inc.
Rockefeller Center
1230 Avenue of the Americas
New York, NY 10020

SCRIBNER PAPERBACK FICTION and design are trademarks
of Macmillan Library Reference USA, Inc., used under license
by Simon & Schuster, the publisher of this work.

For information regarding special discounts for bulk purchases, please
contact Simon & Schuster Special Sales at 1-800-456-6798 or
business@simonandschuster.com

DESIGNED BY ERICH HOBBING

Set in Goudy Oldstyle

Manufactured in the United States of America

1   3   5   7   9   10   8   6   4   2

Library of Congress Cataloging-in-Publication Data
Zappa, Moon Unit.
America the beautiful : a novel / Moon Unit Zappa.
p. cm.
1. Young women—Fiction. 2. Los Angeles (Calif.)—Fiction.
3. Children of artists—Fiction. 4. Hippies—Family
relationships—Fiction. I. Title.

PS3626.A66 A84 2001
813'.6—dc21   2001020566

ISBN 0-7432-1383-1

The copyright page continues on page 301.

For my mother and trees everywhere.

ACKNOWLEDGMENTS

For their inestimable contributions, I gratefully acknowledge the following: In New York, my editor, Doris Cooper, for making me look like I knew what I was doing the whole time and also Jimmy Vines, the best literary agent in the solar system.

In Los Angeles, my unofficial editor/writing guru/soul-sister Claudette Sutherland and her Live Girls Live minions—Trista Delamere, Emily Schlaeger, Cynthia True, Tulis McCall, and Janel Maloney. Along with special guest appearances by Karen and Henry Scott, Gail Zappa and Diva Zappa, Brendan Smith, Giti Khalsa, Jason Ross, Joe Sehee, Stephen Lisk, Roddy Mancuso, Peter Stuart, Tory & Ahmet Zappa as well as Heather R. Price in Orlando, Florida.

Da business: Pearl Wexler, Deborah Obad, & Betty at Paul Kohner and everyone who helped me gather lyric copyrights! (Andrea Moss, Mary Klauzer, Mary Sowerwine, Dawn Capper, Shira Sokol, and Evan Lamberg in particular.)

For putting up with my many mood swings and for making this book possible on a minute-to-minute basis: God, and my family and friends: Utie, La La, Beeshu & Lisa, Olive, Pat McMahon and J.J., Gina & Kevin Lake, David and Lindsey Strasberg, Kate Luyben, Simbiat Hall, Melissa Bushell, Frankie Miles and Sammy, Sandipops, Bridget Gless, Lynn McCracken, Emily, Lukas, Simon, Niki and Berthold Haas, Mollye, Kevin, Ethan and Miranda Stein, David Baer and the Schermerhorn clan, Peter Turman, Laura Milligan, Greg and Amira Behrendt, Julie James and the nice folk at the Improv, Mike Rap, Janeane Garofalo, Greg Miller and Beth Lapides, Patton Oswalt, Joy

ACKNOWLEDGMENTS

Goring, Doug Benson, Brian Posehn, Gary Mann, Robin & Bianca, Lief & Lone, Jo and Mickael, Lazlo and Adam Small, Alice Warshaw, Ada and Arlene Tai, Jules Blaine Davis, Jeff Garlin and family, Mariel & Ryan, Michael O'Brien, Willie Mercer, Flanagan & Largo, Brian Mendes, Shelley McCrory, Lisa Leingang, Matt Walsh, Peter Crawford, Cynthia Watson, Pamela Wynn, Jason Nash, Sanders Trippe, Adam Werbach, Jessica Tully, Kathy & Amy Eldon, Kent Osborne, Danny Ferrington, Beverly D'Angelo and Al Pacino, Megan Slattery O'Hara, Francis Okwu, Mark Scroggs, Michael Lippman, Why Cook, Kinko's Studio City, Crunch Gym, Glow, Alan at Bristol Farms, Joan's on Third, Tree People, Mari & Winsor Fitness, Tracy Pepper, Gabrielle Roth, Lynne Franks, Famille Barthelemy, Julia Sweeney, Quentin Tarantino, Dakota, Jim Jarmusch, Tiffany Rae Baker, Keith Fischer, Laura Dern & Bellina Logan, Orna Banarie, Jim Gaffigan, Bob Kahan, Gary Iskowitz, Jonathan Kirsch, Handsome Jack, Dena and Blues, Anna Hayes, Chelsea Cain, Justine Bateman, Alison VanPelt, Eric White and family, John Miller, Craig Carlisle, The 2 Andys, Bronwyn Keenan, Dana Rae, Kip Winger, Matt Groening, Owen Sloane, Rob and Marisol Thomas, matchbox twenty, Tom, Jane and Brian Doucette, Dave Abbruzzese, Todd Barry, and Miss Ellen Atlas.

My healers: Maria Bartolotta, Robert Coffman, Theresa Crùz, Laura Hart, Minga, Victoria Mestetsky, and Music.

A special thank you to my writing angels for their kind words along the way: Cameron Crowe, Amy Heckerling, Jeff at Writers' Bootcamp, Billy Bob Thornton, Roy London, Cameron and Alice Thor, Ray Wright, Bruce Wagner, Bill Idelson, June Bauer, Kristin Harms & John Wells, Sandra Singh Loh, Joe Frank, Randy Bookasta, k. d. lang, Alanis Morissette, Jacqueline Maher, Teddy Bloomberg, Dana and Sue Gould, FZ, and the very Canadian Rob Cohen.

ACKNOWLEDGMENTS

In Portland, Catherine Ingram for whom there are literally no words.

And most of all, infinity gratitude to my beloved real-life Otto, Paul Doucette.

The man pulling radishes pointed the way with a radish.

—Issa

CONTENTS

CONTENTS

PART THREE
AWAKE AT LAST

PART ONE
BLISS

ONE
PRE-SENT

"Hooray for Hollywood."

—Johnny Mercer

"Yes," I heard myself say when the total stranger asked me to coffee. "Well, er, um, I'm, uh, I mean, I didn't think, uh, ... well why not" is what actually came out, but in my head it sounded a lot like just plain yes.

OK, he's not exactly a *total* stranger; I mean he has served me hot beverages on a number of occasions, so no, it's not like we've never talked. No one's denying we've swapped pleasantries here and there, in between refills of French roast coffee with just a hint of cinnamon (his touch, in spite of the management's disapproval), so it's probably fine. I liked his defiance and said so. He liked that I brought my cobalt blue mug from home and lobbied for free refills. (Thanks to me, the chalkboard sign with the thumbs up now says "Refills free if you save a tree!") And once I watched him give someone change entirely in ones.

So big deal. I said yes.

At least that explains why I am sitting across from the King's Road Café, in my little '89 silver Audi with the sunroof open, parked at the corner of Beverly and King's Road directly in front of a high-end furniture store and a two-hour meter at 10:01 A.M. on a crisp, windyish day, exactly fifty-nine minutes before Otto is due to arrive. It also halfway explains

17

why I am being forced to watch a pear-shaped bald man check his reflection in the window while he wrestles his wind-blown combover back in place and looks longingly at a black and maple futon.

What it does *not* explain is why I agreed to meet Otto so early in the day when anyone with any claim will tell you I am in no way a morning person.

I once broke up with a man for continually trying to rouse me in the early A.M. to have all-hour intercourse. His name was Angie. He was diurnal. He taught me that word. It means he was the devil and woke with the rising demon sun. One morning, he woke me with a massive predawn erection; I sat up, rested my elbows on Angie's cat fur–encrusted futon, faced this cross-legged man with the Egyptian-style beaded goatee and said, "I am the daughter of an artist. I thought you understood that the day begins around eleven *at the earliest.*" Disciplined Ben had understood this, toy-obsessed Ed did too, even collegiate Liam did in his own redneck way, but not Angie. He just looked away and covered his sunrise lap with a pillow. Behind him the sky had begun to take on an annoyingly yellowish hue. I held my hand up to block out its enthusiastic urgings. Angie's back began to tremble. I softened then and placed my wayward hand on his knee. "You could be a male model or an adorable underweight baby in an incubator, and if you woke me I would still give you a Cuban necktie for disturbing my sleep."

I shift a little in my cracked leather seat and adjust my visor to the morning sun. My God, do I think this coffee encounter with Otto might amount to sex?

I check one of the many clocks next to the Day-Glo hammock in the window of the trendy shop. A bright orange one reads 10:04. I watch a skinny lady with muscular legs and a royal blue satin windbreaker that says "Jazz" in rhinestones jog by. Of course *none* of this explains why I am here an hour EAR-

LIER than I need to be. I tell myself, Relax Mer, you know you just like to get a feel for a place, to tune in to the frequency of a spot . . . Hell, you like getting a good parking space.

Just breathe.

What kind of a name is Otto anyway? Odd-o is more like it, with all that talk about history and physics and light noticing itself being observed. When I asked him what he liked to do for fun he said he enjoys "reading, Ping-Pong, and creating an internal double of himself energetically, yunno, to let off steam." All this before handing me his number written in black ink from a disposable fountain pen on the inside of a custom-made matchbook with the First Amendment typed inside the flap. He does make the most perfect head of foam I've ever seen. "Low fat is key. Nonfat is bullshit."

I hold my hand to my stomach. Surely he understands romance is out of the question, since we are meeting during business hours. I think I might be sick. I look at myself in the rearview to see if I look sick.

Instead I find a stray eyebrow that I can't pluck or pull, so I lick my finger and smooth it back in place. Relax, Mer, I tell myself again. This time I say it like my Scottish yoga teacher, "ReeeeLOXshh," which makes me always want to say "bagel and cream cheese" in my best Sean Connery right afterwards.

Over the last year and a half, since the Jasper Husch Incident, I have come to realize that I am a nervous person, especially when I am subjected to my first, official—dare I say it—"date" in over nine months. A year ago I would not have even noticed this guy, looks, foam skills, and all. Six months ago his kindness didn't even *register.*

I hate that word, date. It makes everything sound tough and chewy. Date. Like all the sweetness and moisture of life has been sucked from your bones and, well, in a way it has, if you are forced to get back out there and . . . *date*. Why couldn't it be called a cloud or a pudding? Something bouncy and hopeful. I'm going on my first pudding in over nine months since the Jasper Husch Incident. That sounds a lot better. Funny. Like a Nancy Drew Mystery, with accompanying illustration of the shadow of a man fleeing down an endless spiral staircase along with a small, incriminating pool of pudding. I smile; Otto is so nice.

I was wearing a pale blue calf-length rayon dress with little white painted moons along the hem, an orange shawl, and pink platform shoes that fine Wednesday. He was standing behind the counter of my favorite coffee joint, the Mom & Pop Kaffeehaus, like he always did, this time wearing a pair of too short navy blue vintage cords, brown suspenders, and a Rainbow Brite T-shirt. "Otto Guthrie," he said extending his arm over the counter, which I accidentally shook at the wrist. "Nice to meet you," I said awkwardly pumping away, "I mean officially for real." When I released his arm he backed away slightly, and massaged the wrist back to life with his spare hand. That's when I noticed how nice his hands were. Are. I mean really noticed. That's probably the main reason why I didn't just turn and run screaming out of the building. Then he said, "Hey, what's your name, anyway?"

I froze and fixed my eyes on a ball of tinfoil hanging from a thin red piece of twine Scotch-taped to the ceiling. It was one among many, a local artist's tribute to clouds, displayed in a row above loose tea stored neatly in glass jars.

"America. America Throne." America Thrown was more like it. I scanned his eyes for any recognition of my famous name and the famous dead father that went with it: "B. Throne, painter, writer, poet, political activist, renaissance man, genius," the papers said, "dead of an aneurysm at age fifty," but nada.

"America Throne," he repeated, swirling it around in his mouth like a fine wine. "Hippie parents?" he said after a small eternity. I decided he was either clueless, had a good poker face, or didn't care. I thought, Cool.

"Yeah I guess," I said. It was either that or blurt out my entire defining history, complete with those last few minutes I spent with my father, the only other man I loved best in the world, besides Jasper, who had broken my heart so completely.

But I didn't. Why? Because I've had *therapy*.

Then he said, "Hey, can I take you out sometime? I know you like caffeine" and I said "Great" meaning awful, and he said, "How's about Friday?" and then a blushing silence passed between us and then he said "America Throne, huh," and I said "Yup" while swinging my arms and pressing my lips together like I was about to get a bassoon lesson.

Which brings me to here: me parked in my little car, playing the scene over and over again in my mind's eye, while I case the joint like a shitty private eye exactly fifty-six minutes before the rest of my entire life begins.

Across the street I watch a waiter in black jeans roll down the awning to give the pine tables and chairs and its few customers some shade. In a little while the place will be crowded and sun-assaulted.

I check my mirror again, this time to see if I'm still cute. Then I tug on the little St. Christopher that hangs on the rearview from a pale blue ribbon. My mother gave it to me a long time ago. She had been traveling through Europe with my father on a second honeymoon, well actually a first considering they had been married for close to sixteen years without a first. She went into one of the little churches in France or Spain or Italy, someplace in the middle of nowhere, and lit some candles. Outside they sold trinkets and mementos. She wrote me a postcard and told me about it. I still have the card, the Blessed Virgin with a flaming sacred heart. Apparently it had been blessed by the pope to protect its owner from the dangers of travel. I was about to get my driver's license. She got my dad to sign it, too. "Bugs and Fishes," it said (meaning hugs and kisses), "Mom and Dad."

10:07. In less than fifty-three minutes, if he's on time, Otto'll arrive and take his seat at the King's Road Café. After a while we will get into a deep conversation, and swap family horror stories. The old me would have told him with a humorous detached irony about the birth of my stillborn baby sister Shiva Plum when I was nearly three and leapt right into how my mother would not even begin to smile again until the birth of my brother Spoonie, "the miracle baby," two years later. I would have launched into my jealousy of the wunderkind with the golden curls and longer eyelashes than my own, the one who restored laughter to our house but who stole all the attention. I might have told him about dropping out of school early because we traveled so much from one grand opening to another and about the financial roller coaster we endured as a family, living on the tidal wave success of one sellout show and living through the cinched-belt failure of another. Sometimes we'd save money by staying behind while my father traveled first-class to exotic places, to be seen at an important event promoting coffee table books of his art with their lucid, acerbic text criticizing everything from Elvis to processed cheese.

I would have told him how my father's worldwide fame and respect the globe over seemed incongruous to my anger about his notorious but covert affairs and about my mother's resulting bouts with depression; how in my eyes she both craved his attention and desired her own life, but remained unsatisfied pursuing any achievements on her own.

This would naturally lead me to expound on how difficult it is to be hippie royalty *and* try to find your own identity in the shadow of a certifiable self-made "genius." About the complexity of emotions involved, growing up the daughter of an artist while living in a fishbowl, citing a particular incident during my mother's photography phase. It seemed to me her artistic statement involved taking photos only when people were miserable and didn't want their photos snapped, as demonstrated by the one of me taken when I was seven. I'm standing shirtless in my underwear in our lavender and wood-paneled kitchen holding a soft fabric dolly that Spoonie had just defaced with fake-blueberry-scented permanent Magic Markers. Only a few moments before she began snapping away I begged her to give Spoonie up for adoption as punishment for his heinous crime. In my fury to be taken seriously I slammed my hand down on the kitchen counter, my small fingers accidentally grazing a pool of leftover salsa. In the photo I am holding my favorite dolly by a limp leg, rubbing my red swollen eyes with my chili pepper fingers, and screaming. Not only did Spoonie go unpunished, but I was scolded for even daring to dream that Spoonie be given up for adoption. My only true consolation came a few days later: After seeing the finished photo of me, my father was so entranced with the purity of my pain and discomfort, he exerted great effort, working several days without sleeping, eating, or spending time with us to capture me in a 6' x 9' oil portrait. He would later entitle the piece *Pure* for a show of the same name, "as if to illuminate the beauty of our true natures in honest response to pure stimuli—genius!" according to one reviewer. Though my father did not care for reviews or opinions of the "humorless masses," it is among his only works which won him international acclaim, comparing him to Bacon and Schiele, two painters he greatly admired.

At the show I wore a frilly red dress like a Spanish senorita, complete with a red hibiscus bobby-pinned behind my ear. The portrait of me hung resplendent sandwiched between a woman at the height of orgasm in a piece called *Ecstasy* and a matador just at the moment before plunging the death blow dagger into a bull.

For a few wonderful minutes my father paraded me around on his shoulders.

One lady with raccoon eyes recognized me and asked if I was "the pure one." Proudly I declared, Yes! Unfortunately within earshot of several photographers. My father affectionately squeezed my leg while the flash bulbs went off. They hurt my eyes, but I was on top of the world. The painting sold for $30,000, shocking for that day, so that night we all slept at a fancy hotel to celebrate and I got to order anything I wanted from room service. Since I was the inspiration, my father presented me with a white rabbit fur coat with a champagne-colored satin lining. The next day our photo was in the newspaper.

This would all lead to my confession about being a late bloomer, which is polite for poverty-level trust funder, which is polite for loser. Then, without warning, I would stop stirring the sugar at the bottom of my too bitter espresso, and become very still, my eyes drifting past him, and I would bravely describe seeing my father die quite suddenly in the arms of a woman who was not my mother.

Otto might have looked down thoughtfully at his empty cup then and reached for my sweaty tear-soaked hair, brushing it away from my face and telling me something terrifically understanding like "I wish I could take your pain away" or a fatherly, "There there, everything's gonna be all right" or maybe, like Jasper, he'd freak out and bolt because I am so emotional, leaving me to pay for his uneaten sandwich.

I dig my pinkie finger into a perfect little doggie hole where Tulie has scratched and dug her little doggie nails into the passenger seat. My mother always says, "One day you will like all the damage that little dog has done because when she is gone, they will be sweet reminders of creature comfort."

10:08. I reach into the bottom of my purse in search of a stray Chiclet. Anything to *do* or *chew* to settle my stomach and its building nausea. Or worse, what if Otto is my future husband and I don't even know it! What if he *isn't* my husband? What if he's just a ship passing in the night? A stranger. A fling or something awful in between. Would I even be able to tell? Is everything just a choice? A science experiment? A cosmic consequence based on random accidents I have mistakenly called Collected Data? What if I have to go on a hundred—no, three hundred—more puddings before ending up *alone.* They say if you haven't found someone by the time you graduate high school you will be in a kind of loveless inferno until you are in your forties and *have* to settle. No soulmate for you, America Throne. Bad America, bad.

I close my eyes, count to five on the inhale, count to five on the exhale. "I am a river and those are just mind thoughts calmly rushing by. Stop it, Mer, just stop." But I don't.

What if he drives a jalopy? What if he takes the *bus?* Who cares about cars and stuff like that? That kind of thing only matters if you're going to have kids. He could be crazy. He could be getting a master's degree in Crazy. Jesus, *what if he's a murderer!* What if I am on stakeout and he's A MURDERER! I shouldn't be here to see this. Drive away quick, Mer! I have never wished for hand cream more in my life.

I count to five again. Relax relax relax, that is just your fear talking. I pound my breastbone lightly, saying, Calm calm calm, only love lives here. Then I reach for my cell phone. Maybe there's still time to catch him.

Oh God, I don't even have his number. What kind of a responsible person leaves the house without the wherewithal to cancel everything at a moment's notice. I feel my palms go all sweaty. Drive away, Mer!

I reach for the key in the ignition. That's when I see him walk in. Walk in! This is so my life. What kind of loser shows up for a date an hour early?

I scrunch down a little lower in my seat hoping he hasn't

seen me. He's wearing jeans and boots and a bandana around his head. He looks handsome. A little too handsome. I watch him signal to someone inside and then choose a table outside in the sun. I watch him sit down, hit his knees on the underside of the table, stand up, pull his chair back, hit the customer's chair behind him, apologize, sit back down, slide forward and bump the underside of the table with his legs again.

I think, Drive away, Mer, but I don't, because he has a rose in his hand. A big, fat, orangy-pink straight-from-somebody's-real-garden type of rose.

TWO
BUGS AND FISHES

"You forgot to carry the zero."

—Built to Spill

In the dream someone hands me a bouquet of roses. I am Miss America and I am being crowned on a stage in an opera house with red velvet curtains. In a dress made of clown noses. One of the judges, dressed in a long black robe like a courtroom judge, hands me the flowers. People in the audience are laughing and applauding. They are all dressed like nurses, including Jasper. My brother Spoonie and my mother are there, too. As I turn to wave to them, I see Jasper sneaking out a side entrance. For some reason I know he has given me a fatal disease and he wants us to die from it. Separately. My heartbeat quickens and I run toward the exit after him. Just then the bundle in my arm turns into a squirming baby. I look down and find it's a girl. I know it is my dead sister come back to life. I am so happy to see her that I lean in to kiss her, but she starts to turn blue. I look around for help but there is no one there. I realize night has fallen and I am in a forest dense with spiny trees and fog, and I am utterly lost. I start to cry and when my tears fall they turn to rose petals. Now I am in an industrial kitchen decorating the baby's coffin with icing instead of paint. I write "Bugs and Fishes" in pink along the edge where the hinges are. Just then the baby's eyes blink open and her mouth forms a perfect "O" as if she will speak. "Don't be afraid," she coos in a croney old voice.

• • •

I woke up on my back, sweaty and frightened, hands clenched at my chest gripping a handful of nightgown. I heard an owl in the giant pine tree outside the window. I fixed my eyes on the white painted beams along the ceiling overhead and listened to the sound of my pounding heart. I caught my breath. Oh yeah, our new place.

It was our third night there. In the morning Jasper would fly back to San Francisco, finish one last illustration job for yet another Internet billionaire, pack up his painting studio, cats, clothes, and furniture, along with everything else he owned, and hand the keys and the lease over to his deadbeat friend Benny in exchange for help loading the rented moving truck. Then, Jasper would drive back down to make Los Angeles (and me) home once and for all.

I turned my head to make sure Jasper was still by my side. Lying next to me, beatific in deep REM, was the best boyfriend in the world. His long eyelashes looked like feather dusters set against those milky white eyelids. One of his perfect hands cradled his perfect hairless cheek while the other perfect hand lay pressed between his perfect thighs. I swear, Jasper could sleep on the very edge of any bed without ever falling off.

I rolled onto my side and inched toward him. I curled my legs under my nightgown, stretching the white cotton so that it pulled tight at my lower back and hips. It felt a bit like a hug. I listened to Jasper's breathing, watched his lungs fill his upper back, watched his freckly shoulders rise and fall in the moonlight.

Why couldn't I have a good dream like the one where I'm a long distance runner? I love those dreams. They are better than flying dreams to me. Sometimes I cross a finish line. Sometimes Jasper is there to greet me. Sometimes my father is there in a pair of skintight snakeskin pants, when he was at his happiest.

Something about an even, measured pace and knowing I have the stamina in body, mind, and spirit to continue going and going forever and ever.

I made my body into a crescent to match Jasper's shape, curled my flesh and bones into his, two cozy spoons. "Baby I had a bad dream," I said nuzzling my way into Jasper's ear.

"Try to fall back to sleep."

"Baby I can't," I whispered into his night-smelling shoulders. I had to exhale the other way because Jasper hated it when I breathed on his naked back. Not me. He could breathe his stink breath directly into my nose and it would still smell like honey kisses. "Baby? Are you still sleeping?"

"Go get a drink of water," he groaned, "that always works in the movies." Jasper amazed me, he could be dead asleep and he would still manage to say something clever.

I got up and pulled my favorite brown and grey stripey wool sweater from its bedpost resting place and wrestled it over my head. My long brown hair hung in loose braids against the wool—silky smooth against scritchy-scratchy. I aimed for the kitchen, bare feet against hardwood floors through an obstacle course of half unpacked boxes. I kept my fingers extended, trying to get a feel for the new space in the dark. I could hear Tulie making licking noises in her crate. That made me feel safe.

In the kitchen, leaning against the door frame, I fumbled around the wall for the lightswitch. It still smelled like paint, pale pink walls with red trim.

I turned on the Jesus nightlight I had found at a junk store on Vermont and examined the necessities I had managed to liberate in the dark from a box I had labeled "Essential Living": my kettle, a strainer, an "I Heart SF" mug that Jasper bought me as a gag one afternoon while we played tourists down at the wharf, and a lone chamomile teabag.

I love the ritual of making tea. The alchemy of water and

tea leaves, heat, and a love-worn teapot passed on from one generation to another and so on. As I waited for the water to boil I imagined big ships since the beginning of time carrying important cargo, spices and teas from exotic places, just so I could drink it a million miles away. I sat on an ice-blue rag rug from Ikea, hugged my knees to my chin, and listened to the gas pilot hiss as it glowed.

Our third night together in our new place, I thought proudly. Even in the dark I could see that the house had already begun to come together.

We, well I, had managed to find the place for a mere $2,500 through a friend of my mother's. A real steal.

The house itself was an old, rustic, wooden one-bedroom nestled in the canyon. It used to be one of several getaway cabins for movie stars back in the twenties and thirties. Even though we were only fifteen minutes from Hollywood, the broker with the chipped, fill-in nails told me that in the olden days it took forty-five minutes to get there via trolley, past orange groves and ranch houses. The roads weren't even paved. This was considered going to the mountains! Nothing but miles of dirt back then. Now the place boasted our own canyon store and dry cleaner's! In less than an hour I had put down the deposit (plus first and last), signed the lease, got the keys, arranged for a moving truck, and called Jasper.

I didn't mind paying for it all up front myself because in the first place I was the one who found it and I wanted to secure it, and in the second place I had the money saved up anyway so I figured he could always pay next month's and square the rest with me when he collected on an upcoming art show. After that it would be fifty-fifty. I mean, we were in this for keeps, so no big. Then Jasper flew down for a quickie visit, gave the final thumbs-up, and helped me paint.

I glanced at the iris-colored flame beneath the kettle and stuck the end of my braid in my mouth.

We weren't planning on making the move to live together this fast, having been together only a year and a half, but this place was too good to pass up. I admit, I pushed Jasper a tad; even though it was only a one bedroom, I assured him there was plenty of charm here to make up for the space we would be missing, and as soon as he saw it he agreed. Plus he would be closer to the better galleries and the people with *real* money to buy his art. Besides, we had a genuine wood-burning fireplace now and were planning to convert the garage into Jasper's painting studio, since having a "public transport only" boyfriend meant we needed only one parking spot.

I thought, My God, soon we will probably be married! Isn't that what comes after living together? I wasn't exactly thrilled at the idea of being married to a painter, like my mother, but at least I knew the ropes: the creative highs and lows, the pouting, the thieving gallery owners, the pretentious buyers, the awe over Jasper's art. Next would come children and buying a house together! I imagined our children now, a boy and a girl, each with Jasper's long limbs and caffeine-free groundedness and maybe my hair and aesthetic.

Tulie let out a little yawn. I looked over at the brightly colored Mexican blanket that covered her crate near the breakfast nook Jasper and I painted periwinkle. The kettle began to whistle so I reached to turn off the gas, catching it before it cried out in agony.

I watched the steam rise up to meet the new ceiling as I poured. Then I sat back down again, this time cross-legged, and pulled the lacy edge of my nightgown over my knees and thought about how good Jasper's *Star Wars* action figures were going to look lining the cabinets of our new kitchen.

I held the cup in my hands to warm them, felt the steam rise up and wash over my nose and eyelids and forehead, leaving a fine dew in the baby-fine hairs that framed my face. I took a sip of the yellow water, then pressed the cup to my cheek. I liked how my features, though individually kind of funny, formed a pleasing incongruity when arranged all together. Jasper claimed that I most resembled Princess Leia. Sometimes he said Bjork or Alanis. That's because I usually keep my hair coiled up about my ears like fuzzy wintery muffs, or hissing cobras lying in wait, depending on my mood and the company.

I looked up at my God Wall, a portable altar on framed corkboard in the breakfast nook. In the dark I could just make out the postcards and magazine tear-outs I had collected over the years. Images of lovers, pioneers, poets, postwar survivors on street corners, at the beach, poised on a crescent moon, or in elaborate costume. One postcard is by far my favorite, and depicts an old-fashioned classroom circa 1880, the names of the children written in thoughtful cursive on an old school blackboard, names like Sam and Harry and Jane and Mary Swope. Maybe I like it because people have always made such a big deal about me being named America.

I traced a lone chicken pox scar with my finger and thought, It will be light out soon.

Inhaling the night-blooming jasmine that wafted through the little screen window, I leaned against the newly painted built-in kitchen cabinets and just listened.

I didn't even care that I looked like an ad for coffee sitting by myself, grinning dopily, save the slats of sunlight on my face. On and on they chattered, our new birds. Our new sounds.

Our new home, I thought happily.

I climbed back into bed. Once safely under the covers, I wriggled out of my sweater, and let it fall to the floor. Jasper exhaled deeply. I curled in close to him, pressed my hands together in prayer. I thanked God I was me, America Throne, the struggling-to-get-her-career-together owner of Tallulah the all-black, all-gas French Bulldog; best friend to one Sadie McGuire; daughter of Camilla and the famous dead-before-his-time genius painter Boris Throne; sister to the deceased Shiva Plum and the very much alive bursting-with-hormones-and-musical-talent Spoon "Spoonie" Throne. Blessings to us and the lives we touched. And of course, Oh Lord, an extra special thank you for sweet, poetic, lanky Jasper Husch with his art and his downright global awareness. My proof that life is good and worth living.

What is it about being so truly loved that makes you feel invincible to the outside world?

"Baby?" I whispered, poking my head out from under the covers to check if he was sleeping.

"Hmn?"

"Goodnight." I kissed his back.

"Go back to sleep, Guava," he said before rolling over and away from me onto his perfect hairless belly. I loved when he called me by my pet name.

He pushed some of the covers back and let a leg dangle out, and gave another nostrilly sigh. I rolled onto my back and closed my eyes. Then I heard what sounded like a cat being eaten alive by an owl or coyote. I opened my eyes and turned on my side inching my way closer to Jasper.

"Jas?"

"What?"

"I can't sleep."

"Think of something good," he said before turning on his side and disappearing into his little corner of the universe. Yes, think about something good. I scooted toward him a little more, faced his back, and smoothed my nightgown over my knees. You are something good, Jasper Husch, I'll think about you for a while.

•   •   •

On our first date, he took me to see the giant sequoias and instead of kissing me, we lay on our backs and pressed the crowns of our heads together under a canopy of trees that went straight up into toothpick points in the sky. I felt so happy to be so small, so insignificant—we were insignificant together.

I now stared at his starry shoulders now, a smallish Milky Way of freckles. I found Cassiopeia, the Big Dipper, the North Star. "You are true north," I whispered as my fingers lightly tickled their way up the nape of his neck to his latest Art Boy hairdo. I gently tugged on one of his white matted dreads, feeling the brittle clump between my thumb and index finger.

Suddenly I am five and my father is unsuccessfully attempting to untangle "rats' nests" which have taken over the back of my fine, honey-spun hair because my mother is still too grief stricken to get out of bed. My daddy is in charge of me. I have just gotten out of the bath. He wraps me in a fluffy purple bath towel and plops me on a metal chair with a squishy yellow seat. He turns the chair so we face the mirror in the pink-tiled bathroom. He frowns. Armed with a black plastic comb he sprays some baby-smelling oil into the hair pile he will inevitably have to cut to expedite things instead of unfastening every strand one at a time.

I felt Jasper twitch beside me, exhaling long and deep. I wanted to say I love you and hear him say it back, but he was already long gone. Inwardly I said it anyway. Then I turned over and thought about the little blue face and what it said about not being afraid.

"Afraid of what?" I wondered before falling into a dreamless sleep.

THREE
COLLECT CALL FROM ZEUS

"Freeze, don't move, you've been chosen as an extra
in the movie adaptation of the sequel to your life."

—Pavement

At 7:10 in the morning I woke to probing fingers attempting to harden my nipples. And even though Jasper and I were unbelievably in love, it made me mad for like eight reasons. For one thing, I didn't like the way he poked at them. It made me feel like a pet store kitten with an eye infection being poked at by someone who had no intention of buying me. For another thing, he totally could have let me sleep for at least forty-five more minutes before driving him to the airport in rush hour traffic. He could have stalled the realization that came with the full light of day, that I didn't want to be the national spokesperson for crotch cream.

Caress me, massage me, lick me, but for God's sake don't poke.

I mean it's not like he didn't know I hadn't slept all that well the night before. Besides, Jasper KNEW I didn't like morning sex. I was certain I had told Jasper about Angie because during that same conversation he had confessed to dumping that one girl for her squirting orgasms.

And even though getting up sooner meant we could start our new life together sooner, who wakes someone wearing a nightgown and big granny-style undies to have sex? Especially when I was almost thirty and still sponged off my family's melting glacier of a fortune and was forced to audition for a yeast infection ointment radio spot to earn my keep. Especially since I was seven to twelve pounds overweight about it.

Even at twenty-nine and born to a genius who made a patchwork living comprised of painting or writing whatever struck his fancy to elicit strong emotional reactions in order "to wake up the sleeping dogs and free one of the humiliation of simply being human," I was yet unable to pick a career. (An utter failure by Los Angeles standards.)

I had no other choice but to accept my mother's offering of $2,000 a month. I had already bounced from yoga studio receptionist to actress to personal assistant to gallery slave to voice-overs. Having inherited my father's artistic nature and my mother's changeability, I looked for jobs that required the minimum amount of work for the maximum amount of money so, like them, I could pursue my heart's desire . . . whatever that turned out to be. Of course my mother, who believed herself to be a sainted patron of the arts, generously dubbed me "a late bloomer," swore up and down it didn't bother her to wait for me to make my fortune. Though she never expressed a desire for repayment, I always felt an unspoken pressure to make a gazillion dollars to pay it all back. Voice-overs seemed to me to be a good compromise. You could make at least seven hundred and fifty bucks a pop just for standing around in a small padded recording booth trying to sound like a baby, a chain-smoking phone sex operator, or a mall-obsessed helium hottie.

Plus you didn't have to wear makeup to work and you could remain completely anonymous.

It made me feel mad and glad at the same time to be a poverty-level trust funder, happy to be able to lean on my family for support, yet able to do little more than pay my rent and bills. I kept meaning to learn how to manage money and cut back, but then there was the house—first, last, and deposit— not to mention the moving in together, the furniture, paint supplies, and of course groceries for the moving in together . . . it adds up, living together.

Didn't my almost live-in boyfriend understand that the sleep he was poking into probably contained vital information which would inform the rest of my natural earthly life as to my actual PURPOSE? My God, did he think I WANTED to be the spokesperson for itchy tweeters? On top of everything, I had to pee like a racehorse!

So, even though I was in no mood whatsoever, I let him continue his advances. You do that when you're in love. My backup plan? The alarm clock would be going off any minute, putting a defining finish to the A.M. frolicking since Jasper couldn't miss his flight if he was to make his fancy magazine illustration deadline. Jasper always enjoyed the challenge of a last-minute big money request; he liked the pressure and the crazy hours and the new contacts and the free exposure.

While he poked at my nipples like a handyman testing a new doorbell, I checked my glands both fearing and hoping for a sore throat. Normal. Too bad. I couldn't bear the thought of selling the nation crotch cream. But, Jasper always said it was better to do something and make some money than to do nothing and make none. Still, what did he know about the struggle for career identity? He'd known he wanted to be a painter since before he was da Vinci in another lifetime. And, just like my father, he didn't care if he made five dollars or five hundred dollars so long as he was doing what he loved.

Jasper rolled over on top of me spreading my legs open with his. I reached my hand into the drawer of our little yellow bedside table and felt around for my diaphragm and a single serving of sperm killer. Jasper removed the wrapper of the applicator tube and squirted some gel into the little rubber cup I held in my hand, then I pinched it in half and inserted it. It was so cold it made my stomach muscles tighten. Then he tossed the applicator aside, pulled my arms above my head, lifted up my nightgown, parted my underwear to one side, and—missing—pressed his giant early morning erection into my belly.

Now I *really* had to pee.

On the second pass my face reddened, not from passion but from extreme concentration. I could tell he was in down and dirty passion mode by the way he moved. Up and down, down and up. He moved his hips in slow grinding circles with speedy jerks pressing into me on the upstrokes. Ow ow.

While he kissed my neck, I turned my head and checked the clock. It was only 7:17. The alarm wouldn't go off until 8:00. I panicked! Jasper bit my ear. If my checkbook, the Burbank airport, and my bladder weren't all breathing down my neck I might be into this.

Think, Mer, think. Aha! To put an end to my escalating urinary situation I playfully pushed him off of me and seductively licked my way past his belly button to his best feature. In this ass-up position I felt some relief. Sucking on him and tasting myself I discovered I was somewhat pasty. I found this a bit ironic considering my itch-cream job potential. I looked at the clock. 7:19.

Suddenly, he pulled me up by my armpits, positioned me on top of him. My eyes began to water. I checked the clock. At 7:21, accelerated jerky thrusts kicked in. At 7:24, the two of us twisted and contorted our bodies in various positions, him in passion, me entirely in search of comfort. I checked the clock, 7:25. Damn! If I were under water I'd be dead by now. Moaning and low groans and grunts kicked in at 7:27.

Then, at 7:29, he pulled my legs up and over my head rather suddenly, lurched forward, and came, screaming, "I don't want to have a baby!" That's when I accidentally kicked him.

"OW! Christ, Mer!" he said rubbing his jaw.

"I'm sorry," I said, wriggling out from under him. "Let me get you a cool towel." I ran to the bathroom, turned on the cold water to drown out the sound, and relieved myself. After almost a year and a half I was still too shy to discuss bodily functions with Jasper, let alone allow him to hear me pee.

I wondered if the erotic art I was inundated with in my youth had raised a prude.

"Are you bringing the towel or what?" I pretended not to hear. "You aren't fooling me in there, you know." Over my porcelain din I could hear Jasper clomping around. I heard the zipping of a suitcase. I pulled up my undies and turned off the water.

In the bedroom I caught him piling clothes into a small brown tattered suitcase. He had already climbed back into his faded navy blue boxers that lay crumpled in the corner only a few minutes earlier. I snuck up and hugged him from behind. "Why are you packing?" I said, passing my hand seductively over his deflated crotch.

"Because I'm gonna need some of this stuff this week," he said, pulling away. He made his way over to the chair in the corner to where his grey T-shirt and brown cords lay and slipped them on.

"Just leave all that here."

"I'm gonna need a suitcase, Mer."

"Yeah, but why are you taking your clothes."

"Because I'm gonna be up there for at least a week. Besides you know these are my favorite things."

"At least a week? You said a few days at the most."

"Yeah, well, I got an extension on that one job."

"You didn't tell me that."

"I'm telling you now."

"Why can't you just come down earlier and do it all here?"

"Because it's easier to just use everything while it's still set up. Plus the cats have a vet appointment they can't miss on Tuesday."

"Oh," I said trying not to sound disappointed.

Jasper hopped on one leg now while he pulled up a green and purple argyle sock. Then he put on his grey runners and, standing, stuffed his hands in his pockets to make sure they lay flat against his thighs. Fine, I thought as he walked past me to zip up his suitcase, I don't need this, not today. Today I needed all of my positive energy to save the orphanage called my bank account and our new life.

I took a speedy shower and slathered vanilla and sandalwood-scented lotion on my legs. Towelless I dripped my way back into the bedroom where I retrieved a flowing magenta floor-length patterned skirt embroidered with tiny mirrors, a black spaghetti strap baby-T, an olive cardigan, and my black suede Boston-style Birkenstocks from an open box. Indian Hippie Chic. While I brushed my teeth I let Tallulah potty potty potty on our steep ivy-covered hillside.

"Good girl, good Tulie," I said, validating her good behavior in a new setting.

I spit and rinsed in the kitchen sink, tapped my toothbrush two times like I always do and accidentally dropped it down the garbage disposal. Just then I heard our Ganesha alarm clock belt out its droning "Om Namah Shivaya." "Jasper?" I called but he didn't respond, so I freed the toothbrush, washed the bristles with liquid Joy, dried my hands, went in the bedroom, whacked the white plastic elephant on the head, grabbed my hand-woven purse, walked outside, and locked the front door.

Jasper was waiting for me in the car.

Leaving with more than enough time didn't look like it would make a difference. My car eked along behind another one so in need of a smog check I couldn't tell you its make or model. Somehow I managed to get over into the turning lane and make a right on Riverside. I picked up some time speeding along the four-lane surface road.

Jasper hadn't said much since we left the house, just stared out the window and watched scenery whiz by. Foliage, trees, and shrubbery in a hundred varieties, from olives to oranges, from Kelly green to greenish grey. Past double-decker mini-malls, shops boasting pizza and falafel and frozen yogurt, yoga and hot tubs. Past a piñata shop with a paper R2-D2 and C-3PO. I thought about my ex-boyfriend Ed and how ironic it was that Jasper was going home to fetch his *Star Wars* action figures and how adorable I thought Jasper was for that, whereas with Ed, I found it pathetic. Maybe it's because Jasper's were still sealed in their plastic packages and treated like salable collector's items rather than actual toys. Jasper liked playthings, but he was a man. I reached my hand over and gave his spindly fingers a squeeze.

"I'm gonna miss my flight."

"You'll be fine." I stepped on the accelerator, sped through a light turning from yellow to red. I unconsciously popped in an old mixed tape Jasper made for me when we first met. He looked at me then looked away.

Traffic moved slowly even once we arrived at the tiny Valley airport. I didn't have time to wait at the gate with him as usual since I had to get from Burbank to Culver City fifteen minutes ago. I caught myself hoping the session would run over, then felt disgusted with myself all over again.

As I pulled up to the small white zone, I kissed Jasper more on his ear than his cheek as he turned toward the seat lever to reach for his suitcase out of the back.

"Oops," I said.

"Sorry," he said, rubbing the eye closest to the wet ear. Then I watched him wrestle the suitcase past the automatic seat belt. Even in a hurry, he moved so slowly it could make a person go strawberry-flavored batty. He pulled his ticket out of his hemp shoulder bag.

"Baby I gotta go," I forcibly cooed. He shot me a sideways look and continued to gather his belongings at his own meticulous pace.

"Sorry about this morning," I said, watching an airport policeman signal for me to get moving. "I'm just really stressed right now."

"I know," he said and we stared hard at each other for the briefest of seconds.

"I love you, Guava," I said, gearing up to merge left.

"Me, too," he said, closing the door. I pulled out and glanced back. He looked like a disheveled punk rock college professor standing there in the white zone. I waved like a maniac, staring back at him in my rearview, but he had already turned and begun to walk inside. Just then Eddie Vedder got cut off in the middle of singing "Don't call me daughter . . ." letting me know side two of Jasper's tape had completed itself, so I ejected it, and turned on the radio in time to hear some lady DJ say that a massive forest fire in Bali had wiped out a batch of patchouli trees. Good riddance. I hated the smell of patchouli.

Careening over Beverly Glen Canyon at daredevil speeds, taking it all the way to Motor, then Washington Blvd., I still managed to get to my appointment fifty minutes late, but the gods took pity and gave me a parking space right out front. My stomach growled.

I flew up the stairs two at a time to Suite 207 because the elevator wasn't working and apologized to an angry black-haired smoker, who I nicknamed Captain Issues because she berated me for being late. "It's a national, you know."

She bade me follow her down a dingy corridor with beige carpeting and ushered me into an all-beige room with a ratty looking couch, a mic stand, and a music stand with the pitiful copy highlighted in orange.

"Are you ready?" I had not even had time to put my purse down and she already had her headphones over her ears and her finger on the record button.

"Uh, yeah I guess so." I dropped my bag on the floor.

"Slate your name."

I leaned into the mic. "America Throne."

She threw her headphones back, said, "Please don't lean in," and returned them to her ears. Her hair looked even greasier in all that fluorescent light. "Slate your name again and begin."

I cleared my throat. "America Throne."

"Take one." She nodded.

I began, "Did you ever feel so uncomfortable you could cry? Down there I mean? Now try new doctor-recommended Itch Begone and say good-bye to that embarrassing odor and discomfort!"

"OK, let's try that again, this time stress 'Down there' a little more and really nail the beat between 'new' and 'doctor-recommended.' Try to sound sexy and have fun. Take two."

When I did it the second time all she said was "We'll let you know."

Outside I was assaulted by chirping birds and daylight galore. It was so bright I had to squint. My stomach growled again. I was starving. Now what? I held my hand up to shield my eyes and looked around. The Greazy Spoon looked somewhat inviting with its neon "breakfast served all day" sign.

I sat down at a table with a blue-and-white checkerboard tablecloth and fake plastic flowers. The place smelled like burned bacon and burned coffee. An erasable sandwich board described their daily special: potato deluxe, health baked with all the fixins', which I ordered from a woman named Shawanda with four-inch-long brick red nails, a diamond stud on one index finger, and a tiny portrait of Jesus' face in the center of the other. It reminded me of the funny character drawings my father used to make on the underside of my toes with a black-inked fine-point felt-tip pen: men with bowlers and bow ties, pretty ladies with long curling eyelashes, a big-lipped moose dressed for a tea party, a hobo with a black eye.

What arrived a few minutes later was a small microwaved potato split down the center and drenched with margarine. On the side, "healthy" parboiled frozen stir-fry vegetables, a side of plain nonfat yogurt instead of sour cream, and some freeze-dried chives.

I thought about my father leaving Russia as a boy of twenty, before he changed our name from Tronov to Throne, sneaking through to Italy via Yugoslavia; he had never seen so much food. When he got to the Land of Sauces he was amazed to encounter four different kinds of sour cream! When he finally got to America, he saw twenty kinds and thought, Poor Italy! He came over here and never looked back. It's one of the few stories I know about his childhood. He said his parents died when he was young, but when anybody asked, like me or Spoonie or a reporter, my mother always made a face at him that made me think he might have been lying. Sometimes I wondered if there was some smothering, perfume-laden Russian grandmother waiting to nurture me to smithereens or a stern grey-bearded squinty-eyed grandfather who beat my father with a belt and that's why my own father simmered with rage but never raised his voice once in the whole time I knew him.

I wanted to send the potato back but I happened to see a homeless man outside digging through a garbage can to retrieve what appeared to be bagel remnants.

I signaled to Shawanda for my check and knocked on the

window hoping to catch the bum's attention: In five minutes you'll have a jackpot! But Shawanda blew our big chance at getting into heaven because she was too busy learning how to use the overblown computer system, and Sir Hefty Bags moved on.

She was still busy adding the tax when I saw a well-dressed very determined David Schwimmer type enter the restaurant to ask if they needed any servers. "No," she replied, but maybe he could leave a resumé, which the guy promised to do, even though we all knew he wouldn't. He caught me watching him so I smiled, but he just looked down and kept walking. He looked sad. Fuck him, I needed a job, too.

Driving home I thought about the guy from the restaurant and how he probably left feeling rejected. Then I thought about Jasper—in a week he'd make his very last drive down the Five, unless of course we were visiting friends or what-haveyou. I felt invigorated. Going home to unpack boxes had suddenly begun to sound like a vacation.

"Any messages?" I said to Tallulah as I made my way to the answering machine with no blinking red light that I could see quite clearly from the front door. I leaned in closer, wiped a bit of dust off the speaker part. "Right-e-o."

I slipped off my shoes and made my way to the bedroom to make the bed. Tulie followed me and licked my foot. I flopped down into the unmade heap. Tulie whimpered. "Up!" I said, giving her permission to cuddle with me. The smell of Jasper on my sheets had made me generous. I held them to my nose.

The first time we made love, it was in Jasper's bed. I was shocked to meet someone who did not wash his sheets for weeks at a time. Shocked that I agreed to have sex with such a one. Not only agreed to, but actually craved. I remembered how the faded purple flannel sheets felt from weeks of neglect, how my mind resisted but then softened to falling deeper into him, weeks of him, showered and un-, dreaming, sweating, crying, breathing, masturbating, lying still. I remembered feeling creepy at first, then like an animal, like my most human natural self, and this made me fall utterly in love with him. Because he had stretched a part of me beyond my previous capacity and perception of myself. He had surprised me, and no one does that. Then I thought about how good his orange leather chair would look in the living room and whether or not we should buy a porcelain or metal toothbrush holder and if it should be installed on the wall or if it was better to use a glass and rest it on the edge of the standing sink. Or maybe we could mount one of Jasper's old paintbrush tins instead or maybe it would make a better vase, and if it was better that his drafting table face toward or away from the neighbor. Time to finish unpacking, I thought, but first a cup of tea.

I stood up, stretched, spotted the plastic wrapper from our stilted escapade, picked it up and tossed it in the wastebasket.

As I moved toward the library slash breakfast nook slash office, I noticed a fax in the dusty machine's fax tray. My first in our new house!

I thought, Maybe it's an appointment sheet for another voice-over audition, or perhaps I booked the crotch cream job and my agent is sending over directions to the recording studio, or maybe it's a flyer for some job fair or workshop to help me figure out what I want to do with the rest of my life. Or a love letter from Jasper!

I smiled as I watched the ancient machine chug out its insta-message, and froze.

If this were a movie, the camera would zoom through the night sky, past the Hollywood sign set against the backdrop of purple mountains' majesty, past twinkling city lights below, past telephone wires and treetops, Jacaranda, Cypress, Oak, past Eucalyptus, Cactus, Magnolia, Maple, Elm, and Palm, and into the open window of a quaint one-bedroom house nestled in the hills.

There'd be a slow pan around the living room revealing a brown leather couch strewn with pillows in brightly patterned fabrics and a comfortably cluttered kitchen table that could easily double for a desk. Past a single gardenia in a little blue shot-glass, past a handmade pear-scented candle, past an old tea tin full of pens and colored pencils and a sleeping dog with shiny ebony fur on a gingham bed near the floor heater. The camera would pause briefly at the fax machine resting on a white wooden bookshelf while the sound of a tea kettle screamed ominously in the background. Foreshadowing? Yes.

Then the camera would travel down a hallway toward a girl with long brown hair whose face we don't see. We would follow her to the kitchen from the heart down. The heart. That's very important. You wouldn't notice how small her breasts are at first because she'd be wearing her favorite cotton nightie, the one that makes her think of blue sky and fluffy white clouds.

The camera would follow her hands now as they turned off the gas stove. Her hands, because if this were a movie, especially, say, a French one, you'd already be won over by her hands. Why? An extreme close-up would reveal short nails, and a little white scar on her left index finger, and a sole beauty mark near the center knuckle of her right. Hell, you'd fall in love with her on the spot.

You'd notice the care and grace with which she'd scoop loose Earl Grey tea from its chocolate brown tin into her favorite grandmother's sterling silver teapot.

You'd think, I hope nothing bad happens to this person because she makes things from scratch.

As the steam continued to rise, the camera would pan up and you'd see her face. The face the boy once claimed to love even though "sometimes things just don't work out," according to the fax. But she doesn't know that, not yet.

If this were a movie she'd make her way into the office sipping her tea in the big porcelain china cup with the red and white flowers and matching saucer, half&half and two sugars, and we'd notice the page in the fax tray.

Now the camera would stay on her face as she crossed to *it* and began to read. There'd be an insert of the tea's milky steam spiraling and evaporating into nothingness. Then a shot of her eyes darting across the page, then of the fax in her shaking hand, only you'd hear the boy's narration, his deep voice resonating directly from his wide, flat hip bones:

America, I found this in a book of channeled information and it says things better than I ever could: "Souls come together not to remain together but to grow and move on. Loss is natural like the setting sun or the falling leaves, and always leads to new beginnings. Detachment is a hard lesson to learn. Even animals cling together in their little nests because they are afraid. O Earth Human, do not be afraid of death. For there is no separation though it appears to be so on the physical. In reality, it is more akin to simply having entered another room." Please don't call me. I have entered another room. Love always, Jasper Husch.

We would hold on a close-up of the girl's face and then, in slow motion, the cup and its contents would fall to the floor and the sound of the girl's heartbeat would be louder than thunder. The camera would be above her now, pulling back back back, as though the perspective belonged to her soul having left her body. And the camera would hold on the girl, head tilted back in a silent, anguished scream, arms outstretched like Jesus.

Black out!

FOUR
A FEW MINUTES LATER

"Baby's got blue skies up ahead. But in this, I'm a rain cloud,
You know she likes a dry kind of love."

—U2

But this was not a movie, it was real life and I was pissed.

"Hello?"

"I got your fax."

"Oh. Good."

"Is this some kind of a joke? Because I said I was sorry about the whole sex thing. You know I am stressed about money right now . . ."

"Look, I don't want to get into this with you on the phone. It's not about yesterday. It's about . . . Sometimes things just end. Sometimes people just don't get along—"

"But we do get along!"

"No we don't. I'm sorry but we don't. Maybe in a few years we . . ."

"In a few years? What are you talking about? Jasper? Are you still *there*? Fine, then I'm coming up there."

"Mer, don't."

"Then you come back here."

"If I come down there this thing will just drag on and on."

"This thing! This *thing*? Do you think it was easy for me to make closet space for you? Jasper?"

"It's over, Mer. I gotta go."

"It's about the cats, isn't it. You are mad that I don't pet your cats enough."

"It's not about the cats."

"THEN WHAT IS IT?"

"Just calm down."

"Answer me! Please? The least you could do is say all this to my face."

"It's the living together, it's the fighting . . ."

"That's it? That's what you're afraid of? The fighting? So what, big deal, we have dumb fights. That's all part of loving someone. I hate it, too, but so what, no big, you're worth it. We're worth it. Jasper? Guava? Why won't you answer me?"

"Look, I'm just not ready. You are and I'm not. We have gone as far as we can go. I'm not ready."

"Baby, please, let's just try it. *Pleeeease!*"

"It's over."

"Then why do I have a pile of your stuff in our new house? Jasper? Jasper? Talk to me! Jasper? I LOVE YOU!"

"Please don't call me. I gotta go." He hung up.

My knees buckled. I let the phone drop out of my hand as I slid down the wall. Tulie came over and started licking my face, but I pushed her away.

Chocolate. I needed chocolate.

FIVE
SAN QUENTIN

"Twist. Twist."

—Korn

Along with my Visa, I put a big pile of it on the 7-Eleven counter: a Snickers, Mounds, Chocodile, a Cadbury Fruit and Nut Bar, Skor, four Chunkies, and ten miniature Reese's. I read somewhere that chocolate has some of the same chemical effects on the brain as love.

"Hello my fire-end, hello my fire-end," chirped the man in the turban with the long woolly beard behind the counter. "Why are you crying Prettygirlyou? No tears, my fire-end, no tears. Fiviteen dollar minimum on credit card my fire-end," he said cheerfully ignoring my overwhelming sorrow, just like Jasper.

"What?" I said, staring at the Irish Cream logo on the cappuccino machine. I knew it didn't taste like it looked.

"Fiviteen dollar minimum on credit card." I looked back at him. He pointed to a handmade sign, black Magic Marker on taped-up yellow legal pad paper turned sideways, to prove it.

"Fine, fifty dollars worth," I said, slamming a fistful of Milky Ways on the counter.

"What?"

"Charge me fifty. Fifty dollars worth," I said, maniacally piling more and more candy on the counter: Clark, Mars, Peanut and regular M&M's, a bag of Hershey's Kisses, Hostess Cupcakes, a Charleston Chew. "Voila!" I said like a top athlete

51

completing a high-bar dismount while he punched in the numbers.

"That's only thirty-seven eighteen."

"What?" I said, leaning in to get a better look at him. I stared hard at how his mustache seemed to come directly out of his nose. It made me wipe my own nose on my sleeve.

"It is true, thirty-seven eighteen, my fire-end," he said merrily, smiling. He was in despicable contrast to me and my chocolate dilemma. "See, my fire-end?" He pointed to the digital numbers in the tiny window display on top of the machine. "See? Three. Seven. One. Eight."

I added two bags of chocolate-covered mini-donuts. He chuckled.

"That won't do it."

I added another fistful of Reese's Peanut Butter Cups.

"Nope," he said gleefully, brown teeth appearing under his nosestache.

"Look," I said planting both hands firmly on the counter, "if it wouldn't be too much trouble, could you just ring up what's here." I slid my credit card a little closer to his stubby fingers.

"So, no fivitee." His eyebrows came to a woolly point.

I stared at him. "No, just ring up what's here."

He matched my stare, then turned back to his little cash register, and slid my card through the narrow slot along the side. "OK, it is your life." Then he handed it over for me to sign my cyber-signature. "Any relation?" he said, beginning to smile again.

"What?"

"To the famous important painterwriter?"

"What?" I said again in utter disbelief.

"Any relation?"

"Yeah, I'm the daughter."

"Oh my goodness, oh my goodness. I don't belief it. I don't

belief it." He looked like a duck in a shooting gallery, running from the inside of the hot dog station to the edge of the magazine rack. "Why didn't you say? I am a painterwriter, too! I am a poet because of your father. He was genius! Genius from heaven above." He pointed toward heaven above. I noticed a fluorescent bulb needed changing.

He reached forward, gesturing wildly. "I am a fan par-tic-ular-ly of his deconstructionst phase in the late eighties. From the show *The Media*? Do you know it? How he would name a work something clever and then paint the portrait AFTER-WARD like that one I love so dearly called . . . *Hasty Brush-strokes, Hyper-real Colors Reveal an Intense Yearning for Speedy Justice*. I mean, his was political and sexual and gratuitous and sub-tle and personal and deep and sad and transcendent and var-nar-ball honest and aesthetically pleasing and hard to stomach and, and . . ." He acted every emotion out while he continued counting out my father's attributes on his nimble little fingers.

This is like a reverse stickup, I thought as I backed up, arms raised in surrender. Please sir, leave me alone, I pleaded with my eyes.

He put his hand over his heart. "The daughter of Boris Throne. I don't belief it." Then he leaned his elbow on the counter. "Yunno, I saw him read his short story 'Kent's Tiny Pony' in Carnegie Mullen at Pittsburgh, Pennsylvania. Sorry, in, at, at, in. Sorry, I am nervous. He was . . . ," he became solemn for a moment, almost presidential, then finally managed "ORIGINAL." For a moment he was speechless. We shared an awkward moment of silence and before I could ask for my goodies, the dam burst. He was crying. Wailing really. "There will never be another one like him."

Venomously I thought, I'm the sad one, not you.

Then as mysteriously as it began, the crying stopped. He touched a finger to the corner of his eye, wiped his mustache three times, and said, "Hey, what is the brother working on? The brother does music, right? I read about the son named Spoon."

This was all a bit too much.

"He just . . . well . . . uh . . ."

"How 'bout your-self? I read somewhere that you are trying some acting?"

"Uh, yeah, voice-overs, actually, because I like my *privacy*."

"How's that going?"

"Terrific. I mean look at me."

"Yeah," he said holding his belly mirthfully. "I guess it pays the bills, huh?" He pointed to my forty-dollar chocolate spree spilling across the counter, then leaned in conspiratorially. "What was it like? Growing up with Boris Throne for a father? That must have been a trip." He took a hit off an invisible marijuana cigarette.

I looked at him indignantly. "Oh, God no. He didn't do drugs."

"No?" He made a face like I'm not buying it.

"No."

"No?"

"No!" I was getting angry.

"Really?" he said, head in an all-disbelieving tilt. He leaned in close, whispered, "You can tell me."

That did it. I wanted to shout, "Well, my earliest memories are of women on all fours posing nude on our kitchen counter while I tried to eat my organic puffed brown rice and apple juice in peace. And of naked men in various yoga postures hanging off my goddamned jungle gym. I couldn't distinguish which ones my dad wasn't fucking. Or how about this little gem? My father and I never shared a meal together alone even once. The one time we were scheduled to have dinner, just the two of us, a crazy stalker-type fan, like you, sir, came over and my father took pity on him and let him dine with us, which is probably why I chose such a narcissistic asshole for a boyfriend and why I have no boundaries with a stranger like you."

Instead I just smiled politely and said, "It was nice, may I please have my receipt?"

"Go, my fire-end," he said, tearing up the little yellow slip of paper. "It is my gift. Take it. A gift to the sad daughter of my mentor." He waved me out shouting "Good-bye my fire-end, good-bye!"

I sort of half-ran and half-limped back to my car like a bad guy with a leaking bloody bullet wound away from the red and white and green fluorescently lit tribute to my father at the corner of Tujunga and Ventura.

The fax lay crumpled in my empty passenger seat. I picked it up, peeled it apart, smoothed it with my chocolate fingers, and reread it. It was worse the second time around.

Driving north on Laurel Canyon, brown bag on lap, I reached into my goodie bag and began cramming chocolate in my mouth like the scene in that TV movie where Meredith Baxter Birney has bulimia. Then I turned onto the 101 and looked for the sign that said Interstate 5.

The sun had begun to disappear behind a massive row of mountains. Blue assaulted by orange and deep purples and rosy pinks, a real shiner.

I sped west on the 101 past palm trees and the middle class, safe in their suburban homes, past their conveniently located massive shopping centers and movie complexes, my windows rolled down and Tori Amos blasting on the CD player. My St. Christopher danced frantically in time to the music.

My plan was to drive directly to Jasper's house and just talk things through, calmly, face to face. I knew if he could see me, he would change his mind. I popped another Reese's into my mouth, stepped on the accelerator until the needle said ninety.

It was almost completely dark now. The Valley's hillside began to twinkle. I checked my messages. Maybe Jasper had called to say he had come to his senses. It would sure save me the trip. I couldn't get a clear signal so I sped up. Then I thought about Tulie and about how no one had a spare key so no one could feed her or let her out. That's when I realized I had missed my chance to merge onto the 405 heading north, so I honked and signaled my way to the Sepulveda exit.

There, I couldn't find the proper on-ramp I needed, so I made an illegal U-turn across an island and five lanes of traffic.

That's when I saw the cherries.

"Ma'am? Ma'am, can you hear me?" said the doughy police officer as he tapped at my car window. He lightly touched the gun at his hip. "Ma'am, can you tell me what happened?"

I was parked on the corner of Ventura by a liquor store, under a green neon sign that made a terrible buzzing sound overhead. It wanted to say Joe's, but the J was missing. "He, I . . . He hates my dog . . . His cats . . . Maybe in a few years . . . Like *HE'S* the spiritual one." I handed him my license, registration, and the fax I still had wadded up in my hand. I just stared blankly into space while my mind played the rewind game.

I wanted some air, I just wanted some room to breathe. That's what I wanted to say to the nice officer with the child-bearing hips, that I was suffocating, you see, that it was vital I get some air. To tell him, even though it looked like an illegal U-turn across traffic into a bus zone, in actuality a bit of breathing room was what I was after, but the words wouldn't come.

I just sat there thinking about the Incredible Hulk. I thought about the alienation he must have felt keeping himself contained like that, and the satisfaction he must have felt truly letting go. I worried I might let go like that this very minute, and never come back.

"Ma'am, can you hear me?" Of course I could hear him, but I was miles away, trying not to burst out of my clothes.

Protect and serve, protect and serve, his hips and legs announced as he walked back to his patrol car. I watched him smooth the thermal paper flat in the palm of his hand, glancing sideways at me from time to time.

A handsome, dark-haired man wearing a western shirt with red embroidered roses caught my eye as he walked past my car. He stared back at me for the briefest moment before stuffing his hands in his jeans pockets and disappearing around the block.

For some reason I thought about endangered animals and homeless people and Tom Hanks and how much he loves his wife and says so every time he's interviewed. My mind was a staticky radio dial searching for a clear signal.

I heard a woman dispatcher's garbled mumblings then.

The officer spoke into a black hand-radio and waited while she spit out more incomprehensible info. Finally the officer looked down at Jasper's letter and read. Then he looked back at me, looked away, and passing a leather toe over the asphalt, folded the white thermal paper in half, in half again, and walked toward me.

He leaned his arm on the roof of my car. "I'm still gonna have to give you a ticket."

"OK," I said, but it wasn't. He handed me the ticket along with Jasper's fax.

"Sorry about your loss," he said, leaning in close enough for me to smell his aftershave. The word "loss" blinked in time with the turning lights on the top of his sedan. Gee they're pretty, like the little chili pepper lights in Jasper's bay window. Tears shot out of my eyes like missiles. "Any relation?" he said, handing me back my driver's license.

"Cocksuckingfaggotasspieceofshit . . ." I said, nodding in the affirmative.

He gave the roof of my car a comforting pat, then winked at me. "Things will look different in the morning, just take it easy."

At home, the wailing continued. Like it was a business day, and this was my job. To grieve.

It came out of me in desperate hurls, a kind of soundless frozen scream followed by a spattering of deep guttural growls, and then the moans, like a ghost. I was being haunted, yes; I was haunting myself, because a ghost is what I had become. A fat ghost. That is what Jasper Husch had made me in the blink of an eye or however long it had taken him to craft that fax. A chocolate-eating, fat phantom.

The wood of the door frame felt cool against my skin. The decorative edge around the peephole dug into my flesh and made little indentations. I leaned into it a little more.

Did he have to go to Kinko's to Xerox it? Did he have time to browse through a couple of books before selecting the perfect passage to let me know our entire relationship had come to an abrupt halt? Did he not understand that a year and a half equaled a lifetime in this disposable world?

I thought, A facsimile—how fitting because Jasper was an extreme likeness to a boyfriend, but not an actual one, not anymore. I thought we had figured it all out. I thought we had resolved his fears about our differences. I mean, he had a key to *our house*. Didn't that mean anything? I pulled at a wet strand of hair and put it in my mouth and locked the door. Click click and I was in jail, just like that. That's when I named the place. For fun. I nicknamed the adorable little cottage we were *both* going to live in San Quentin because, now, my entire house was a prison of aloneness.

Tallulah stared up at me with her big bulgy eyes. She sniffed my leg before giving it a light lick. I knelt down and pulled her face close to mine. "I was going to let you starve to death and die, for what?" Fucking asshole.

Then I made my way to my big empty bed, picked Tulie up and let her burrow herself deep under the covers. I climbed in, lay there perfectly still, stared at the ceiling. Lights out, Prisoner 1-0-7-3-3, Red Fern Hill Drive. Lockdown in cell one. Guilty of loving a manchild in the first degree, sentenced to life without him, no parole.

If I had known that yesterday was the last time we would ever make love I would have tried to enjoy it more.

I raised the covers up around me, smelling the last particles of Jasper I would ever have access to, pulled them close, like so much lead. I promised myself then and there never to call him again. Who in the hell did he think he was? I didn't need him; he wasn't *good* enough for me. He'd have to *beg* me to come back.

And even if he *did* beg, I vowed never to take him back, ever, not after what he did.

I thought, If I can just get through these next few hours without calling him, it will be smooth sailing.

SIX
BLACK SUNDAY

"Mother stands for comfort."

—Kate Bush

But my mother phoned. At 6:19 A.M.

I had left the ringer on silent but the message volume at eight in case Jasper called to reconcile, and now I was being assaulted by my mother's shrill soprano.

"Good morning, Mer, this is Camilla calling!" This was an annoying tactic she had been using since my early twenties to get me and Spoonie to treat her like we were all terrific pals. Pals who obeyed her. "I just wanted to let you know Spoonie is playing a concert this evening." I thought, A concert? Try "gig," Mother.

"Oh! A birdling just landed on the railing! Well I'm not entirely certain it's a blue jay but it is undisputably blue. You know that blue sweater thingy with the tassels and the shiny fringe your aunt gave your grandmother that she hated but wore anyway when your aunt visited because she felt guilty that night they had dinner at the Magic Castle? It's *that* shade of blue. Yesterday two of them appeared and ate the new cat food I put down!" I buried my face into my pillow. My mother blabbed on until the machine cut her off.

Since my father's death my mother has become an early riser. Maybe this made her feel like she could get a jump on things. She enjoys the peace, the light, the *ozone*. "All of the nutrients your lungs will ever need are all right there." She likes the fact that no one else is up and that the whole world belongs to her.

A few minutes later the machine made a series of clicks, then came the booming voice again.

"Hello? Mer? Oh I thought I heard you pick up. It's Camilla, darling. Anyhoo, Spoonie is playing a concert tonight at The Butterfly Club and I am going to need the guest list. OK, love you, bye-bye." It's The *Dragonfly*, Mother. She finished up the endless call with one large wet smacking sound. I closed my eyes, anxious to get back to my sorrow, knowing full well that the grieving process can take up to more than half the time you were actually together. Only, a few minutes later, the machine click click clicked AGAIN.

"Jesus!" I said out loud. I tried to close my eyes but the sun was stinking up the place with too much sparkly happiness.

"Mer? Did you just try to call me? No? Well anyway, I forgot to tell you I need that guest list by four, so let me know who's coming. I just need to know so I can let them know. OK, love you, bye-bye. Mmchwa! Oh, also, I wanted to let you know I set up a lunch for you and that agent I was telling you about. I told him you are not at all happy with your current agency and he said he'd be willing to help you find better representation as a favor to me. I never liked that agent of yours, anyway. His ears are too small. Bad listeners, men with small ears." I looked at the clock, 6:27, then rolled onto my back. I slammed my palm into Jasper's side of the bed, then reached for the pale blue Princess phone on my little yellow nightstand.

"Mother!" I said loudly straight into the phone without putting the earpiece next to my head, "I do not need a new agent! I just signed with this one and I've already been out on at least seventy-two auditions!" A lie. I tilted the phone to hear her response but she was gone. I slammed the phone back on its cradle and curled my body into a fist. The answering machine clicked again. Guess fucking who.

"Oh, and bring Jasper."

I sat straight up, held the phone with two hands. "Mother, I am asleep!" I was yelling now.

Calmly she replied, "Mer, how can you be asleep if you are talking on the phone?"

"Why are you calling me at this hour?"

"I thought you'd have your machine on."

"I do have it on, Mother. What do you want?"

"No, I mean I thought you'd have your phone turned off, it's so early." I closed my eyes, tightened my jaw, exhaled loudly through my nose.

"It's just that . . ."

"What's the matter, do you have a cold?"

"No, Mother," I said slowly, softening somewhat, "I've been crying. My eyes have practically sewn themselves shut."

"Oh. Do you have a plunger?" My eyes blinked open.

"It's too early for mind games, Mother."

"Don't talk to me like that. I only called to say it would be lovely if you and Jasper could attend Spoon's performance this evening and show your brother a little support. I don't need to be treated like an animal just because you're sad and want to take it all out on someone." I heard the sound of running water, then a sandpapery scrubbing, Brillo against porcelain. It made my teeth ache. I pulled my comforter around me.

"What do you mean 'like an animal'?" Tulie made a scraping sound from inside her crate. "Shut up!" I shouted over my feathery barricade. I scrunched back under the comforter and held the receiver very close to my mouth. "Jasper and I broke up."

"Well, good riddance. How about Sadie, will she be coming tonight."

I pulled the phone away from my ear. Stared at it. Then my eye caught sight of one of Jasper's button-down vintage shirts hanging limply from a wooden chair in the corner of our room.

"Ooof," my mother said suddenly as though wrestling something large, and losing. Then I heard a sound, metal grating against metal. "Nobody really liked him anyway. His forehead was too small. No imagination."

"What do you mean 'nobody,'" I roared. "He had a massive forehead!"

"Ooof," my mother said again.

"Jesus, what exactly are you building over there?"

"Don't Jesus me, you sound like an inner tube tire. I don't need abuse from you, Madame, not when there is a lovely, civilized little blue jay perched outside my window waiting for his breakfast. Good-bye, Mer."

"Don't hang up!" I felt dizzy. "Mother, I'm sorry, it's just that I'm very upset about the breakup."

"What for?" Scrape scrape.

"What do you mean what for? For kicks, Mother. I'm upset because IT'S FUN! WHAT IN THE HELL IS WRONG WITH YOU?"

"Good-bye, Mer," she said curtly.

"Mother, Mother, PLEASE DON'T HANG UP! Please?" I pleaded, more docile, "I can be calm, I can be calm." Silence. Tentatively I said, "It's just that I would really appreciate it if you would be careful never to mention his name to me ever again. Ever. Like, as long as I live."

"Mer, the Dalai Lama says our sole job is to be happy, so I ask you, why waste your energy being upset?"

I stared at the phone. "Because . . . because . . ." I was stumped. "Because I feel *shitty*? I mean if I just lie down and accept this, Mother, why not join the army or a cult or or or . . ."

"Now you're just being silly, which I prefer by the way, but don't take this all out on me. I am an innocent bystander simply calling to ask my daughter and her boyfriend . . ."

I tightened my hands around the receiver, pretending it was a very thin neck. I watched my knuckles turn white, then gently held the phone back up to my ear and calmly asked her, "Are you trying to kill me, Mother?" I poked at the holes in the phone. "Are you trying to drive me absolutely insane!"

"Spare me the melodrama, America. I need to know who you are bringing *before* four, if you are coming. I know Spoonie would really appreciate the support, so if Jas . . ." I felt my face go bright red. I was surprised the phone didn't catch on fire. "I mean, if anybody changes his mind it would be nice to see you *both* down at the venue."

"It's not a venue, Mother, it's A DIVEY BAR!"

"Good morning to you, too. Good-bye, Mer." She hung up.

I held my breath and pressed the top of my head into the bed as if preparing for a somersault and stayed that way long enough to calm down. Tears rolled into my hairline in great buoyant drops.

Goddamnit. Every time I want to outright hate her, I always picture two things: her suddenly clutching her heart and dying *or* her face that day as we watched the men in rented light grey suits lower my father into the ground. I picture how the muscles around her mouth tightened and pursed, and how her chin jutted out and quivered. The blue of her eyes flat, eerily dull, and how the tears fell down her cheeks in perfect streams, like rain on a pane of glass. That was the only time I ever actually *saw* her cry. A woman who sheds no tears? What kind of a life is that? Oh, I heard her a few times, when I was little, behind closed doors, when we had no money, when my father went away for long trips and she found a hotel receipt for a Mr. and Mrs. Throne when she had stayed behind to watch us, or upon discovering a scarf she did not purchase for him stuffed in a jacket pocket. Once, on my dead sister's birthday, I heard my father's murmurings, then a door slam and then his footsteps down the hallway, past my room, toward his painting studio. He didn't come out until my mother brought him something hot to eat.

I sat up and called her right back.

"Hello," she chirped, "this is Camilla speaking."

"Mother, why did you hang up on me?"

"I didn't."

"You didn't."

"No, Mer, I didn't."

I looked around the room, shook my head in disbelief. Abort, abort! She's in *New York Times* crossword puzzle mode. Slowly I asked her, "Then how did I end up with a receiver in my hand and no one on the other end of the line?"

"If you remember, I said good-bye." She explained with equal slowness, enunciating every syllable. "The conversation seemed to be over because you stopped talking."

"I was *listening*, Mother!"

"Well, you made a snorting sound."

"Breathing, I was breathing. That's what people do, they breathe. Jesus." Silence on her end of the phone, a standoff.

I wanted to say, What, no apology? Yeah, maybe Jasper and I can get back together just as soon as the breakup fairy pulls the stinger out of Jasper's ass—he'll wake up and we can all live happily ever after so Spoonie has an audience. Terrific understanding of *my* feelings, Mother! But I didn't. Instead I rolled my eyes. "I'm sorry, Mother."

"Well, yes, OK, fine. I need those names by four."

"I know, I know. By four."

"Good. Well, I love you."

I swallowed my pride, "Well, I . . ."

"I absolutely must run, an exploding sink calls. Bye-byeee," she said, sounding victoriously chirpy.

"I . . . I love you, too," I said to the dead phone in my palm. I placed it on its cradle, calmly inhaled, then let out one sharp elongated burst of a scream. I could tolerate my mother when Jasper was around.

I was so tired I felt drugged. I crossed my hands at my heart and tried to prepare for sleep the way a pharaoh might prepare for mummification. Lying on my back gave me pause to consider how much I hated the curtain ties I had made. There were other terrific things to think about, too, like how to afford my new place without my own money or an actual job and what in the hell I really even wanted to do for a living and what's so great about living anyway.

When Jasper loved me, in my old house, he left poems everywhere he knew I'd look: on my answering machine, in my grandma's teapot, in the refrigerator by my half&half, next to my computer, on my bathroom mirror, near the phone by my bed, on my pillow. He would hold me until I fell asleep. When we stayed at his place we would watch movies until the sun came up, pausing to make love, or eat hippie TV dinners. Aflood with memories of where we made love, laughed, cooked, danced, fucked, painted, in windowsills, on bathroom floors and kitchen table tops, where we made still more love, ate, made even more glorious love, experimented sexually. I thought, I am so glad I did not let you shit between my legs. Fuck you for even thinking that was something even remotely acceptable to propose, but you found a way to shit on me anyway didn't you, you fucking maggot!

I heard the phone make another series of small clicks. I leapt for it. It's him!

"Hello?"

"Do you have a plunger?" said Spoonie through a groggy yawn. "Camilla's on a rampage." I hated it when he called her that. I sighed loudly.

"Oh, hi, Spoonie."

"Do you?"

"What?"

"Have a plunger. Camilla wants to know."

"You do realize I live eight miles away and that a plumber might be somewhat closer."

"Camilla says it only requires a plunger."

"Doesn't *Mother* have one there?"

"Just forget it. If you're not gonna help I gotta go."

"Uh . . . sorry. It's just that I feel like I am on the verge of a nervous breakdown here and I really . . ."

"OK. So, are you coming tonight?" I shook my head in disbelief, thought, Is my *entire* family insane?

"No, I can't. I'm suicidal. Jasper and I broke up."

"So then you're *not* coming tonight?" I bit the inside of my mouth.

"Look, I'm just not feeling all that well . . ."

"OK, whatever." He sounded disappointed.

I let out a sigh. ". . . But I'll try to come."

"Cool! Try to come early because I really think you'll like the opening band. They're called Rows Five Through Seven. They're really good! Kinda like fusion grunge mixed with symphonica, like Bach on an all guitar and Twinkie binge."

"I said I'd *try* . . ."

"Hey, I invited Sadie but maybe you could call her and remind her and maybe get her to bring that actress chick."

"What actress chick?"

"That *one*. The one she's working with. The one with the boobs." I rolled my eyes. "Oh, and Camilla needs the guest list by four."

I bared my teeth. "Yeah, she mentioned that."

"Try to go a little easy on her. She's *cleaning* again." I stared at the phone. Cleaning meant she was upset about something. From the time we were little, Spoonie and I had already come to associate the smell of Comet and a clean sink with emotional betrayal or financial disarray: her missing my father and fighting with him long distance or a deal made with a shady dealer under my mother's radar. I could hear my mother in the background, calling out to Spoonie for assistance. Suddenly I felt bad that the weight of her universe rested on his shoulders because he still lived at home. Then again, he got the same allowance as me and none of the stress of my expenses. *And* they got along.

"Do you know what it's about?"

"You know Camilla. She's full-on top secret, but I'll try to pull a *Murder She Wrote* and get back to you. So, see you tonight?"

"Yes," I said, painfully aware that I was a bad child for not asking my mother about her life more and helping her out, like Spoonie did.

"Well, bye," he said yawning.

"Bye."

I hung up, rolled onto my side. I pulled my down comforter up over my face and tried to relax. Just then I heard a loud-ass neighbor start up his loud-ass saw outside.

"GODDAMNIT!" I screamed. I kicked my legs. I was having a full-blown temper tantrum. I stood up suddenly and began to pace. I mimicked the sounds I heard outside and buzzed around my room arms outstretched, like an airplane. Saw saw, buzz buzz, right wall, left wall, and back to the bed again while some new neighbor "gardened." I flopped back down on my bed and kicked some more. This time on my stomach.

The smell of gasoline wafted its way into my solitary confinement. I thought, Permanent rest, gas chambers and electric chairs, death by lethal injection and Jasper. Then it hit me: Why should Jasper get to sleep peacefully if I couldn't? I mean no one else was treating this like it was real or any big deal so why should I?

"You have reached Jasper Husch Fine Arts and Illustration. No one is here to take your call so please leave a message or push star to send a fax now."

"Hey baby it's me, are you around? Are you a square? OK, call me when you get in. No big. Love you." I hung up and lay back and eased my head gently into my downy pillow. It felt good just knowing I had made contact.

I called right back.

"Baby are you there? I really need to talk to you so can you please pick up? Guava? OK, well call me back OK Baby. I was wondering if you wanted to come down for Spoonie's show tonight. Baby? OK, well let me know. My mom needs the guest list by four. Thanks. Bye."

"Baby, it's me. Are you up yet? Honey? Jasper? Baby, please pick up if you are there. Baby, are you there? Pick up pick up pick up pick up pick up I know you can hear me. I know you are screening. No? Baby, it's important. I really really really have to talk to you. I was thinking maybe you'd like to fly down and see Spoonie's show tonight and then we could sleep in late tomorrow and get up and have breakfast in our new kitchen together, and then we could drive back up together and pack your stuff up and drive it back down together, whaddya say? Baby? Baby, please don't do this to me. Jasper? No? Fine!"

I slammed the phone down.

"Pick up the phone, Jasper. Pick up the fucking phone. Pick the fuck up, you fucking piece of shit. No? Fine. Since I can't talk to you, let's recap. Two days ago we were in love. *Yesterday* I put you on a plane headed back for San Francisco after not the best, OK fine, rather awful rushed sex, but I was stressed because I have exactly $200 to my name. Plus you *know* I don't like morning sex, plus I will have you know that my mother is cutting my allowance back so now I am *totally* stuck with this place and no money and no job. And I mean honestly, Jasper, I could not have gotten wet if I wanted to, not with only $200 to my name. Plus, thanks to you, I'm totally stuck. Maybe you are used to having no money, Jasper, but then another job always rolls on in for you and *leads* to something. Because your artwork is in demand, while I, jack-of-all-trades yet master of none, could starve to death in this town riding bareback on my father's coattails! Are you hearing any of this?"

The machine cut me off.

"Let me tell you why $200 is a bad amount of money to me. OK, so yes, I know *everyone* has concerns about money and career and such, but not everyone is a C-level celebrity, Jasper. Not everyone had a head start and *still* can't pay her bills or figure out what to do with my life. You might expect this from a homeless woman or a grocery check-out girl or whatever . . . Hey that's pretty funny, they're both bag ladies! Anyhoo . . ."

"Fucking machines, listen, I know this sounds weird, Jasper, perhaps even harsh, but I always wished I were raised a bottom feeder, like you. Like my parents. That way perhaps I'd *understand* that the bottom isn't so far to fall. You guys don't seem to freak out over things like having no money. If I were raised with nothing, like all of you, perhaps I'd be *motivated* to achieve, like all of you. When you are raised rich like me you do not have a desire to succeed because you have seen it all. You *know* money is not the answer, certainly not the key to happiness. The only reason to work is so that you can afford *not* to, so you can live happily ever after with the people who matter to you. That's where you come in, Jasper Husch: You matter. So while I was here busily trying to figure out a way to make money so you wouldn't leave me so I wouldn't have to rely on you so much, so that, so I could have my own self-esteem so you wouldn't leave me, you decide to leave me. And because why exactly?" The machine cut me off *again*.

"Baby, please pick up. I'm sorry I keep leaving these long messages I just really love you and I really want this to work out so call me, OK? Bye. I love you."

I lay back feeling like I had been beaten by a pillowcase filled with a cement skyscraper so I sat up and called him right back. It rang and rang so I hung up. Then I lay back and wiped my nose on my comforter.

Just ignore him, I thought. Yes, avoidance. Avoid all people. Avoid everything. Especially feeling. Try to sleep. Try to sleep it all off.

I lay perfectly still and congratulated myself because I, unlike Jasper, could commit to things, like lying down.

A few minutes later though I had to get up to pee.

In the bathroom, I caught my reflection in the mirror and started picking blackheads instead. I tore off a piece of toilet paper and began squeezing like a demonic facialist. I bent my nose flat for more surface access. Twenty minutes and an inflamed face later I looked like a heavyweight boxer who had lost. I scolded myself, "Stop it, Mer, you are out of control! You'll get through this. Just make it through the next seventy-two hours and the hardest part will be over." *Then* I peed and made my way back to bed. Only I ended up getting sidetracked at my living room window.

There, from the corner of my eye, I saw a hummingbird. I stood still now and watched it hover outside the window near my lilac iMac, dip its beak into the face of a red hibiscus, dart away, and move to suck the nectar from another veiny flower. Then, the hummingbird, representing joy in Indian folklore, paused by my window, held itself perfectly in place, and crapped. It pooped out a massive hummingbird poop, a grunt about a third its size.

I thought, This is so my life.

Later, around dusk, after ordering and then consuming three sides of mashed potatoes, biscuits with molasses butter, a side of cornbread, a Caesar salad with caramelized pecans, and fried okra from Why Cook, I climbed into bed and passed out only to wake up in the middle of my brother's encore feeling jet-lagged and guilty for having missed Spoonie's show. I then leapt out of bed like a night fisherman checking his lobster traps to find *eight* messages!

Spoonie called to tell me that Sadie and I were on the guest list plus one.

My mother called to see if I had any names for her.

My mother called to find out if I wanted to drive with her.

My mother called to see if I had left yet.

Sadie called to say she was very worried about me, was sorry she missed my calls, but thought I knew she was away all weekend and that she'd see me down at Spoonie's show.

Sadie called from a pay phone to say she wasn't on the guest list and where was I.

Sadie called to tell me she got in anyway and where was I.

Sadie called again to say that she was home now and that she loved me and that she was really worried about me. "Mer Mer Mer? I'm really worried about you. Whatever you do, *don't watch TV*. Promise me you'll call me if it ever gets that bad."

SEVEN
RADIOACTIVATE

"Cancer for the cure."

—Eels

Public access is the only way to go.

For around fifty dollars you can buy a half-hour time slot, and make your own TV show devoid of any content or professionalism, and beam it directly into people's homes. At least that is what I concluded from my living room sofa hours after watching a lady marinate a chicken in orange soda—"An old family recipe; it literally comes right off the bone!"—after watching a guy sing songs about all the signs of the zodiac, and *well* after the lady who looked like a dancing bear dance like, well, a dancing bear.

I marveled at the fact that although I shared the same desire to have my artistry seen and appreciated, whatever it might turn out to be, these pitiful outcasts were organized enough to take the three days of required training time, to learn how to work the camera and lights and editing equipment and pull off all this mayhem, whereas I waited around for my agent to call and tell me when and where my next rejection would be held and how much money I wouldn't be making when I didn't book the job.

Presently a man was making a belt buckle out of turquoise and found objects.

My phone rang. I thought, Please let it be Jasper! But it was only Sadie.

"Mer? Mer? Mer? Mer??" I hated when she did that. She always says my name like a scratchy cat meow. Calls it affection. I didn't pick up.

Mainly because the man on the TV was smiling now. He was missing four teeth at the back. I hated happy people and Sadie was always happy.

Sadie is my best friend. We have known each other ever since we both dropped out of a still-life painting class at Parsons almost nine years ago. I wanted to impress my father, so every Sunday A.M. I would trudge all the way out to Pasadena, set up my shitty easel, and fail to capture the beauty around me. As it turned out, watercolors are a nightmare, but we both had massive crushes on the gentle instructor, Larry Gimmel. We confessed it to one another that first morning on the trek from the parking lot. I gave her half of a lemon poppyseed muffin, and in spite of our shared crushes, she told me I had some black things in my teeth.

I trusted her instantly.

Once inside the gardens we began to feel the inspiration. Larry told us all to select a spot and paint, as best we could, exactly what we saw. The gardens were set up so that you had the opportunity to visit Japan or France or Brazil or merry old England via the plants.

We both chose England and started with some climbing roses. My roses climbed all right, and then they kind of jumped, and ultimately ran. My painting seemed to be crying. I blamed the color palette which insulted real life, not taking into account that I had no depth perception, no sense of light or shadow play, along with zero perspective. Everything rested on the page with equal import and flatness. At least Sadie's interpretation expressed a bold commitment. She was not bound by the tradition of reds and pinks for the blossoms, she chose greens and greys, arranged them in abstract sorts of blobs, and then selected black for the background, which she painted *after* the flowers were done. Her "roses" sort of hung in a suspended blackness, a portrait of a sad infinity.

I felt like a failure. I felt like it was an indication of my sanity and accuracy to perceive reality correctly because I could not convey it with my hands. I wanted to be like my father. He could deliver the world exactly as he saw it.

With his head cocked, and his mouth in a half-pout, half-frown, Larry seemed genuinely concerned. He gave us both the same note: start with one color and get the relationship right with it first before inviting other colors to join in. He demonstrated effortlessly with a little palette knife, creating a rich world using only *green.* He painted some foliage and a little winding path over my mess, and I swore I could see all the way down that road and into the depths of Larry's soul.

As we made our way back to the parking lot, Sadie confided she really had tried to paint the roses at first but then thought about her goal, Larry, and how sucking was a good thing. "The worse the painting, the more the notes. The more notes, the more Larry." Larry turned out to be gay so we both dropped out.

Now Sadie does set design for movies, mostly indie horror films. I like having her for a friend because sometimes she has no work for weeks at a time and we goof off. It's much better than having friends with real jobs.

"Mer? Mer? Mer? Pick up, I know you are there." I didn't pick up. "Mer? Mer? Mer? No? OK. Tallulah? Tallulah? Tallulah? OK, well tell your owner to call me back when you get this." The machine cut her off.

I watched the guy with the old-man hands show off his belt buckle mastery in an extreme close-up. It was truly ghastly, that belt buckle, a tangle of twisted metal, like a small bus accident, but with a coral and turquoise inlay.

The phone rang again.

"Mer? Mer? Mer? Please pick up, I know you are there. I know you can hear me. You are probably just sitting there listening to this. Mer? Mer? I've thought about it. You are probably just experiencing pre-thirty jitters." I stared at the machine, tried to send an electric shock through the wires, hoping to singe off her perfectly messy bangs. Failing, as she kept right on talking, I faced the TV and watched an ad for baby lasagna with renewed interest. Little layers of noodles and tomato sauce and something brown stuffed in tiny jars. For newborns. "Promise me you're not watching TV, Mer. Are you? Mer? Mer? Please call me. OK?"

He's probably at Benny's. I imagined him at Benny's little shit-hole apartment in the Haight now. I hated Benny. Benny was a jazz musician with a dyed blond beard who I was convinced was secretly in love with Jasper, who of course denied it endlessly.

I aimed the remote and switched channels, landing on a skinny man in a purple unitard with long stringy hair and an equally skinny beard. I watched him show off his "invention," a custom-crafted Velcro apparatus which he boasted "perfectly duplicates the experience of floating in water while remaining on land." He assured me that by making minor adjustments to the fifty or so foam circles, "a baby or a legal giant could feel like he was floating on a distant ocean while safe in the comfort of his own home." While a phone number flashed on the screen encouraging me to "Act now!" I wondered why he invented it, wondered if he was allergic to water, wondered if a person could get seasick in her living room. Then and there I made a pact with myself to avoid men with beards entirely.

Ha ha ha! My belly shook with mirth just thinking about how much Jasper would have enjoyed this and how much power I had over him by not calling to tell him about it and how much enjoyment I was having on my own without Jasper. I thought about how easy it was going to be to give up the most perfect lover I had ever had, the gangly boy who cried at movies and laughed at my jokes. To give up his beauty, intelligence, and creativity and not miss having him in my arms for even an hour.

The amazing thing was that part of me was actually proud of Jasper for listening to his inner voice because I know that's the hardest thing in the world to do. I just didn't understand why his inner voice had instructed him to dump me while mine insisted we have a batch of children asap.

The phone rang again. Bless Sadie's heart.

I turned the machine and ringer volume off. Time to focus on checking out.

On the boob, a man from India with thick grey fingernails that curled and curled and touched the floor. He had been growing them since 1956. He kept the creepy gnarled Hand in a long black sack. His wife had to turn the Hand over every half hour when they slept so it didn't cut off his circulation because his precious useless Hand was so heavy. I got mad at her devotion to his insanity. She reminded me of myself.

I looked around my new place. The whole house seemed dead, like all the air had been sucked from the rooms. I thought, Being broken up isn't so bad. Losing all desire to work or eat anything other than items extracted from the cacao pod seems to be working out fine. There's lots of great stuff on TV that I normally would have missed had I been burdened by a healthy loving relationship. *Now* I could catch up on a bunch of stuff being a happy twosome had kept me from, like doing my taxes and getting a job and alphabetizing my entire CD collection. I couldn't catch my breath.

That's when I felt it. Glurp. A warm wetness between my legs and the dull ache in my lower back and ovaries. On the TV a lady was running on the beach in a white bathing suit and smiling.

Quickly I wiggled out of my undies and kicked them over to a laundry pile I had started in the living room, the one that

Tallulah had turned into a little nest for herself. "Off!" I snapped as I gave myself a quick wipedown with a kitchen rag. Then I wedged the receiver between my shoulder and ear, wadding up a bunch of paper towels, and held them in place with my legs to catch the flow.

I was ecstatic!

EIGHT
RADIOACTIVATE (DANCE REMIX)

"Take the L out of Lover and it's over."

—The Motels

"Hello?"

"Jasper? It took you so long to pick up I was worried something had happened to you."

"What do you want?"

"Uh, I just wanted to call you and tell you that I just got my period."

"I don't want to do this."

"Well, what I wanted to say was that that's probably why I have been such a bitch lately. And, anyway, I just wanted to say I'm sorry and I, uh, really hope we can work things out because I really want us to get back together. Jasper? Well, anyway, I just thought you should know. About my period. And my bitchiness. Jasper? I really wish I were saying all this to you in person. I just really miss you. I love you so much."

"Are you done?"

"Why are you being like this?"

"Are you forgetting you left about a thousand evil messages lately? This is hard for me, too, you know."

"Why are you crying? Are you fucking someone?"

"I gotta go."

"I'm sorry, I just don't understand why you are doing this to me. I just don't understand why you are doing this. *Please* still love me."

"Stop torturing me."

"I'm sorry. Jasper? What do you want me to do?"

"I want you to say good-bye."

"I'm trying to make sense of things, you asshole."

"I really have to go. You obviously aren't in a place to understand or listen to me so I am going to put the phone down now."

"Excuse me, but I would appreciate a little respect, seeing as how we just spent practically two years together, so just tell me, are you fucking someone?"

"Mer, please. I can't deal with your screaming. It's abuse, you know. Your abusive treatment of me is part of the problem."

"Am I screaming now? No, I'm not. Are you referring to the fact that I express anger at *all*? Because in the entire two years I have known you, you have never raised your voice once and, you know something? You wear it like a fucking badge. You smolder and say nothing and things eat away at you and then you suddenly dump me for no reason, or at least none you can articulate and yet *I'm* the abusive one? Are you gay?"

"Why can't you accept sometimes things just don't work out?"

"Just answer the question, are you *gay?*"

"Why are you doing this? You are ready and I am not. We have gone as far as we can go. You are ready and I am not. That's all."

"Stop saying that!"

"It's over."

"But I said I'm sorry!"

"This is just too painful for me. We can be friends sometime but just not right now."

"Friends? *Friends?* Are you a fucking crack smoker? Just answer that one question—are you high? Are you a crack-smoking *basehead?* I am not your friend, I AM YOUR GIRL-FRIEND!"

"I have to go."

"What about this house? What about your stuff? I met your fucking parents and could still have sex with you afterward, for Godsakes."

"I never told you to get the house in the first place."

"You never told me not to!"

"You never gave me the chance! I have to go, Mer."

"Is this about the sex toys?"

"It's not about the sex toys."

"Because if it is I'll be experimental, if that's what you want. It just seemed like the type of thing you'd introduce ten years into a marriage that's falling apart, but we can do it if you want to. We can do it tonight! Jasper? Are you still here?"

"I gotta go."

"Fuck you. You are going to need a fucking restraining order mister because THIS THING AIN'T OVER!!!"

I slammed the phone down before he could, slumped back down on the couch, and buried my face in my hands.

And why shouldn't I pick a guy like Jasper. Hadn't my dad abandoned me in increments a million times over? I decided I wasn't only mad at Jasper, I was mad at my father, too. And God. I felt abandoned by all of them.

NINE
SADIE TO THE RESCUE

"Running down a dream,
that never would come to me."
                    —Tom Petty and the Heartbreakers

On TV: footage of brave men who flew into the middle of deadly hurricanes to gather data about their severity. "Storm chasers," the narrator said. They showed some shaky footage from inside a noisy cockpit. I could see that the pilot had a wedding ring on.

My own hand was shaking as I hit redial.

He let his machine pick up. I called back around 800 more times, only getting his answering machine. My calls ranged from manic to dangerously calm. I hit redial like a pro, like I was perfecting a dance routine, ra-pa-ta-ra-pa-ta, jazz hands! Until finally the machine didn't pick up anymore. He must have unplugged the phone. I wondered if I was going crazy. I wondered if it was really possible to die from a broken heart. I wondered how long it might take.

I could really feel the cramps starting up. The paper towel rubbed the soft flesh of my inner thighs, making a scratching sound as I galumphed my way to the bedroom. Penguin-like, I flung myself on my bed.

Get a grip, Mer, I thought. Think only bad thoughts. Remember his meat BO, butt acne, and the male-pattern baldness on his legs, not to mention the actual legs. How about the crust in his eyelashes, are you going to miss that?

How about his reign-of-bathroom-terror stench? Can he cook? No, he can't. We know he doesn't bathe. What's so good about him? I screamed at myself inside my head, "SHUT UP! I just love him, OK?"

That's when the doorbell rang.

"Open up, Mer. I know you're in there, I can hear the TV, so open up." Sadie.

I tiptoed back into the living room, and quietly slid the phone a safe distance away. Evidence. Then I made my way to the front door, the tips of my bathrobe ties dragging across the polished hardwood floors. Tallulah followed me with a wagging tail. At the door I adjusted the paper towel wad between my legs, wrapped my robe around me tight, and opened the peephole. Sadie cocked an eyebrow. I pulled on the brass handle and opened the door. My eyes stung from the brightness of the daylight. I blinked and squinted, trying to keep them open.

"Hi, Sade," I said, forcing a smile.

"You look like shit."

"I know." I let my head fall forward.

Sadie rushed the short distance and gently rested my head on her shoulder and began stroking my hair. Her blond locks smelled like honeysuckle. She let me stay like that until her red cardigan was soaked. Some strands from her sweater made my raw nose itch. I backed away.

"How's the transitioning going, mama?" she said. Sadie pushed past me and threw her purse on the couch, spun around to get a good look at the place. She looked at the TV, looked at me, and slapped the poor defenseless Off button. Then she beelined past me and headed for a box in the hall. She dumped out the contents: mismatched socks, a pair of tan suede roller skates I've worn twice, a kazoo, a box of cotton balls, a tin of Band-Aids, a broken wire hanger, an empty CD case. She put the empty box in the center of the living room floor and headed for the black fitted flannel sheet I was using as a curtain.

"What are you doing?" I shrieked.

"Letting the stench of death out." She threw open a window, more light came in. I recoiled like a vampire, "Aaaahhh!"

She scanned the room briefly and headed for the bedroom closet. I followed her. Tallulah followed me. She began gathering up Jasper's T-shirts and boxers and trousers. The green and purple argyle socks fell to the floor. Even with the growing stack in her arms, she knelt down to retrieve them. She wasn't fucking around.

I windmilled my arms. "No, Sadie, what are you doing!"

"I came over here to redecorate and to help you find the will to live."

"That old thing? I lost it a while back." I sounded like an old soused embittered movie actress from the forties.

"Why don't we look for it?" she said, pulling Jasper's clothes off their hangers. "We can just make divining rods out of wire hangers like your mom used to have you do when she couldn't find her car keys." I swung at her and missed. She ducked and the clothes fell to the floor. That was the most exercise I had had in days.

"You know the rules. Number one, throw away everything that reminds you of him." She counted the information out on her bony fingers. "Number two," she made a backward peace sign, "throw away any article of clothing that you would not want him to see you in." I focused on her knuckles. I never noticed how pink her hands were. "Number three—pay attention, Mer—do something new every day, something that you've never done before. Today, I suggest washing your hair. With shampoo." She emphasized the poo part. I wanted her to read aloud from *Winnie the,* and call it a day. "And number four, NO TV! If we must turn to the outside, we deal only in cinema." She swept her palms together swish swish, like she was dusting them off. "I suggest you merely pretend your life is a movie and recast. What you need is a nice rebound screw with a new leading man."

"You're disgusting, you know that?"

"Why, because I tell you the truth? You need a great orgasm from a new guy or a great orgasm and no guy. Either way this calls for screaming O's."

I glared at her. "What I *need* is Jasper back."

"For Godsakes, Mer, he's a Cancer with a Virgo rising and a Gemini moon. You knew it was only a matter of time." She headed unflinchingly toward my bulletin board. I flipped her the bird behind her back. She started extracting photos of him and haphazardly throwing them in the cardboard box.

"Whoa whoa *whoa!*"

"Now now. Trust me on this one, Mer. We are going to have a nice little funeral for him. I will not stand by and watch him suck the life force out of you. From now on this box is a coffin."

"Wait a minute!" I rushed toward her, tried to pry the photos from her dainty fingers. "I don't like the way you're man-handling him."

She fought back hard, guarding them close to her chest. "I never thought he was right for you anyway. Too Passive. Screw him."

I stepped back. "What's that supposed to mean?"

"It's not like anybody liked him. Your family only put up with him because you were *in love*. Please! You put up with this kind of bullshit from someone wonderful, Ben Affleck maybe, but not Jasper Husch." She deposited the photos in the box and headed for the kitchen. I followed her. I could hear Tallulah's little nails trailing behind me.

"But, but . . ."

"The truth hurts," she said, dangling the little tea cup Jasper had hand-painted for me for my birthday last year (when he still cared) from her pinky finger. "But don't kill the messenger." She dropped it in the box.

"Not the cup!" I collapsed in a dramatic heap. I lay down on the cool linoleum of the kitchen floor, black and white squares like a checkerboard. Tallulah licked my hair. I pushed her away. She nudged her stinky chew toy my way and I sat up and leaned against the stove. I thought, Why, God, why me?

"At least he lives in another city. You can make a clean break."

"That 'other city' was my salvation from this hellhole. THAT city is real life. *This* city is illusions and lies." I stood up and followed her around like a basketball safety.

"Then why didn't you move *there?*"

"Because . . . because," I stammered, ". . . my work's *here!* I mean honestly, Sadie." She shot me a look that bored straight through to the core of me. We both knew I could do voice-overs anywhere. Maybe she was right. Maybe I fucked it all up. Maybe Jasper wasn't the one who was afraid of commitment. Maybe I was. I don't know how long I was silent. "Just get out," I said wearily.

Sadie made a face and started to say something but then thought better of it. She just turned, walked into the living room, and grabbed her purse off the couch.

"Sorry," I said.

"That's OK," she said, pretending to be interested in her car keys, "maybe I'm being too rough." I watched her study the teeth of a shiny silver one, fingering the edge of it. Then she put them in her sweater pocket and looked at me. "I just hate seeing you like this. You deserve someone who's going to see what I see in you. What everyone sees. He's a fucking loser, Mer." She looked at the white plaster ceiling and wiped mascara from underneath her lids with her middle fingers, then examined them for damage. "Of course if you guys get back together again, I fucking love the guy."

I managed a small smile.

She took a tiny step toward me. "Just promise me, if you can, promise me, whatever you do, you won't call him. At least let him come to you." I looked down at the floor, noticed a knot in a floorboard. It looked like a woman screaming.

"OK," I said.

"Promise?"

I looked up at her. She was staring into my eyes now, searching for weakness or potential betrayal or at the very least some squirrelishness. "Promise."

"You will feel so proud of yourself if you don't call. If you give in you'll feel like shit and he'll be the winner and he doesn't get to be the winner, so we have a deal, OK?"

I looked outside my kitchen window, spotted a dead butterfly in a spiderweb. "OK, OK, I double-promise."

She ran over and hugged me. "I gotta get back to work but I will check on you when I get a free minute." She giggled. "I'm supposed to be on a run for paint thinner." Then she pulled a small parcel out of her purse. It was elegantly wrapped in heavy-looking brown organic paper, twine, and some dried purple flowers. She tossed it on my couch. It landed upright. She turned back to me, a big mischievous smile spread across her face. "Did I mention how happy I am that we are both single together?" She was actually jumping up and down.

"Sadie, uh, hello, painful breakup alert!"

"I know I know, but whenever you are ready to hit the town, just say the word." She hugged me again and we both heard a wet thud. We looked down. The homemade pad had reached its critical mass and lay bloody side up on the floor. "What the hell is that?" Just then Tallulah came over to sniff the bloody mound. We both burst into hysterics. "No!" shrieked Sadie gleefully.

"Off!" I snapped, still laughing. But Tulie picked it up and tried to make a clean getaway. I grabbed her by her collar and she dropped it. Sadie kicked the thing with her foot. It flew under the sofa. We erupted again. I held my sides. Sadie brushed away streaming tears from her cheeks. With Sadie's help moving the couch, I was able to retrieve it with the broken hanger and deposit it in the trash.

"This is so *Happiness*!" Everything was a movie to her. She air-kissed me on both cheeks. "I gotta go. Try to stay cinematic, Mer. And for Godsakes, don't call him! Make this *your* decision." And she was gone, a rainbow after a hard rain.

I stared at the door for a moment. I could do it. With Sadie's help I could do it. The *new* plan was to make him come to me. He'd have to sweat out *me* not calling *him.*

I climbed back into bed.

"Jasper, it's me, are you there? No? OK, I love you."

For a moment I berated myself about being weak, but I let myself feel awful for only a few minutes. Instead I reminded myself to stay cinematic about all of this and decided, cinematically speaking, that I had been in the equivalent of a terrible car wreck and gone through the windshield and was now hospitalized in critical condition, and if, in my dementia, I cried out for my dead husband, so be it.

TEN
HELL OR HIGHWATER

"I am the widow of a living man."

—Ben Harper

Inside Sadie's package was a book with the title, *How to Get Your Mate to Marry You or Move On*, "written" in a blood-red curlicue font. On the cover was a seventies-style soft-focus photo of a gold wedding ring dangling from the thorn of a red rose. I sighed dramatically before flipping to the three book-marked pages' worth of adventures she had planned for us over the next three months to keep my mind off of one Jasper Husch, super-villain. The list of activities ambitiously included white-water river rafting, karaoke, tap dance lessons, horse-back riding, a cooking course in Italy, a painting course in Spain, an archeological dig in Israel, miniature golfing, go-carting, therapy, and yoga.

Ick.

On the inside flap of the flimsy paperback, in pink sparkly ink, she had inscribed, "This book is my BIBLE! Love, Sadiepop." I adjusted the giant sanitary napkin between my legs and burrowed a little deeper under the covers.

In chapter one of The Book, written by Dr. Karl Sage, Ph.D. (see smiling photo of plump doc inside back cover), he stated, "If the person wishing to make positive change to repair broken bonds and restore The Love Within™ can not show three simple days of self-restraint, i.e., not calling long enough to Let Love Lick Its Wounds™, then the fractured relationship is indeed irreparably doomed."

I read on.

His program was a one-two punch: Out With The Old & In With The You™: "You must be on strictest watch for ninety days." I thought, Can I give Jasper Husch ninety days? No problem. "In addition, try new things! Do something you've always wanted to do Once And For You™. And for both your sakes, have fun because a happier you means a better weeeeee!" Next to all this was a tiny photo of the jolly doctor with someone whom I presumed to be Mrs. Sage. On a roller coaster with their hands in the air. I scratched at it with my finger, smelled the cheap paper. Jasper and I never did dumb fun stuff like go to amusement parks. I read on.

In chapter two of The Book, it stated that there needed to be a masculine giver, a feminine receiver, or else both parties had to remain androgynous in order to ensure Lasting Love™. The FemRe was supposed to respect her mate's ideas and wait for the MasGi to cherish her feelings. It made no difference if the receiver was male or female but no relationship would work if you had both. I thought, Of course! I had been the masculine giver *and* feminine receiver all along. It was uncanny, I was a *type!* If only I had found this book sooner, Jasper and I would be sending out applications to preschools.

I would know if the relationship were salvageable within nine short weeks. Perfect, I thought, secure in the knowledge that Jasper would crumble because, even if Jasper managed to avoid me for eight and a half, my birthday fell within the nine-week window. He wouldn't be able to resist my birthday.

In other words, Mer, make *no* overtures of any kind and *wait* for Jasper to come to *me*. OK, can do.

Several testimonials in The Book bolstered my confidence because "literally dozens" of the RMs™ (retrained males) actually turned around and proposed within the first thirty-seven days when they felt their female counterparts retreat. Ah, but would I say yes? Maybe yes, maybe no. Maybe yes. I let out a little squeal.

When you broke it down, all I had to do was get through the next eight weeks and twenty-seven days. That would be eazy-breezy-telekeneezey! I figured about 4,000 complete listens to an Alanis Morissette album plus sleeping in late would pretty much do the trick.

In some rare but extreme cases, Dr. Karl recommended total abstinence for The Wounded Heart™ in the form of lengthy silent retreats to derail and totally incinerate "those feelings and patterns which magnetize only pain." I shuddered thinking about all the losers that had it *that* bad. Out loud I said, "That will never be me."

Then, without hesitation, I got up and ran to the bathroom to look at myself in the mirror, to look myself straight in the eye and make a promise to myself that very minute: America Ludmilla Odin Throne, you will get Jasper Husch back come hell or highwater, even if it means having the discipline *not* to call him. You will find the strength to have zero contact with him at all costs.

I got goosebumps. I felt like a spy on a secret, important mission to save the world. I felt like I had a purpose! Then I kissed the mirror, spotted and dealt with a blackhead I had missed, and climbed back in bed.

"Hello?"

"Hi!"

"I asked you not to call me."

"I know, I know. I just called to tell you I won't be calling you anymore, well at least not for a while."

"You're calling me to tell me you aren't going to call me?"

"Well, uh, yes, when you put it that way . . . I just . . . I just don't want you to think I'm abandoning you or anything because I'm not. It's just something I need to do. For me."

"OK."

"I mean . . . I just need to disappear for a while . . . Yunno, to take care of me. Also I thought you might want to get an extremely helpful book called . . ." I looked at the book now, turned it over in my hand, shitty font in shitty ink on shitty paper; suddenly it all seemed so pitiful. I felt all the blood drain from my body. "Well, it's kind of got a cheesy title, something like *Getting Love* or *Moving On* or something by this guy Dr. Karl Sage . . . Anyway, never mind, but, yunno, it's pretty helpful . . ."

"Well, good, thanks."

"So how are you."

"I gotta go."

"Yeah, well, OK, me, too. Well, take care of yourself."

"Yeah, you, too."

"Well, bye."

I slammed the phone down so hard Tulie jumped.

I sunk down under the blankets, covered my eyes with The Book, and decided to sleep it all off like a bad dream, but not ten minutes later my mother stopped by out of the blue "just to say hello as I was nowhere near your neighborhood!" I let her in and retreated to my feathery cocoon.

She was wearing a Chinese dragon print dress and red lace-up high-heeled shoes. She managed to look somewhat put together, save some blotches of pink cream all over her face. "What the hell is that stuff?" I said, climbing deeper under the covers.

"Calamine lotion mixed with calendula and aloe. Camphor is great for tightening the pores. That's a terrific book you're reading. Really helpful," she said, pointing. Then, she pulled out three chocolate cream puffs from a waxed paper bag, three because she was superstitious and could only eat things in odd numbers, and arranged them on a plate retrieved from my kitchen. She sat down at the edge of the bed. Her roots needed dyeing. Since my father's death she had made a commitment to a certain shade of auburn. Firehouse Red I believe they call it.

"You went out like that?"

"Who do I have to impress? Fuck 'em if they can't take a joke." She bit into a cream puff and recoiled like she had been socked in the stomach, trying to catch the white goo that snuck out the back with a cupped hand. "Mmm!" She held hers out for me to take a bite. "Don't you want?"

I made a sour face and rolled over onto my side.

"I'd really love it if you came over and helped me organize your father's room." I hated when she called it that. She meant his art studio. The way she said it made it sound like it was the fifties and they were divorced but still lived in the same house. I didn't answer her.

"America, you really have to pull it together here and stop being so selfish." The cream puff clunked as it landed on the dish. I felt the bed give way a little when she stood up and left the room, taking the delicate china plate with her. I heard the fridge door open and close with a vacuum kiss, the jingling of car keys, her high heels against the hard wood floor, Tulie's nails click clicking behind her, then the sound of the front door opening and closing and a car engine starting up.

Fuck you, I thought.

Then I made my way to the kitchen and retrieved the puffs. I set the dish aside and lined them up on my kitchen counter, leaned against the stove and ate them one after the other. That's when I saw the envelope my mother had left lying on the smooth white tile. Enclosed was an article she had neatly clipped from the *L.A. Times* about how the depression of one family member negatively affects the rest of the family.

That, and my blood money check for two thousand dollars.

ELEVEN
AUGUST

"Thank you disillusionment, thank you frailty,
thank you consequence, thank you silence."
— Alanis Morissette

Sadie brought more clothes than she needed for the first three crucial nights. Unsure as to whether I could endure the remaining sixty-two days, eleven hours, and forty-eight minutes, I enlisted her expert help.

Dressed in grey sweats, a white tank top that said "Bitch Goddess," and blue Converse slip-on tennis shoes, Sadie transformed my living room into "a safe workspace." She lit a candle and spread out a bunch of newspaper and art supplies, including a blank spiral sketchpad, glitter, crayons, colored markers, glue sticks, and a stack of magazines for collaging.

She pulled two cushions off the couch and motioned for me to join her on the floor. Reluctantly, I sat down. She put a black disposable fine-point felt-tip pen in my hand and began. "Chapter one, question one: What did your Primary Annihilators™ (your parents) teach you about love and how is this similar to what you learned from your current partner?"

"I really don't see how writing any of this down will . . ."

"Just do it, Mer. How do you think I was able to get over Jeep The Creep so fast?"

"Sadie, you were comatose over him for almost a year." I watched her nostrils flare ever so slightly.

"Yes, well, without this book it might have taken me three. See how I did mine?"

Sadie showed me her journal with the sparkly gold glitter cover. She had graphs and pie charts and collages and quotes and affirmations and articles and photographs and dried leaves and a calendar of tasks including things she had eaten, a happy face sticker for good days, a frowning face sticker for bad days. She had gone the extra mile and had a little gold star on the pages for the days she masturbated, pink shiny hearts for what she called "duty dates," red ones for real dates, and silver hearts for "wink wink nudge nudge" dates. Mostly her book had all four. "For extra credit," she said wickedly, "it just helps take the edge off." It's strange how you think you know a person—Sadie with her book and Jasper with his lies.

"Ready?" asked Sadie, book poised.

"Wait, what was the question again?"

She rolled her eyes. "Just write down what you hate about Jasper in one column and what you hate about your father in the other." I really didn't see what loving Jasper had to do with my father—the only thing they had in common was their profession and perhaps their disappearing-act life-style.

"Sadie, this is bullshit."

"Mer, how do you think I got my amazing job and why do you think I now have the patience to hold out for my dream man. This isn't just about dating, it's about finally living." She flipped her hair behind her ears. "Now start writing."

I stared at the blank page, took a deep breath, then wrote:

THE THINGS I HATE ABOUT JASPER HUSCH:
1. His slowness
2. His silence
3. His underground anger
4. His selfishness

5. His false self
6. His false love, e.g. Guava
7. His lack of communication
8. His star fuckerness
9. His timing
10. His fear
11. His lack of cleanliness
12. His wishy-washiness
13. His lack of commitment
14. His money hoarding
15. His lack of follow-through
16. His spiritual cluelessness
17. His lack of loyalty
18. His lack of sensitivity
19. His sex toys
20. His cats

Then, on the other half of the page I listed:

THE THINGS I HATE ABOUT MY FATHER:
1. His quiet rule when I came home from school
2. His lack of attention to me in my life
3. That I heard my parents have sex all the time and that I was mad that I even knew what an orgasm was at such a young age and worse, that I knew what theirs sounded like, my mother gurgling and pleading like she was dying while my father never made any noise because he had no way of communicating because we couldn't express our disappointment or anger or even joy because strong emotion made him uncomfortable. Plus I have no personal photos of him because I knew how much it bothered him when fans wanted his photo so I never asked. Plus he always gave Public Face in photos anyway and I

wanted his private face. Besides, he thought he was ugly and I look like him so I thought I was ugly, but I also look like my mom but he must not have thought she was pretty or valuable or why else would he cheat on her so much? And maybe that's why I chose men that needed to be babied and coddled and then felt weird when they tried to do nice things for me like when Jasper bought me my favorite toothpaste without needing to be asked I mean we had zero boundaries growing up so how could I be grateful for tiny gestures like the time I gave Jamie Nye a blowjob out of gratitude because he pulled a chair out for me and got my coat he wanted sex and I wanted him to leave so I blew him.

Thanks dad.

I looked up at Sadie seriously. "Next question please." My arm was a windup toy that needed to keep going.

That night Sadie slept beside me in my big bed built for two and I managed my first restful night's sleep in days.

By day three, we had already been to the museum, miniature golfing, and spent a drunken evening karaoking Billy Idol songs until three A.M. I got a standing ovation from three Korean businessmen after a heartfelt rendition of "Rebel Yell." Even though I was sad and missed Jasper like crazy I just kept thinking, "Let love lick its wounds let love lick its wounds." I imagined Jasper licking his big lazy-ass paws after eating the fucking gazelle I killed.

The rest of August went like this:

Tuesday August 15: Go to batting cages with Sadie after work.

Wednesday August 16: Get manipedi with Mother in fancy salon. End up buying $120 worth of skin care products I won't use.

Thursday August 17: Go on voice-over audition for more legroom on commuter flights.

Later go on date with self and play Ms. Pac-Man at local bowling alley. Get hit on by guy who sprays disinfectant into returned bowling shoes.

Friday August 18: Go roller-skating in Venice. Start to feel like old self a little. The self I was before I ever met Jasper.

Later go to pier to ride Ferris wheel. Catch obnoxious couple make out in front of me. Feel like piece of shit because Jasper doesn't want me; despise sloppy couple in precariously dangling car for being in love. Wish their death but fear my own for wishing theirs. Think about Jasper's hairline, behave.

Back on ground, eat cotton candy, feel better.

Saturday August 19: Have picnic with self in park. Finish rereading section on Trying New Things. Deeply understand importance of putting my energy back into ME. When get to part about starting with things I've always secretly wanted to do but was too afraid to dare try, realize answer is *art*.

Decide to keep journal chronicling all the hours Jasper and I endure apart, complete with watercolors, photos, and favorite poems. Take entire weekend to work on with impunity because in heart *know* that someday Jasper and I will be together again and he would more than appreciate how I kept the faith alive, in spite of hardship of time and distance apart.

Take (and later glue in) several Polaroids of myself. Start to get a little crush on self. Under sexy photos of self dressed like Vegas showgirl write "You may be seeing this now and feel bad you hurt me but don't because making this journal has helped me love *me*. P.S. Can you believe you wanted to leave all this?" Feel, I am really changing for the better in ways I cannot see.

Monday August 21: Zip over to casting office on Sepulveda for voice of Morticia Addams–type widow on black comedy cartoon kid show called *Good Mourning!*

Pop in nearby crappy frame store, buy and later glue postcard of Chagall's *The Lovers* on the top of secret journal. Get brainstorm! Decide to *send* said journal to Jasper to remind him of how happy we once were. Remember vital to keep secret from Sadie. Congratulate self because not phoning. Remind self to suggest we both keep one and send it back and forth to keep our love alive together.

Go to OfficeMax and spend rest of savings on necessary materials. Stay up staring and gluing in photos, saved notes, movie and concert stubs, etc. Start to get a little crush on self.

On inside flap of top secret love vigil *livre d'or* write (and even mean) "No matter what happens, even if we are not together, I just want you to be happy." Sign it Bugs and Fishes, Mer. Fall asleep with smile on face.

Tuesday August 22: Have awesome sex dream we are back together. Get up in best mood for the first time in weeks. Go to Kinko's to FedEx IT. Do *not* tell Sadie.

Wait by phone for reply.

Wednesday August 23: Wait by phone for reply. Wonder if he is out of town? Wonder if FedEx guy lost it in the mail? Worry if maybe it fell out of truck? Wonder if someone stole it and saw the naked Polaroid. Call Jasper and leave message asking if he got it.

Later see Spoonie's band and secretly check messages from club seventy-two times. Come home to NO messages. Eat chocolate. Pick skin. Scream at Tallulah. Fall asleep in pool of snot in too-squishy pillow.

Thursday August 24: Wait by phone for reply.

Later have coffee with Sadie at French café on La Brea. Notice bald girl there is so pretty. Bet Jasper would want her. Bet Jasper is fucking someone exactly like her now. Hate her. Spill guts to Sadie. "Writing is contact. Now you have to start the whole nine weeks over!" Fuck. Fuck. Fine. Cry so hard on drive home, almost get in accident.

Come home to a steaming pile of shit. Wonder: Does my house smell like dog? Is that why he left me? Drive to store for ammonia. Eat entire bag of miniature Reese's. Refuse to brush teeth. Fall asleep watching late night talk shows.

Friday August 25, 4:00 A.M.: Discover Jasper has switched over to voice mail. Leave screaming message demanding return phone call, even though cannot disturb his sleep the way he disturbs mine. Burn. Bombard Jasper with messages, e-mail, and faxes demanding collage love journal back, plus all previous letters, photos, etc. asap.

Call Jasper and apologize for screaming messages. Calmly explain he has until sunrise to put things right with me, otherwise no more me, ever. Reiterate sunrise to accept my offer. Hang up and scream at Tallulah for making licking sound.

Friday August 25, evening: Call Sadie and confess everything. Beg her to sleep over. While waiting for her to arrive, pretend I am a dead body at scene of very bloody crime. Pretend I am also the detective. Speak into invisible tape recorder in fakey Raymond Chandler-esque accent: "The body has been identified as belonging to one America Throne; note the cellulite on the thighs like the wing of an airplane caught in a severe hailstorm and birthmark on her ass that looks like Italy."

Receive sudden influx of Pompeii imagery. Think: All that beauty and then Whammo! volcanic surprise. Recognize I am severely depressed when I use phrases like Whammo. Wonder if I am going crazy.

When Sadie arrives, get extensive lecture. Resolve to focus on me, my work, and to, gulp, try *exercising* for a change.

Later burn arm on oven rack trying to make baked potato.

Saturday August 27: Begin Day One all over again. Go on dumb voice-over audition for Charging Bull Beer. Be forced to say "¡Ay caramba! It's double hopped!" Imagine Jasper being speared to death by bull's tusk or antler or whatever they call it, hopelessly paraded around in a colosseum outside Madrid.

Come home and take small walk with Tulie around block three times in a row. Feel strong. Decide: Will never take Jasper back, *ever.*

Hear Tallulah stretch and relax, letting out an adorable high-pitched little breathy yawn. Thank God for her. Cry because I love her so much. Hold Tulie close even though making soul-crushing licking sound.

Later get phone call; find out booked dumb beer voice-over. Begin working on Mexican accent. Eat Mexican food for dinner.

Monday August 29: Record radio spot. Feel like a human again. Smile at people. Take a walk for the first time in eons. Notice the way light hits plants and trees. On drive home hear my and Jasper's song. Sing along to Journey's "Open Arms." Go home to zero messages. Resist *strong* temptation to call Jasper and beg him to come back now that I'm making the sweet green again. Instead doodle self-portrait in black ink on white paper.

I am a fat skeleton monster lady with spots and scales and

flippers and pimples and ingrown hairs and rolls and rolls of stomach fat. I have squinty piggy eyes with dark junkie circles under them and my teeth are rotted, blacked out, and covered in chocolate. I am waving hello with one hand and clutching a wad of steaming shit in the other. A giant erect cock is sticking out of my ass, bloody at the end where I tore it away from Jasper's body. I stand childlike under a palm tree and some twinkling stars. Underneath it all I wrote: *Another Fucking Day In Paradise.*

TWELVE
RADIOACTIVATE (RADIO EDIT)

"Can you help me I'm bent."

—Matchbox 20

"Hey Jas, it's me. Are you there? Pick up if you're there."

THIRTEEN
ROCK BOTTOM JESUS

"It is time for you to
stop all of your sobbing."

—Pretenders

Spoonie received a threatening call from Sadie that I was on
deathwatch and had to be monitored constantly. Because I had
screwed up and had to start the ninety-day plan over AGAIN,
she informed him that it was his duty as a brother to take me
out and "show Mer a good time," including drive *and* treat. I
wanted to go to a desert island where artists didn't exist and die
from eating too many overripe papayas.

Instead, Sadie suggested the W Hotel for high tea, based on
a recommendation she received from the ditzy lead actress of
Beddy Bye for Betty, a horror film about a baby-sitter who gets
stalked by the demonic children she sits for. Since Spoonie had
a crush on the vixen lead, even though he despised idle Hollywood chatter hangs, he thought it sounded like a good idea.
Besides, Sadie promised a meeting with the starlet in exchange
for his good behavior. So, when Spoonie pulled up in his inher-
ited cherry red convertible T-bird (given to our father in
exchange for one of his paintings), and honked twice, I halfheartedly ran down the steps to greet him.

His wheat-colored Beatles haircut was still wet, framing
his face in damp, photo-ready points. He was wearing big
droopy Hawaiian print shorts and a white V-neck. It could be
below freezing outside and he would still be wearing shorts. I,

however, was bundled in a grey cashmere sweater and a pair of jeans. For additional warmth, my long brown hair hung down my back like a shawl.

I missed my brother. We used to be close when I was the only female he worshiped.

"Hey," he said.

"Hey," I said pulling the passenger door open and sinking into the matching candy-apple red leather interior. I gave the door a little slam. It didn't close.

"Camilla wants us to help her clean out the office, so I thought we could go over there first, help her out for like an hour or so, and then . . ."

"Uh, hello! What about Operation Rescue Mer? I'm kinda not feeling up to going through a bunch of old fan mail." I was feeling bad enough as it was. The last thing I wanted to do was hang out in my mother's depression going through my father's belongings, so that we could haul it over to some mothball-infested old-sweater depot so I could bump into strangers *wearing* my dad's shit. I gave the passenger door a firm tug. It still wouldn't close. "I mean, can't we go later?"

"Yeah . . . We can . . . It's just that—" His voice cracked.

I looked at Spoonie. He bit his lip, his childhood body language for something's *really* wrong. "What? What is it?"

"I shouldn't tell you this but, Mustard."

Mustard is our code word for Big Trouble.

Once in tenth grade I had made the mistake of telling Spoonie about a guy I liked who had never tried mustard before. I have always found it charming whenever people have a marker in time that delineates who they were before an event and who they were after, whereas Spoonie finds it instantly pitiful. He couldn't believe that Geoff Smith was so sheltered so as to never have been exposed to mustard. "It was practically used as a lubricant in our household!" Spoonie had said, holding his sides. "Or does he even know what a lubricant is?"

Mustard?

Spoonie took a deep breath now. "I overheard Camilla talking to the accountant and she can't afford to give us money anymore and hasn't really been able to for a while now."

"What's that supposed to mean?"

"Any money she gives us comes from her own savings. She takes it as a flat-out loss. She has to clean out the office so she can figure out what stuff to sell. Like on eBay. Otherwise, she's gonna have to think about selling the house."

"What? Why doesn't she just . . . Does she know you know?"

"No, you know how she is. Even if we confronted her she'd just deny it. As I was leaving she asked me if we'd help her sort through some things to take to Goodwill. I just think we should help is all."

I hooked my hand over the passenger door and lifted the door handle and pulled it toward me. It still wouldn't close. I was really irritated now.

I looked at the clock. 2:00. I felt like a bad child for even thinking of myself at all, but I wasn't exactly anxious to feel worse than I already did AND have all of us staring into the financial abyss (pretending like we didn't know what was really going on). I told myself, Maybe it'll be good for me to reach out to someone else in my time of need. Anyway, by the time we get done helping her we'll still have plenty of time to get tea and make it downtown to visit Sadie without hitting *too* much traffic.

I turned my body sideways and tried to slam the door firmly with two hands now. Spoonie had to get out and open it from the outside and slam it for me. Finally it stayed put. I thought it was funny that it forced my lazy-ass brother to have to be a gentleman.

I looked up in time to see Tallulah's head peering out through the living room window, her front paws resting on the sill. Her ears stood straight up like little black windsocks. She whimpered, "Don't go!" Probably a warning, I thought.

As we sped along Mulholland I prepared myself for the onslaught of chaos and that dizzy feeling I always get as I round the corner and see the front of my family's home: the curling arches of the wrought iron gate vaguely "attached" to a twelve-foot section of an unfinished redwood fence. We couldn't get zoning permission to build the continuous twelve-foot-high wall to surround the house that we actually wanted, so we had to improvise and create the *illusion* of a perimeter. The freestanding structure is now a painted tribute to some of my mother's favorite birds and stands exactly next to four drooping nine-foot blooming cacti on one side and a smallish grove of bamboo on the other. As one arrives, one sees swans, red-tailed hawks, pelicans, owls, starlings, cardinals, hummingbirds, peacocks, and blue jays soaring in the sky, poised on fountains, or perched on low branches overlooking a lake view. It's the kind of thing one drives past and says "What were they thinking!"

I am already annoyed at the thought of setting foot onto the gravel driveway, greeted by our five dogs, two overly friendly Saint Bernards, Lola and Isabelle, a brooding collie named Toast, Erazzmatazzmus, our pug, and a shaky miniature whippet named Mr. Dash, as well as their corresponding piles (which Spoonie refers to as "the security system").

Even with a full-time gardener, Spoonie and I have to cover our mouths and noses with our shirts and make a run for the front door.

"Come quick, Mer! I'm receiving an entity named Cornelius and he has a message for you." My mother was standing in our cluttered, bric-a-brac kitchen next to her psychic teacher Madame Barbara, a woman with Cher-esque jet black–permed hair that came down to her ass. She looked like a midget vampire, save her white Nikes which crept out from beneath her black and purple floor-length gypsy skirt. I glared at Spoonie. My mother always did this, insisted she needed help right away then scheduled something else to prevent either rebuttal, incident, or follow-through.

"I thought you needed help cleaning out the *office*," I said.

"What? Oh yes, all right, in a minute. But first I want you to come in and let me give you both a healing. Madame Barbara has been patiently wresting my third eye open, and with only three sittings, already I'm seeing past lives. Come on in my bedroom, Mer, I want to give you a transition reading."

"Camilla thinks she's psychic," said Spoonie, rolling his eyes.

"Your mother is very psychic for beginner," said Madame Barbara in a fakey sounding Transylvanian accent.

"We all *are*, darlings, if we are willing to open up and *listen*." I could have spit. The last thing I needed was my mother blowing a sanity fuse. She had already graduated as a head chef from her Eat-the-rainbow-for-a-healthier-chakra course and was a master in Mindful Defensive Driving taught by an ex–stunt driver turned Buddhist in some doomsday course about escaping LA should the big one ever hit. "Madame Barbara has studied with shamans and has enabled me to meet my inner wizard!"

"Mother, do you understand that I was dumped via a fax full of *channeled* information?"

Madame Barbara chimed in, "Ooh, find out channeler. You always vant make sure channel iss pure so channel information iss reliable."

"The reader *is* the filter, you know."

"If filter is *bed,* then information is *bed.*"

Spoonie picked up a box of our father's stuff and thoughtfully cocked his head. "Wait, Camilla, so where do you want this?" he said, trying to intercept my mother's escape-hatch plan.

"Uh, actually, put it in the garage so I can go through it again later. Ooh! Cornelius is showing me men dressed in twenties-style bathing suits and curlicue mustaches popping up like jack-in-the-boxes."

"Quick! To *eeling* room!" encouraged Madame Barbara.

"Seriously, Mother, I thought we were coming over here to move boxes."

"Mer's right. What about this one? What should we do with it?" Spoonie pointed to an overstuffed box full of my father's clothes. I recognized a pair of striped hip-waisted trousers and a frilly shirt from the days he would work in costume to blaring melancholy music: Bach, Satie, Howlin' Wolf, John Lee Hooker, the Bulgarian Women's Music Choir . . .

"Oh," said my mother reluctantly, "why don't you load this into my car so I can take it to Goodwill." She looked at Madame Barbara who nodded silent approval. Spoonie mouthed the word *eBay* when my mother wasn't looking. "Take the easel, too, and then come and meet us in my bedroom so I can give you a healing, too."

Watching Spoonie lift the easel made me instantly nauseous. Before I could stop myself I shouted, "Don't sell the easel!" Spoonie shot me a look of death. For a moment tension hung suspended in the air like a high wire trapeze act. "I meant donate . . . because I want it."

My mother cleared her throat. "Sure, of course. You take it, Mer. Now come with me for your healing." Then she quickly grabbed my hand and led me down the hallway past Spoonie shrugging helplessly, past a teak daybed littered with satin pillows, past an altar of seashells and beach glass, past candid black-and-white photos of Spoonie and me as children, past three narrow bookshelves full of our old bedtime books, and past a wind chime with four misshapen emerald green–glazed discs—"planets" from my mother's pottery phase that bore our names: Spoonie, America, Boris, and Camilla in careful black brushstrokes, and a tiny blue one that said Shiva Plum.

My mother stood in the doorway of her bedroom now. Light shot through her dyed red hair from a window near her bed. My eyes drifted past her and focused on a cactus with three black blossoms and a prickly dangling limb precariously held in place by a wire hanger; I looked at my mother again. When she said, "Please remove your shoes and be seated," I obeyed.

Madame Barbara was already battling a black meditation cushion on the floor near a theme rug honoring the animals of the Serengeti. I positioned myself a good distance away from Madame Barbara, who was now skillfully adjusting several items on a converted breakfast tray—some feathers and teeth, the jawbone of a fish, a chipped crystal ball, and a small plate with several cubes of jack and cheddar cheese on toothpicks. She touched everything the way someone with an eating disorder might, arranging and rearranging everything like hors d'oeuvres at a party.

"Go on, Cherushka, ask your mother question."

"This is ridiculous."

"Just ask me," my mother pleaded. She looked so sincere, so passionately dedicated to healing me, even in her own dark time, that for a moment I really believed she could.

I scratched my forehead. "OK, when will Jasper and I get back together?"

"It's over," said my mother matter-of-factly.

"What?" I said bristling.

"She *vont* you to ask *divverent* question. I already tell her is over." I couldn't believe my ears. I couldn't believe my mother was allowing this woman to say such preposterous lies to her and now to me. In our own home. I wanted to storm out of the room, dragging the black-haired ghoul by her cheek implants, but my mother smiled at me so sweetly, I stayed. For her.

"I ask for you," Madame Barbara clucked, "*Meester* Cornelius, spirit guide, *meesteerious* information giver, please tell this girl lady how is coming *so-loose-eon* for broken *art*." She winked at me, congratulating herself on her expert question asking, then she popped a piece of cheese in my mother's mouth. Then, placing a witchy hand on my mother's arm for support, she said, "Now, Marushka, tell Cherushka what you see."

My mother closed her eyes and licked her lips several times before announcing, "Cornelius is showing me some men wearing animal pelts. Dirty men with dirty faces and metal helmets. They're Vikings!" Her breathing became irregular now.

"*Vat? Vat* is?"

"They have raped her and now they are taking her, carrying her on some kind of a pole by her hands and feet, like a . . . like a spit, to roast her. No! They want to sell her on the black market." Even though my mother's eyes were closed, I watched her eyeballs move back and forth very rapidly, under the skin of her lids, blinking several times as if she were enduring a waking nightmare.

I remember going to the grocery store with my mother. She'd hitchhike with me on her hip. I'd loop my arms around her pale neck and study her profile like a prized statue in a museum. People would stop because she was so pretty, with long flowing hair and big doe eyes. Or maybe because of the way her hips leaned forward on her pretty, muscular legs. No shoes. Definitely no bra. She looked fourteen. She still does.

Her feet used to be black and callused from walking everywhere barefooted, walking around on hot asphalt in the middle of summer with no shoes, even when she'd have to come to my school for parent/teacher conferences because Spoonie and I were absent so much. Her feet were hard, like hooves, and her toenails were painted magenta. I can't see magenta without thinking of my mother's toes.

"Good *vork!*" said Madame Barbara coolly, popping cheese into her own mouth. "*Zis* is feeling tone of current predicament. Now ask your inner *vizard* to give you *so-loose-eon.*"

"All right," said my mother meekly, "I'll try. Now the Vikings are untying her from the pole. They blindfold her and place a rose in her mouth and take turns spinning her, spinning her, spinning her!" My mother flung her eyes open suddenly, and lunged forward, throwing her arms around me, as if this was all too much to see and to bear.

"Is good. Is very powerful message."

Upon hearing this affirmation, my mother sat up and brushed her flaming mop away from her eyes, still panting slightly and smiling at me like she had just given birth to something miraculous.

"That's it? That's the message? That's the '*so-loose-eon*'?"

My mother just shrugged. "I guess so."

"Mother, you're like the Magic 8-Ball of psychics. How am I supposed to interpret this?"

My mother looked at Madame Barbara for approval. Madame Barbara patted my mother's hand. My mother sat up a little straighter, looked at Madame Barbara again, and, gaining confidence, said, "Well . . . whatever you're going through, I imagine the solution will . . . involve . . . a rose."

Madame Barbara took the opportunity to pop another pasteurized cube into her cavernous trap. "Maybe *iz vo-man's* name or *lo-case-eon*," she said, talking with her mouth completely full.

"Like the Rose Bowl, which is what we have to pass on our way downtown to see Sadie," said Spoonie who snuck in when I wasn't looking. He stood in the corner with his arms crossed and motioned for me to get up with his pointer finger.

119

"Wait! Mother, do you realize I count on you to be a stabilizing force in my life? How can I when you are practically insane."

"Mer," said Spoonie, lurching forward and gently lifting me up by my arms.

"No, Spoonie, this is bullshit." I watched as Madame Barbara oafishly tried to sidle out of the room on her hands and knees in an effort to retrieve her shoes, but not before grabbing an entire handful of cheese cubes.

"Can I help that Cornelius wants you and Spoonie to help me clean out the office. He says there's a psychic healing waiting there for you, should you decide to receive it! He's showing me a beautiful rose garden this very minute."

"Mother, do you even hear yourself? Did you forget that I am in a suicidal depression? Do you know how awful it is to be left behind by a living person? I'm planning on marrying him!" Spoonie held his breath.

"Then why don't you call him up and simply tell him how you feel."

"I ALREADY HAVE! HE DOESN'T RESPOND!"

"Then why don't you give up all this moping?"

"What a great idea! Why don't you have your inner wizard wave his magic wand and make it happen?"

"Mer," implored Spoonie, "please don't."

"No! She is a fucking grown woman, Spoonie! She doesn't need to fabricate a fucking internal kingdom to try to get control over everything and everybody just because she's too afraid to actually *ask* us for help in this world. Too afraid to *actually* share."

My mother fell still. After a few moments she wiped her eyes with the back of her hand. Finally she turned to me and said, "If you don't want a healing, that's your problem."

That's when I slammed the door and headed outside, and sat on our sloping hillside staring into a half acre of gully behind our house. I sat on the ground, pulled a handful of dried grass, and began tossing it a blade at a time. I watch the movie in my head: I'm nine. We are in our old house. Spoonie and I have just finished picking fruit in our "orchard," three pitiful fruit-bearing trees, a loquat, a plum, and a crab apple. My father is outside putting dry ice into a plastic container. He has rigged some contraption to make smoke come out of the head of some devil-looking guy on the wet canvas he is drying in the sun. "Look!" we say to him, holding our plastic bags open with sticky fingers to show him our loot. "Not now," he says, trying not to burn his fingers. He has one checkered sleeve over his hand and is reaching for a piece of dry ice that has got stuck between the back of the drying canvas and the container resting on a stool. Spoonie does not notice the yellow jacket that rests on the edge of the glistening plastic bag he holds. I swat it away with my own hand and quickly jump back, toppling the wet painting to the ground. "Is it ruined?" I say, burning with terror and humiliation. "Is it ruined?" I ask again. My father says nothing, only quietly turns and heads inside, careful to close the screen door behind him.

I'm twelve. We move into this house. I miss my old friends. I tell my father I am moving to Hollywood to become an actress. So he writes a story about a twelve-year-old girl who is lonely and wants to move to Hollywood to become an actress. He calls her Amelia, after Amelia Earhart because he used to call me Air-Heart because whenever my father was working too much, I pretended to flap my arms and fly around the room to get his attention. The story gets made into a movie but I don't get to play the part of myself because they have to shoot it in Canada to save money. Plus no one has the time to be my guardian. But my father goes, to oversee production, and has an affair with some eighteen-year-old who plays the part of fake me while we stay behind. My mother has to be hospitalized because "his art is more important than his family." A nurse has to come live with us because my mother still won't get out of bed. That's when my father finally comes home.

I'm eighteen. I move out of the house, paying for rent with my allowance. It's my first place. I decorate with hand-me-downs and things I find in junk shops and flea markets. I am starting to see what I look like to myself. My father doesn't come to visit or even call me because he doesn't have my phone number.

I'm twenty-six, the men are wearing cheap grey suits when they lower him into the ground. The pretty lady I don't recognize can't get her umbrella to close. My lips begin to quiver.

I looked up now, stared hard at my father's tree house of an office with its winding spiral staircase and its bare-faced neutrality. To it I confessed that I picked the fight with my mother on purpose. I wasn't ready to go in there.

I heard crunching footsteps in the leaves behind me just then. It was Spoonie. "Do you still want to go for high tea?"

The sun was already beginning to make its descent. I figured it was probably around 3:30. By the time we got over to the W, we would surely hit rush hour traffic trying to get downtown. "Nah, fuck it. Let's just go see Sadie. You can take me for tea tomorrow."

"Tomorrow I work."

"Fine, Saturday."

"I have rehearsal. How about Tuesday?"

"Yeah. Fine. Whatever."

Spoonie started up his engine and we sped along Mulholland in the afternoon sun in complete silence. He waited until he turned right on Highland to say, "Camilla's right, you know." He turned on his blinker and got in the left lane to merge onto the Hollywood freeway.

"Are you trying to hurt my feelings?"

"Mer, Jesus, I'm not gonna lie to you. I talked to Jasper myself. He told me." His words were a slap.

"What do you mean? You talked to him? When?"

"Well, you knew I needed to talk to him because he's done some artwork I'm thinking about using for my album cover . . ."

"Excuse me, seeing as how the circumstances have changed, oh I don't know, only *slightly*, I would have thought you'd have changed your mind."

"Look, he's having a hard time, too, yunno . . ."

"Whoa whoa whoa, I don't believe this . . . I would *never* do that to you."

"Do what? What did I do?"

"Are you high? If someone broke your heart and ripped it out of your chest, broke it into a million pieces, spit on it, and then set it on fire, do you really think I would call them up, see how they are doing, and then help them get some *work* out of the whole deal?"

"Don't be stupid. I would never expect you to stop being friends with someone just because we broke up." I glared at him for three exits, Gower, Melrose, Western.

"Because *I'd* never put you in that position!"

"Shit happens; get a fucking job."

"Fuck you!"

He switched lanes at Alvarado. I crossed my arms. "That's your real problem, you know; you have no purpose, no vision for your*self*. You take money off Camilla and define yourself by whoever you're dating."

"What the fuck are you talking about? You get the same allowance I do; you just have a job at the dumb paint store to HIDE the fact that you're just as privileged as I am. Look in the mirror sometime, privilege boy." My hair whipped around me like a stampede. I tried to wrestle it into two knots about my ears.

"At least I save my money for my real career, thank you very much—while you're out buying furniture or ordering food, waiting around for someone to give you a job, I'm investing in myself.

"I'm just saying get some job, any job until you figure it out. A pet store, Starbucks . . . If nothing else, it'll boost your esteem." I shook my head in utter disbelief. We could have been strangers on a train for all he knew about me, or cared.

I faced him now. "If I'm such a fuckup and you're so great, why don't you move out!" He tightened his grip on the steering wheel, wouldn't speak. I turned away from him and rested my chin on the passenger window. I could smell the leather oil from the side panel. The ends of my hair snapped at the corners of my eyes as we drove past a mural of anguished faces and raised fists. In the painted crowd I could pick out Rosa Parks, Malcolm X, Dr. King, Che Guevara, Gandhi, and that guy with all the grapes. They knew what I was talking about.

"What?" he said.

"I didn't say anything."

He changed lanes again, exhaled loudly. "Look, I didn't take time off work to fight with you."

I turned and struck like a cobra. "No, you just took time off to meet Lila. The whole world stops for a beautiful woman, doesn't it, Spoonie. You're just like Dad!" A lie. His jaw muscles tightened.

He veered suddenly, careful to avoid rear-ending an Alfa Romeo that darted out in front of us, then downshifted. "All I'm saying is get over it, Mer, the guy's totally moved on. Sometimes things just don't work out."

I closed my eyes and swallowed hard, felt the cool of the wind against the stinging heat of my cheeks, and tasted salt.

FOURTEEN
OTTO-EROTICA

"Ooh these little earthquakes.
Here we go again."

—Tori Amos

When we arrived downtown, I headed, on foot, past a silver and white meal truck, past rented trailers with humming engines, past train tracks, cracked windows, and abandoned warehouses in the opposite direction of Sadie's set.

My father used to have a loft space down here. That was in 1979, when I was ten, during his loner phase. He used to get dropped off and stay for weeks at a time. No phone. I would help my mother prepare picnic baskets of goodies for him: liverwurst and mayonnaise on sourdough toast, tomato soup, sardines and smoked oysters in oval tins with a little key. Sometimes he would eat only one thing for weeks so he wouldn't get distracted. While he was gone I pretended he didn't exist or lived in Siberia. We had the house to ourselves. That's when we could make all the noise we wanted. But when he came home we had to "Can it, kiddos" during the day because he was too sensitive to light and sound and needed to sleep. The art show was called *One*. It was a flop.

A plastic bag blew past me. I kept walking.

Past old lampposts and alleyways strewn with trash until I came to the Mom & Pop Kaffeehaus, a trendy art gallery slash coffeehouse. A welcome mat was embedded in the sidewalk. "Come on in," it said. I did.

Inside, mounted on the back wall was a giant painted portrait of a punk rock mom and a biker dad with a handlebar mustache. Their eyes glowed with tiny flickering orange lights. On a little gilded plaque underneath, it said: Mom and Pop. The floors were polished concrete. The light picked up the odd stone or a splash of spattered paint. A local artist's tribute to the human vagina, in dried beans and pasta, was on display in crudely made plywood frames. Derivative, I thought, probably a fan of my dad's. In the corner, Billie Holiday made the jukebox's neon rainbow blink on and off.

I walked up to the counter where a handsome dark-haired guy in a tattered woven cowboy hat, grey T-shirt, and army pants made a perfect pitcher of frothy foam. He looked familiar. I couldn't help but stare. "That's for here, right?"

"Excuse me?" I said, confused.

He turned and caught my eye and I blushed. "Oh, I thought you were the other guy." He looked a bit like Tom Hanks, only hairy. I noticed a massive wad of black chest hair protruding from his neckline. "What'll it be?" he said as he placed two large cappuccinos in blue ceramic mugs on the counter.

"A hazelnut latte," I blurted. It came out sounding southern so I pretended to be looking for something in my purse, sneaking a look at the hot guy behind the counter as he ladled thick white foam with a teaspoon without watching what he was doing.

Just then a skinny man in painter's pants, John Lennon glasses, and saddle shoes put a wad of money on the counter next to the tip jar that said SUPPORT COUNTER INTELLIGENCE and scooped up the two cups. "Keep the change." His voice was higher than I thought it would be. "By the way, dude, your band completely rocked the other night." The hot guy behind the counter smiled and nodded and said "Thanks." Any crush I could have on either one of them dissolved with the utterance of the word "dude."

The bespectacled stranger smiled at me as he turned to go. Out of the corner of my eye, I noticed he had a rose patch on the butt of his pants. I felt faint. Why wasn't I wearing more makeup or something less boxy? Could either of them see my sweat stains? Could they tell I'd been crying? I pushed the thoughts away. I did not want to feel new feelings about guys.

"Two-fifty," said the hot counter guy as he faced me.

"You look familiar," I said, knocking over a sugar dispenser. Fine white silt covered the counter. "OhmygodI'msosorry. I was aiming for my drink!"

"Whoa," he said, scooping it into his cupped hand. "No problemo. Do you need some sugar?"

I thought, More than you know. "No, I'd better just drink it like this. I don't really trust myself. I've had a pretty shitty day. I've had a pretty shitty month actually. My boyfriend just dumped me." Idiot. The words hung in the air like rotting meat. Like that squirrel that got trapped in the bush outside Jasper's back window. We found it upside down, tangled in a patch of thorns. It must have struggled for hours before it died.

"Then this one's on me."

"No, that's OK." I reached inside my purse.

"No, really. Maybe that way you'll come back and you won't be a stranger next time." He put the blue ceramic cup on the counter along with something sweet wrapped in a napkin. I pulled a strand of hair from one of my loopy ponytails and blushed some more. He smiled. On the juke, Janis Joplin belted out "freedom's just another name for nothing left to lose." I took this as my cue to go.

I got as far as the first table when he said, "Oh hey, take a flyer!" He was stretching sideways across the counter. His shirt pulled up a little and I could see a small patch of black hair against the smooth pale skin of his stomach just below his belly button and a massive sweat stain under his right armpit. I leaned in. He smelled like metal, like a man. "Here," he said handing me a small red piece of paperboard with black writing on it. I grabbed the corner of it, careful to avoid skin contact; I blushed. "My band is playing Thursday night. Come check us out." He slinked back in place. He rested his elbows on the counter and flopped his chin in his hands. He tapped his face with his long fingers and smiled again. I blushed some more and put the flyer in my purse without looking at it. I smiled quickly, then looked at my shoes, which were now pointed toward the door.

"Bye," I said, when I was safely outside.

"Bye," he shouted back.

The sun was setting now. It bathed the dirty buildings in golden light. I thought of the colors in the little paintings my father made in his travel-size watercolor books during his trips to Italy. I walked back with my testosterone-infested cappuccino and the wafer the cowboy gave me for free and realized I had accidentally stolen the blue cup. I wasn't even about to go back there, not after all the dumb stuff I said about being dumped.

"There you are! Shit!" Sadie said loud enough for people with walkie-talkies to stop and stare. I could tell Spoonie had told her everything by the way she embarrassingly fawned all over me like a cuddly octopus. She grabbed the napkin with the remainder of the wafer out of my hand and stuffed the treat in her mouth. "I was looking everywhere for you. I wanted you to say hi to that producer I was telling you about but he already left. He totally wants to meet you. I showed him that photo of you in my wallet." Then she leaned in close and whispered, "Divorced."

I was insulted.

"I happen to still be in love with someone, Sadie. I can't even *think* about somebody else." I let a punishing silence pass between us, then smiled.

Sadie looped her arm underneath mine and pulled me toward a standing wooden structure at one end of the massive darkened echoey converted soundstage. "Come along." Just then a hot guy wearing a massive tool belt sauntered past us and smiled.

"Jesus, it's guy central down here!"

Sadie smiled and waved at him and then pretended to be waving away something smelly in front of her nose. "Passaroo, I tried. He's Ack Dack."

"Sadie, as if! What's Ack Dack?"

She rolled her eyes. "Ack Dack. ACDC. Yunno, he swings both ways which is slang for don't bother because he's bi."

"Sadie!"

She swatted me lightly. "Sheesh, don't get your knickers in a twist!" she said, leading me over big extension cords held down to the concrete floor by thick black electrical tape, toward a large plywood structure. We peered around the side of it. "Voila!" she said, showing me the set she had masterminded: a children's bedroom dripping with a thick red gloppy syrup, over twin bedspreads and clothes and children's books and brightly colored building blocks.

The bloodbath had other sentimental touches like strewn shredded teddy bear parts and limbless Barbies and a pink music box turned on its side. Its tiny dancer clumsily twirled in time to the sad, twinkly droning. The overall effect was haunting. I was impressed. It looked exactly how I felt.

Sadie then led me through the fake seventies-style, blood-coated living room set. There we ran into two more hot guys in paint-splattered overalls painstakingly making two chalk outlines on the blue AstroTurf carpeting. Two actors dressed like plainclothes cops smoked while they waited patiently to dust for fake fingerprints.

"Wanna sit down?"

"Sure."

"Not here, this is a hot set."

We headed toward the catering truck now where we found Spoonie deeply engrossed in a conversation with the double-D, slightly more attractive female version of Peter Lorre in a powder blue sweater set. She had a bloody knife sticking out of her right shoulder, which really complemented the gash above her eye and blood-drenched hairline of her shoulder-length black hair. They looked nauseatingly adorable.

Then, in a loud whisper, Sadie said to me, "I really think you might like Jym, at least for a rebound screw."

"Sadie!"

The actress turned and spoke up now, soft as whipped cream, "A-B-C, 1-2-3. You always have to replace a someone with a someone." She smiled warmly and offered up her hand for me to shake. Instead I shot her my most evil look and, before I could be introduced, loudly said to Spoonie, "I'll be waiting in the car."

Later, when Spoonie and I drove away from the faux massacre in silence, I realized that, without Jasper, my life had been reduced to hocus-pocus and fake blood. I looked over at Spoonie.

"That wasn't cool back there, Lila is really nice." He looked peaceful in his twenty-two-year-old hormone-infested rock-'n'-roll universe.

"Why don't you just date Tulie, at least she has a personality."

He looked at and through me, as evolved people who happen to be your wonderful, smarter, more together, handsome younger brother tend to do and said, "I see someone's in a better mood."

FIFTEEN
CAMEL GATEAUX

"F.U.C.K. is that how you spell 'friend' in your dictionary. Blackon black, guidebook for the blind . . ."

—XTC

The view outside my window was a pointy pagoda-like roof and a guy banging away at an old car. That's what my neighbor does for a living. Hits that car. At least that's what I deduced on my first day of being thirty, as I watched a shirtless, ultra-tanned white-haired Frenchman test to see if the metal on the one side of his maroon Ford truck from the forties was as loud as the metal on the other side.

It was.

I had managed to make it to day sixty-five without so much as a hiccup. My plan was to stay home and pamper myself; that way I'd be close to the phone when Jasper called. For my birthday.

However, my hopes of sleeping in late were dashed. I sat up on my knees, rested my elbows on the windowsill, reached under my nightie, and pulled the left side of my white cotton undies out of my ass. At least it wasn't alarm day.

That's when he enjoyed playing the "what if" game. What if I jiggle the door handle, does the alarm go off then? Yup. What if I put my foot on the back bumper? Yup. What if I sit on the hood? Yup, again. I didn't know much about car thieves, but I couldn't imagine them casually leaning against the passenger window, which, as it turns out, also set it off.

My head throbbed in time to the automotive beating. Bang bang bang. One for every day Jasper had not called or written or faxed. It didn't matter, though, because today was my birthday, he'd call.

Entering thirty with a bang, I thought, as I made earplugs out of Kleenex and slunk down onto my belly. My pillow smelled like my new peony and seaweed–scented shampoo, a recent purchase on a "Me Date" at Fred Segal's, along with a prebirthday impulse pair of shiny yellow patent leather trousers I planned to wear to dinner with my mother and Spoonie later that night. I had bought them without bothering to try them on.

The phone rang.

Jasper!

"Hello?" I said, accidentally jamming Kleenex farther down my ear canal. "Ow!" pulling the tissue free. "Hello?" It was only Sadie, calling on a staticky cell phone.

"Am I the first?"

"Yes," I sighed, "you're the first." I examined the twisted pointy end of the tissue for any amber-colored residue.

"Oh goodie, then I'll sing! Happy bir—" Her cell phone died. I stared at the phone for a moment before placing it back on its cradle. I waited, then picked up on the first ring. "Mer, I'm heading over the canyon, this phone's about to die, so what's the deal? Are we still on for seven?" I set my dirty tissue on my bedside table.

"Yes."

"A *real* seven? I know your mother's involved."

"Yes, a real seven!" I was shouting now because she was.

"What are you going to do today?"

I patted down some air pockets in my duvet. "I'm probably just going to hang here and spoil myself rotten, yunno, stay in bed, read, take a bath, maybe . . ."

"You're not waiting around for anyone to *call*, are you?"

"No," I said singsongy, tipping my hand.

"Because he probably won't, and you might want to prepare yourself for that possibility. Because, I mean, he hasn't called you in over . . ."

"Well I think he will!" I said defensively, pulling a loose thread from the edging of my pink cotton nightie near the armpit.

"Yeah, and it might rain popes. Anyway, I'm just saying . . . Why don't we go out barhopping and get you laid?"

"Sadie!"

"Hell, get us both laid. Have you been masturbating regularly?"

"Sadie!"

"Semi-regularly?"

"Sadie!"

It was true, I had been wholly unable to even think about pleasuring myself. For what? I'd only fantasize about Jasper and what would be the point? It depressed me, but mostly I feared I'd die of heartbreak *and* be caught in a gutter with my hand down my pants. I stared at the peeling pansy sticker on the little yellow chest by the side of my bed. Inside that drawer was a small purple-and-white tube full of lubricant Jasper had brought home once when he tried to talk me into letting him fuck me with a Coke bottle.

"Are you still there? I guess that's a *no*. Mer, do you even want to get better?"

"Yes, I do, but . . ."

"Well, eventually you're going to have to *kill* that super piney feeling and the only way I know how to do that is new Boom-Boom. Yunno, replace a cock with a cock. Like those squirrels. How 'bout a male prostitute?" What squirrels? Her phone cut out. She called right back.

"Goddamnit, cell phones are annoying! Sorry Mer, I'm

analog now. You don't have to sleep with anyone tonight, we could just get some new drive-in-size fantasy going . . ."

"I don't want a new fantasy, I want . . ."

The phone went dead.

I lay there staring at the peeling pansy sticker. I ran my finger over its surface, felt the difference between the paper and the painted wood; then I absentmindedly tore a small corner of it off, put it in my mouth, and quickly spit it out. I opened the top drawer and reached my hand in. I fingered the small tube of lubricating gel.

Suddenly I'm seven. I have just fallen in love with a blue-and-white rubber-soled round-toed sneaker. I like the front nub, its hard round flat surface pressing up against my soft and bony peeing place. Bonk bonk. I kind of smack myself with the front end of the shoe, which only a few moments ago was a convertible car that Barbie was driving to meet Ken. As I knew nothing about sex, save the sounds I overheard in my parents' bedroom, it was merely an awkward bumping that made me feel a little tingly. It would be years before I would discover the pool-heating jets while attempting to push off the side like an Olympic swimmer.

I dropped the tube of clear goo back in its tomb and closed the drawer.

I clasped my hands in prayer. Aloud I said, "Please God, please make Jasper call because I don't want to boink boink diddle diddle myself, not on my birthday." Tulie scratched at the inside of her crate. I got up to let her out. I felt a little ill.

"Good Tulie, potty potty potty," I said as I watched her find a spot on the ivy-covered hillside through my kitchen window while I poured dry dog food into her chipped ceramic bowl. "Good potty."

•   •   •

When Jasper loved me, on my last birthday, he put a whole universe together for me complete with my favorite music, tiny hanging lights, and the scent of geranium oil. He lined the floor with a trail of tea candles that I followed to the bedroom, where he had covered the bed with rose petals. In the middle of the bed lay a single gift, a painting he had made in secret, just for me. Of Tulie wearing a queen's coat and holding a scepter. Then we made love until the sun came up.

I reached over, grabbed the lube from the drawer, wriggled out of my undies, bit the plastic top off the purple-and-white tube with my teeth, spit it across the floor, squeezed some clear gel onto my fingers, and reached my hand down underneath my nightgown. Sadie would be proud. At first my hand halfheartedly probed my dried flower arrangement like a clumsy left-handed seventh grader. After a while I got the hang of it again, and peeled back the soft folds of skin between my legs, and lightly traced circles around the small fleshy arid hills with my gooey index finger. I kept my eyes closed, ground my hips into the mattress in slow circles. The phone rang. I let the machine pick up. It was my mother.

"Happy birthday, baby girl! It's Camilla calling and I have a surprise for you! Are you there, birthday girl? Pick up if you are there. Mer, darling? No? Darn. I wanted to pop by with your surprise! Oh, I'm giving it away." I got nervous just thinking about it.

"Baby girl, are you screening? OK, well, I'll just see you when I see you. I'm not going to tell you what it is, but you are going to love it. Bye-bye." Maybe she was picking Jasper up from the airport! I resumed probing.

But the phone rang again.

"Mommy loves you."

I buried my face in my pillow. Slight turnoff.

•　　　•　　　•

I am full-on masturbating when they arrive. My mother and her "surprise"—an unmarried Asian couple dressed like bankers and a whory-looking younger female counterpart acting as their translator. They had come to assess where the energy in my home was blocked, because, for my birthday, my mother had arranged to have my house feng shuied.

I had no time to wash my hands, only to leap up quickly, slip my undies back on, and blushingly let them in. They tried to insist on "Western handshake" but I managed awkwardly to offer up my sinless hand instead.

"May we come in?" asked the hooker translator. My mother mouthed the words: Are you all right? I blushed, nodding, I'm fine as I led them into the living room.

With a guilty game-show hand reveal, I said, "Welcome!" The couple walked around, tapped out numbers on a flat black compass as big as an atlas, and calculated the four directions in relation to the exact hour of my birth. They kept tsk-tsking at each other as they peered into every nook and cranny of my home, opening and closing doors, studying ceilings and corners, walkways inside and outside the house. After a half hour of intensive snooping they stopped to give me the first of several pieces of "*goo* news."

"They want me tell you, you will never have a *goo* relationship unless you cut down tree in front of house. Otherwise you always single lady," said the slutty translator with the drawn-in mouth and teased-up, brittle, oranging hair.

"I'm sorry, they want me to what?"

The translator made a scissors-cutting gesture with her index and fuck-you finger for clarification. "Cut tree or you single lady forever."

I turned to my mother. "They want me to chop down a more-than-hundred-year-old tree so I can *date* again?"

She smiled, nodding.

The translator made the scissors gesture again. "Cut, then

you happy in man love." They all looked at one another and smiled and nodded. They had all contributed to ruining my life and they were smiling.

"Arso, in bedroom must get rid of bed. Arso, must keep bathroom door close at all time. Arso, if possiboo, sleep in closet if you want have career success, otherwise bedroom fine." The translator bowed. I was outraged. I looked at my mother. She looked serene, as though pleased that the wisest of elders were completing a more than helpful transmission.

The banker couple said something else in Chinese. "Arso," said the translator, "buy fountain and get rid of mirror." The couple looked at each other and shivered, then looked back at me and smiled. "Arso your Neptune in Scorpio say no no alcoho."

"That's true!" My mother shrieked. "We are all allergic to alcohol. It runs in the family!" My mother smiled proudly. The three strangers huddled together and whispered something else. I waited for the translator to garble out some more helpful news. Her eyes widened; she looked at me with what I perceived as real pity.

"What? What is it?" I said.

Solemnly she said, "They want me to tell you so sorry but Neptune arso rule anesthesia, so no no plastic surgery."

I glared at my mother, then looked back at them. "Anything else?"

The translator smiled warmly. "Most important cut tree otherwise no husband. No husband, no kids. No kids, no reason be alive. No reason be alive, no happy grandma." She bowed at my mother, which started a wave of them all bowing at her. My mother blushed and clutched at her heart like she had just won an Oscar.

"Yeah, I get it," I snapped, losing all sense of decorum. I wanted to throttle my mother. Didn't she agree that all of this was a depressing pile of fraudulent insane? A giant, stinking sack of untrue? Or worse, maybe they were dead right. Maybe they all knew what I couldn't admit to myself: that I was destined to be alone, forever.

"Do her fortune!" my mother pleaded. "What about her career? Any chance of success in acting?" They had almost already gotten three-quarters of the way through the front door to leave. The old man turned now and took my hand before I could refuse. "What about her acting career?" my mother said again.

"Oh no, very bad. She bad at business and she bad at acting. She bad at relationship and she bad at know how to be happy."

My mother's face dropped. "That's what I always thought."

I stomped my foot. "Well, is there anything I *am* good at?" I heard myself say, giving *all* my power away, "What *should* I be doing?"

"Work with color. You very *goo* talent for art. Paint bedroom color of *rose*, very healing for you." It sounded like lose. I thought, Unfuckingbelievable, what is it with these con artist people and their fucking roses? "*Goo*-bye!" they said, bowing and bowing at me.

"Good-bye," I said smiling. This time they insisted on Western handshake and won.

I wondered if I would go to hell and if it was justified payment for such awful information. I actually thanked them before they drove away, but not before overhearing my mother confess that she, too, always thought working with color would be very therapeutic for me. Since fucking when?

By two o'clock I had transformed my house into a mini–day spa. I had steamed and scrubbed and cleaned my pores, shaved my legs, painted my toes, and was feeling a little cute in spite of the fact that Jasper still hadn't called. Yet. Then and there

I courageously decided that feng shui is for Chinese people and not for America the country *or* America the person.

By four o'clock, still in my bathrobe, I had cleaned my floors, sinks, and toilet bowls spotless, curled my hair, and started my makeup.

By six o'clock, the sun had begun to set and Jasper still hadn't called. (I must confess I was starting to get a bit worried.) I picked at an ingrown, ate a loaf of bread and an entire stick of butter in the name of toast, and looked up "break-up" in the dictionary: "Dissolution. Separation of things into its parts. Decay, esp. Death, the termination of an assembly or Partnership." One word away from "break out": "to become infected with a skin eruption"—the thing I couldn't seem to stop doing over Jasper and, oddly, exactly next to "break-through," the thing I wanted more than anything in the world.

Finally, Sadie and seven rolled around. And even though there was still no sign of Jas, I slid into my new pants as Sadie had given me implicit orders to wear something sexy. Sadie kept saying the words "duty dating" like she was the General in the Dating Army in the war against being single. To improve the odds, but hoping for some evens, I slapped on a little shiny red lip gloss.

"How do I look?"

Sadie covered her mouth with her hand. "Oh my God."

"What?" I said as I speed-walked over to my full-length mirror. My plastic thighs rubbed, causing a slight friction burn. I took a long look.

"Very action-based, very *Matrix*-esque," she said enthusiastically. "Now what shoes?"

All I could see was the way the pants made my hips flare, my stomach droop over the top, and that they went straight up my crotch. "I don't know, Sade."

"Well, I do. Come on, you look gorgeous!"

She took me by the arm and led me into the closet, grabbed

a pair of high-heeled purple boots I got downtown for ten bucks, and off we went.

At the fancy Chinese restaurant (my mother chose), I spotted her and my brother and the girl from the set sitting in a large black leather booth. My brother and the actress stood up to let me and Sadie slide in. The actress introduced herself. "I'm sorry we didn't get a chance to talk on set the other day; you seemed a little distracted. I'm Lila." I smiled politely and shook her hand, then glared at Spoonie. Then Lila bent around me. "Hi, Sadieface!"

"What's up, sistamama!" said Sadie somewhat nervously.

Lila pointed. "Did you see that our produ . . . ?" Sadie coughed, shook her head. "Oh . . ." said Lila winking.

I could not believe my eyes. How dare Spoonie bring her to my fucking birthday dinner. A fucking winker! How dare Sadie, too, for liking her.

My mother attempted to make pleasant conversation.

"Isn't it remarkable that we're all single? You, Sadie, and I? Spoonie will probably end up married before either one of you two!" said my mother. Lila blushed. Sadie squeezed my hand. I looked up and through the ceiling, at God, and thought, What makes my mother like that? That's when my mother's cell phone rang. She just handed it to me, nodding knowingly. I froze. Who could it be? Jasper? The president? An *alien*?

Tentatively I took the phone. "Hello?"

"Are you and that nice Jasper engaged yet?" It was my grandma. Calling from her boat in Hawaii.

"No, Grandma," I said, dying of humiliation and embarrassment to be on a cell phone in the middle of a restaurant, "we broke up."

"Men are bastards, always taking their halves in the middle before turning around and dying on ya. The only thing they're good for is the frequent flier mileage. Ha ha ha. Get him some water, will ya Joe? OK, gotta go, someone's choking. Grandma loves you, baby girl. Happy Happy."

I wanted to call my machine to see if Jasper had called yet, but I was completely surrounded, so I just handed the phone back to my mother.

Around and around went the lazy Susan; spare ribs and fried seaweed, orange peel chicken and beef and broccoli in oyster sauce, fried rice and eggrolls, and wonton soup.

Then came the presents. I got a journal and colored pencils and a DVD of Lila's last movie, even though I don't own a player. The card said "Love Spoonie *and Lila.*" My mother gave me a red knit blouson with capped sleeves and a dragon on it (that I'll never wear), a check for thirty dollars (one for every year!), and a hummingbird feeder ("to feed the bird-lings!"). Sadie gave me a giant translucent purple vibrator. As I tried to stuff it back in its velvet pouch, Sadie loudly announced, "It's called the Grape Ape! I got it at the Hustler store!" Just in case the people in the back of the restaurant couldn't see it.

When the chocolate crème brûlée came with the single candle in it, I blew, wishing for Jasper back.

When I opened my eyes I saw wisps of smoke rise up past the blackened candle stem. Then, slowly, tiny sparks began to flicker and the candle blinked itself back to life. I blew it out once more, praying that it would not be so, that I would not have the type of family that would think I would find this remotely funny. The more I blew the harder they laughed. Lila took mini-Polaroids. That's when my mother announced, "If I ever date again, the next boyfriend I have is going to be black." I buried my face in my hands, stared at Lila through the web of my fingers to study her reaction. Spoonie's new girlfriend, who couldn't tell if my mother was joking or not. Instead, she just snapped another photo.

I excused myself, and waddle-ran to the bathroom. Sadie followed too closely behind me. The way those pants were rubbing I could have started a goddamned fire. Sadie grabbed my arm. "Wait, Mer, I want you to meet someone," she said, waving to a blond gangly giant with clunky black Elvis Costello glasses and a soul patch at six o'clock. "Look! It's Jym Court the producer I've been telling you about. Isn't this a coincidence?" Jym waved back and motioned for us to come over.

I shot her a look. "Yeah it sure is a coincidence. How come he brought a date?" Sitting next to him was a gorgeous amazon. I recognized her from the magazines. A model.

Sadie bit her lip, then blew it off. "Who cares about her, come on." As we zigzagged past the ultra-hip in comfortable chic, the pants made an awful friction sound, causing some people to turn and stare.

"Jym, this is America. America, Jym."

"Nice to meet you," he said.

"Nice to meet you *both*," I said. The frail girl's hand went limp in mine, but her eyebrows were perfect. Then we all smiled politely back and forth at one another. Sadie squeezed my hand three times indicating the three-seconds duration of eye contact she required of me. I could only stare at the ground and cross my legs because I was suddenly desperately aware of how much the model wanted us to disappear (a good sign) and of how the fabric of my trousers was creeping up inside me like a karate-chopping hand in reverse.

"Well, again, it was nice to meet ya'alls," I said and bee-lined for the bathroom with Sadie in tow.

As the bathroom door swung open, Sadie whispered, "Now can I fix you up with him?" I don't know if I burst into tears because she was treating me like it was really over between me and Jasper or if it was because she wanted to fix me up with a guy who dated models or if it was because I caught sight of the girl in the mirror who was out publicly and could easily win the award for the deepest camel toe contest.

I feigned illness and waited in a stall until Sadie was gone. I rested my head against celadon-painted walls. Jasper shouldn't have set the bar that high. He shouldn't have painted my dream; that's the kind of stuff people don't recover from, not if they are me. Then I checked my messages on the payphone in the bathroom to see if Jasper had called yet.

He hadn't.

"Do you want me to come up?" Sadie asked when we pulled up to my house just before midnight.

"Sure," I said, meaning no. Even from the window I could see that the red light of my answering machine wasn't blinking.

We sat cross-legged in silence on my living room floor, she with a pillow and me with a battery-operated digital clock and the phone in my lap. Sadie looked at me like I was dying of a massive gunshot wound to the chest and didn't want me to find out.

"He might still call," I said.

"I know," said Sadie.

We watched the clock. 11:56, 11:59, then 12:00.

"Are you OK?" she asked. I nodded. You could hear crickets all the way up the canyon. "Well, I should probably get going." I nodded again. Sadie stood up and went to the kitchen to grab her car keys. I followed her in on my knees.

"Please call him for me, Sadie, for my birthday. I just want to hear his voice. Pleeeease?" I clasped my hands together.

She paced around in my tiny kitchen, then swung around to face me. "What do you expect me to do?"

"I expect you to be my friend. Just call and hang up, that's all I'm asking. I just want to hear his voice. I don't even care if we get his machine."

She crossed her arms across her chest. "What if he answers?"

"Hang up. Pleeease?"

She began to pace again. "This is all a little too *Girl, Interrupted* for me." Then she stopped, put her hands on her hips, and looked up at the ceiling, then back at me. "Ok, I'll do it. On *two* conditions."

I stood now. "Fine, yes, anything."

"One, you go on a duty date with Jym."

I crossed my eyes. "Fine, yeah, whatever, and?"

"And two, that you see Dr. Karl Sage, in person, and do EXACTLY what he says."

"What if he says, Hang in there, Mer, Jasper is totally right for you?"

"He won't."

"What if he does?"

"Fine."

"Fine," I said. Sadie shook her head. "Come on, Sade, I just have to hear his voice. I can get over him if I just hear his voice."

Sadie rolled her eyes, held her hand out for the phone. "What's the number?"

I grabbed my phone, punched in the crazy math, and handed her the phone. We leaned in close. He answered on the fourth ring. "Hello?" he said. He sounded happy. "Hello?" he said again. In the background I could hear a giggling female voice say "Who is it, baby?" It had a British accent. Sadie hung up.

The room was spinning. Not only could he live without me, he *preferred* it. I clutched at my stomach. The muscles in my belly cramped. I felt a rush of hot liquid in the back of my throat. I ran to the bathroom, locked the door, and puked.

Sadie knocked on the door but I didn't answer.

I pressed my forehead to the cool of the tile wall, listened to the flushing toilet settle itself. For round two, I let my hand rest on the rim of the toilet. In my head I watched a *Saving Private*

Ryan-esque movie trailer starring me: Speedy flash-cut images of me kicking in a door of a thatch-roofed hut only to find Jasper and his slut, writhing bodies on satin sheets in OUR bed, and me spraying them with machine-gun fire. I thought, Now I'll just have to pretend you are M.I.A., Jasper. You are dead and I'll never get to see the body to say good-bye.

Only he wasn't dead.

I wanted to scream but no sound came out.

Instead I knelt forward and threw up dinner and my entire existence. Sadie just kept knocking on the door. "Mer, open the door. Mer, please answer me, are you OK in there? Maybe he'll call you tomorrow," she managed brightly "Mer?"

After a sharp intake of air through my mouth, my breath plateaued and settled into small aftershocks of air. I fell still. Finally I stood, opened the door. "He's not gonna call." I sniffled, turning a piece of toilet paper in my hand over and over.

"Well, maybe he'll . . ."

"Sadie . . . don't." She just nodded her head and looked at my shoulder, brushed my hair behind my ear. "Are you OK?"

I stared at the floor, wiped my nose and mouth with my already damp paper-thin tissue, then folded it into a perfect square. "Yeah, I'm OK."

PART TWO
LET THE HEALING BEGIN

SIXTEEN
BOO WHO

"With my naked eye I saw the falling rain,
and I knew if I said it all, I would be free again."

—Luscious Jackson

The bearded man with pointy shoes came out to welcome me. I hated him on sight. Pointy shoes? Please. No wonder they only took photos of authors' heads. Plus, he looked much more jovial in person, all shiny wax-apple smiles and dimpled cheeks. His eyes were actually twinkling.

I was disgusted as I followed Dr. Karl Sage, Ph.D., into his "office," which consisted of a forest green couch full of pillows, a navy blue single bed littered with stuffed animals, and a rolltop desk—a shrine for Kleenex. Against one wall stood a sturdy-looking oak bookshelf. It bragged five shelves of dense-looking tomes; some of the soft covers had titles like *In Search of the Shadow Self* or *Raising Your Own Inner Child* or *Unearthing the Hero Within Using Dreams, Symbology, and Garlic.* There were rocks, seashells, crystals, dream catchers, and a small god's eye with red and green and orange yarn wrapped around two Popsicle sticks. A large window revealed three neat rows of bustling streets and a glimpse of the Pacific Ocean. On the wall near Karl, a couple of official-looking certificates, a painting of a ship on a stormy sea along with some cheesy aphorism about endurance, and a brass clock so I could watch the fifty spendy minutes tick by. On the table next to me sat a digital clock for the good doctor to watch himself grow a hundred and twenty-

149

five dollars richer. The whole room had a masculine nautical hippie feel to it. Not at all my type of setting. I preferred something womblike, in varying shades of cream, egg, and white, with pretty photos of tree-lined roads leading to a distant but hopeful future. Certainly some flowers, maybe even a tea set complete with a small tin of almond biscotti.

God, his shoes were pointy.

Sure, I bought his book and read it cover to cover, but that was me dissecting *him*.

"How are you doing?" asked Dr. Karl with the compassion of a weeping saint.

"How am I doing?" I said, adjusting my buttocks into the too squishy confessing couch.

"Yes, how are you doing right now?"

I crossed my arms across my chest. "I'm doing fine, just fine," I said, inspecting the fabric of the couch. I traced the raised paisley pattern with my mind's eye.

"You seem agitated."

"Do I?"

"Yes." He cocked his head thoughtfully. "When we spoke on the phone, you mentioned several things. Maybe we could start with the breakup and feelings of extreme depression, OK?" I nodded almost imperceptibly. "So, do you wanna tell me what's going on?"

"What's going on?"

"Uh-huh. How's the body?"

I clenched my hands into fists. "You mean other than what I already told you? Other than I hate my life because my boyfriend dumped me and I have no real career and my best friend wants me to stay single forever and my mother drives me nuts and my brother's life is perfect, not to mention that I have fantasies of murdering my dog when she makes a certain annoying licking sound?"

"All right now." He laughed. He had the most intelligent

eyes. I could tell he was really listening to me, really seeing me, possibly without any judgment whatsoever.

Gross.

I fought back tears of gratitude by finding a little resting spot for my tongue in my back left molar. "I want my boyfriend to love me and he doesn't. He doesn't want me. This world is so fucked."

"And what does that remind you of?"

I looked at him, brushed my stringy wet hair behind my ears. Karl handed me a Kleenex which I took greedily. "It makes me think of God and how He doesn't exist, and how even if He did, all He likes to do is ruin everything. All He likes to do is take away anything good."

Karl scribbled something in a small spiral notebook with a fancy maroon pen.

"What are you writing there?"

"This?" He looked down at his notebook. "Oh, these are just my own personal notes, so I can keep track of anything that might bubble up to the surface. I keep them in this filing cabinet right here." He gestured to the file cabinet under the desk. I squinted at him warily. "But you can look at them anytime you like. See?" He turned to show me he had written on the powder blue lined paper: "depression over loss of male love, probably dad" in loopy chicken scratch. "All right now, you were about to tell me what that reminded you of."

"Is that supposed to make me feel safe, you showing me those notes? Fine, my father," I said coldly, hiding my nose and mouth behind the damp tissue. "That's who it reminds me of, my *father*."

"Can you tell me a little bit about him?"

"But what about my boyfriend?"

"Let's start with Dad since that's where the imprinting first occurs. Did you know that's where it begins?"

"Uh . . . yeah . . ."

"What's your father like?"

I eyed him suspiciously. Hadn't he heard of my father? Didn't my name sound familiar? Didn't he know who I was? If he knew who my father was, surely we could get this over with in one session. "My father's dead."

"Oh," said Dr. Karl warmly. "Well, what *was* he like?"

I stared him down. "Oh, he was just a brilliant genius, that's all. Yunno, he painted a bunch of stuff, got a bunch of awards, wrote a bunch of stuff, got a bunch of awards, built a bunch of stuff, then dropped dead, leaving us all behind." He scribbled something down on his little pad. I kept my arms crossed, eyes at half-mast.

"Oh, OK so, he *was* the famous painter. I'm sorry, I know very little of his work. I remember seeing something about him once on PBS or hearing something on NPR. His work was not really my taste, very graphic, very sexually explicit, is that right?"

I nodded. "Some of it."

"You seem angry. What did you mean by 'leaving us behind'?"

"Nothing." I brushed the steel blue carpeting forward with my foot, brushed it back.

"It doesn't sound like nothing."

"Why didn't you like his work?"

"Let's focus on me some other time. Today is just for you. Did *you* like his work?"

"What, the painting, the writing, the elaborate stage designs, the performance art?"

"Sure, any of it."

"You mean as a kid?"

"Yes."

"Well, as far as the art went, I liked some of the colors. Mainly they embarrassed me. The early stuff, anyway."

"How do you mean embarrassed you?"

"Well, yunno, close-ups of vaginas and anuses, people copulating, penises being inserted into vaginas or anuses or ears or whatever. It freaked a lot of people out, including me, and I still had to behave *nice* in public and be *supportive*. At age seven. Some of the buttholes were so close up they looked like flowers, so they didn't bother me *as much*."

"Tell me a little bit about his creative process."

I sighed as though bored. "Well, he'd have his friends come over and sit. Well, not really friends exactly, because my parents didn't have any of those, uh, so I guess students or models really. Well, they wouldn't really sit, mostly they'd be naked on all fours on our kitchen table or stuffed in the dishwasher naked in some yogic posture or something. Then my mom or my dad would photograph them from all angles and they'd either come back and 'sit' some more or become my dad's . . ." Angrily I made air quotes with my fingers, ". . . friends."

"Why did you make air quotations just then?"

"Because. While they'd work slavishly long hours, I'd be downstairs helping my mother prepare food for all of them. His studio is behind the house I grew up in. It's like a tree house with a big redwood deck, and I'd come up there with fancy tea sandwiches we had painstakingly made on a silver tray and I'd find them all naked, all over our things because my dad had decorated the 'set' with stuff from around the house, like my toys, blow-up sex dolls, porn comics, the American flag, our dishes and blankets and forks and clothes and whatever. Once he did a series of acrylics based on nude photos he took of me and Spoonie, when we were tiny. He painted these tiny nude children on everything. Household stuff: soup spoons, plates, a baby doll of mine, an old TV, a can of bug killer. Me tiny and nude on an old black phone. It totally freaked me out that someone else was going to buy tiny me and take me home to their house. Of course critics thought it was some deep commentary on the decline of communication and commodification of society or something. It was pathetic." I laughed. "I wanted to be a secretary when I grew up."

"What else?"

"Nothing else. Just big droopy naked-ass bodies all over all our stuff, just your basic all-American orgy scene." I thought I detected a slight frown beginning on Karl's face. I crossed my legs and shifted my weight onto my right hip. "We didn't have a lot of money then, so we had to kind of use stuff from around the house, yunno, share stuff." Karl's shiny pen moved across the paper. I scratched at a nonexistent itch on my throat. Did Karl think I was weird? Did he think my parents were weird? Was my upbringing weird?

" 'Stuff,' " said Karl.

"Pardon?"

"You mean like your own personal toys and personal belongings?" My face reddened.

"Well, I mean, all for the sake of art, yunno." I nodded and smiled uneasily. Dr. Karl just continued to look at me with a blank face.

"Were your parents naked, too?"

"Oh God, no. Never!" I thought, Phew, I'm in the clear. I continued confidently, "The only time my parents were ever naked was when we were all alone in the house. *Then* they would walk around naked." I smiled.

Karl frowned, shook his head, and began scribbling violently.

"Hey, what did you just write? Is it bad?"

"No, no, I just made a note to myself about some of the things I suspect we're going to be targeting in our work together here—your negative response to explicit visual stimuli, the fact that you weren't protected from inappropriate stranger nudity or inappropriate parental nudity, a lack of object constancy coupled with narcissistic parenting and improper reality mirroring . . ." The room began to spin. I felt claustrophobia, like the walls were closing in and squeezing my helpless history self right out of me. I wanted to run outside and get some air.

"How did all that make you feel? How did sharing your toys with strangers make you *feel?*" Dr. Karl asked, handing me a stuffed koala bear.

"I felt, uh, angry. Is that what you want me to say, I felt angry?" I said, unconsciously pulling at the bear's ear. I was angry with Karl now.

He rested the tablet on his knee. "America, I want you to tell me whatever is true for you. I'm just here to help YOU." Dr. Karl smiled. "If you felt angry then, that's how you felt. Is that how you felt, angry?" I wished he'd stop smiling.

"I wished everyone would die and one day my father did. There. Are you happy now? Are we done?" I had practically twisted the ear of the koala bear clean off.

"Could you talk to him about your feelings?"

"NO! Weren't you listening? I couldn't talk to anybody about anything."

"Was there ever a time when you could? Tell me about reaching out to your daddy. Tell me about your daddy being there for you." I looked outside the big window and stared into the vastness of a perfect blue sky I couldn't feel.

I'm twenty-six, the men are wearing cheap grey suits when they lower my father into the ground. My grandmother's lipstick smudges the edge of her white glove. Spoonie balances on the sides of his shoes. It looks like his feet are praying, only his shoes need to be polished. I don't say any of this to Karl. Instead I push the feelings away and watch a seagull fly past, dropping something it holds in its beak.

•   •   •

"What does all this have to do with my boyfriend?" I said, tearing at the corners of a tissue.

"I don't know yet. What did your boyfriend do?"

My eyes narrowed. "He's a painter."

"Like your father? Look, America, I am going to save you a lot of trouble. What do you want?"

"What do I want?"

"Yes, what do *you,* America, want?"

"I want Jasper back."

"Besides Jasper."

"I want my father back."

"Well. They aren't coming back so pick something else."

"What do you mean?" I roared, pounding my fists into the sofa.

Karl smiled. "Would you like to do a rage exercise to move some of the blocked energy around?" Before I could say no, he motioned for me to move to the floor by the bed with all the rest of the stuffed animals. Somehow I did. "Great," he said. "What I'd like for you to do is to lie down and slap your tail-bone into the ground."

I blew my nose. "What?"

He turned to pour some hot herbal tea from a silver thermos into a coffee mug that said NUMBER ONE DAD. "I'd like to have you lie down on the floor and slap your tailbone into the ground." He turned back to me now, smiling even more warmly than before.

"Yeah, no, I heard you, I just don't . . ."

"It's an exercise I have you do to help unblock some of the trapped first and second chakra energy at the base of the spine. It's actually based on what little children do when they are having a temper tantrum." While he spoke I watched the steam from his herbal concoction spiral up behind him. It made a little wispy halo around the back of his head. "Your survival and identity issues are hidden in your tailbone and this exercise is sort of like turning a little key which opens up a little door there and relieves some of the trapped negative feelings. Compacted rage, self-loathing, hopelessness, despair."

"But in the book you didn't say . . ."

"I work a little bit differently one on one. In fact in extreme cases, I'll go so far as to recommend nine-day silent retreats to really purify the emotional body and face the dragon head-on, so to speak." I thought I might faint. Did he think I was that bad off? Did he think I was An Extreme Case? "Would you like to lie down and try it?"

"I had no idea floor work would be involved. I don't even belong to a gym." Karl reached out to hug me. I hissed like a cornered animal. Karl looked worried.

I buried my face in my hands and convulsed in big 7.5 quakes. Karl handed me a new box of tissues. My hair fell down around me, protecting me like a cage. "I just want to not be in pain anymore. I just want to be able to let Jasper go and be able to move on. I want a different ending, I want my life to begin." I felt Karl tentatively rest his hand on my back. I wanted to swat him away but I didn't.

After a while Karl said, "I'm sorry but our time's up for today but we can get right into this next week if you'd like." He stood up now and moved toward the door. I looked up, panic-stricken, then ran interference by blocking the door frame with my arms.

"But why is all this happening to me?" I said, eyeing him hungrily.

"America," he said, folding his hands politely at his crotch, "sometimes we choose prickly people to make us feel yucky feelings so we can uncover old hurts and be pointed in the direction of our wholeness; that way, we can start to feel our happiness sprout real roots . . ." He exaggerated his face to punctuate words, scrunched up for "prickly" and "yucky," smiley for "wholeness" and "happiness." ". . . because eventually we are only going to be interested in finally seeing our true selves, grounded, in an expectationless reality." The way he said it, I knew it was probably trademarked or would be soon. "But we can talk more about this next week if you'd like."

"But how am I going to get through *today*?"

"How 'bout a homework assignment?" he said brightly.

I made a face. "OK."

"One, make a list of all the things you love about Jackson, the positive qualities you associate with him."

"Jasper."

"Jasper. Then make a list of all the things you love about your dad. See if you can notice any similarities between Jameson and your father, any patterns. This will allow you to see if you can have the positive qualities you associate with them in your life, on your own. See if you can start to give those things to yourself."

"Jasper."

"That's right, sorry. And Two," he aimed his fingers at me like a gun, "take long walks. That will keep the blocked energy moving until we meet again. And Three, I'll let you in on a little secret," he was whispering now, "sometimes when we start behaving like the person we are so mad at, there's a little pot of gold waiting for us at the end of the Anger Rainbow, so you might want to think about picking up a paintbrush between now and the next time we meet. It might be very healing for *you* to start painting. Of course, call anytime. You did great work today."

Me? PAINT?

He unlocked the door. Then he held it open for me like a real gentleman, saying, "America, if you continue to work like you did in this room today, in no time at all you won't even be interested in entertaining situations that aren't in your best interest." He pressed the little grey card with silver writing into my palm, patted me on the shoulders, and declared, "All right now."

•   •   •

The brightness outside stung my eyes. I couldn't stop blinking. The sun made little iridescent prisms in my eyelashes where the salt had crystallized. I thought, So this is how it is. Pay someone not to have enough time for me, then, when I get better, in about thirty years, I will finally make good choices. For me. Yes I felt angry! Angry that my father had all this time for all these freaky naked people who touched all my things and rubbed their stupid smelly-ass fat cocks and cunts all over everything. All over *my* things. I didn't ever want to see those things or those people ever again. And there it was, The Finished Product. The horrible memory frozen in time for the whole world to see and everyone that saw it said it was fucking wonderful, and, oh, how neat that your life was so free, not like society with its soul-crushing *rules*. Lucky you, America, to know true freedom all the time!

I looked at the business card and wiped my nose on the fabric of my long, loose-flowing skirt, then tossed the card in the trash. The sea air hit my nostrils once more and I felt like little sparkles of light were trying to burrow themselves into my lungs.

When I got home I checked my messages. Habit I guess.

Then I flopped down on the floor in the living room, and unconsciously unclipped the black disposable pen from the spiral binder of my journal, found a clean page, and drew a little hairy octopus suffocating a pink-cheeked cherub of a girl, writing the things I loved about Jasper and my father on the long, strangling tentacles:

His appreciation for music, color, air, trees, light, eyelashes, legs, dancing, eating, sleeping, not sleeping, anything fun, his humor, his

159

mind, his commitment to himself and his creativity no matter the distraction, his belief in himself no matter the criticism, his focus, his kindness, the way he was so patient with his freaky fans, his ability to actually enjoy himself, the way he did everything so expertly, in his own way in his own time, his smell, his hands, his hugs, the way he loved me unconditionally, and how happy I felt when he loved me.

Together Jasper and my father owned everything good in the world. Did I think I could provide the same things I associated with being loved by them for myself? No, I did not.

SEVENTEEN
FREE DUMB

"Tossed in to my mind stirring
the calm, you splash me with beauty and pull me down
cause you come from out of nowhere."

—Faith No More

"Based on Jasper's body type, the way his neck lurches forward and the way his shoulders kind of collapse in toward each other, I can honestly say that this relationship was doomed from the get-go," said Karl the following Thursday.

In the photo we are sitting on a low stone wall. Jasper is wearing a pair of ripped-up jeans and a too-small crewneck olive-and-grey vintage wool sweater and Birkenstock sandals with thick orange socks. I am wearing a pink flowy dress with big red hibiscus flowers and a pale blue knit beanie my grandmother gave me. I have my arm around him. I am smiling broadly. Jasper's eyes aren't open all the way and he looks like he just got a whiplash brace off. It's the best one I have of us together.

"Just looking at how skinny his calves are I can see he isn't equipped to handle your anger and intensity. Eventually you would have left him."

"Really?"

"All right now. Today we are going to find out where *not good enough* lives in your body so I want you to just breathe." I sat up.

"Before we begin I just want to say how great it is to realize that I have merely transferred my pain onto Jasper when really it was my father who caused it all along and I'm totally willing to transfer it all onto you so we can get down to business." I smiled. Karl looked at me with a straight face, thought better of saying anything, and silently passed me the Kleenex box.

"Why don't we go inside and just *breeeeathe.*" I closed my eyes again, folded my palms in my lap, and let out a massive sigh. "Now imagine you are on an internal jungle *safari.* You are walking through a dense, but lush, tropical jungle looking for where not good enough lives. You hear the crunch of leaves under your feet. You brush vines out of your way. Ooo-oo-wah oo-oo-wah." He made a distant jungle monkey sound. I peeked an eye open, arched an eyebrow, saw that Karl's eyes were closed, so I closed mine back up again. "Where is not good enough hiding? Oo-oo wah oo-oo-wah. Come out, come out wherever you are! Where does not good enough live in the body. Woo hoo! Come out of your hiding place." I bit the inside of my cheek, thought, You can do this, Mer, just surrender . . . "We are gonna pull you out by your roots today, so don't be shy!" I imagined it, all right, me wearing a pith helmet, hacking through uncharted territory with a large machete, through the tangled vines of all my negativity to get to the glowing bejeweled source, swap it for a bag of sand and run like hell so that the boulder didn't get me on the way out. My mother would *love* this guy.

"Just relax and keep breathing. Now imagine an emotional Geiger counter scanning the landscape of your vessel." I rolled my eyes even though they were shut tight. I thought, Sweet Jesus, he's obviously a quack who tricks you the first session and then completely snaps for round two. "All right now, can you tell me where not good enough lives, America?"

"Uh, it's definitely in my belly." I was feeling kinda bloated from lunch and was expecting a period, so it wasn't completely untrue.

"Great. Now just breathe into your belly and when you're comfortable, tell me what you see." I didn't exactly know how to breathe into my belly; all the same, some images bubbled up, of my chicken Caesar, half order of spaghetti, and three cappuccinos. Then another, of me putting his grandkids through college while my condition worsened, came floating up right behind it. "Anything?"

"Nothing yet."

"You're doing great. Keep hacking!"

I opened my eyes. "Are you sure this really works?"

"Well, you are a little tougher than most, so why don't we send for backup, intensify the quest so to speak. Why don't we have you stick your legs straight up in the air and point your toes toward your nose." I paused, stared at the diplomas on his wall, and swung my legs up above me.

"Good. This activates several meridians along the backs of the legs and inner thighs. Just let the blood gently cascade down your legs and pool into the lagoon in your belly." I felt the blood moving toward my hips now. It made me feel a little queasy. "Just keep breathing, America, breathing and pointing. Let me know when the images start to surface."

"I'm seeing something!" I said suddenly. It was true. "I'm standing in the sun by the stairs near my old public school classroom. I'm ten! I'm running my fingers over my greasy forehead. I have pimples. A ton of them. They just keep erupting. I keep my eyebrows raised to stretch the skin so that the redness disappears. It makes me look like I'm in a constant state of surprise. Everyone notices that I am slowly becoming a large pepperoni pizza. The kids yell out various toppings whenever I walk by." I heard Karl scribbling.

"Go on."

"I'm so self-conscious, I start wearing a baseball cap to school to hide the inflamed whiteheads and scabs. One day I hear my mom and dad fighting because Spoonie and I never see my father who is always in party mode when he's away and too tired to play with us or too busy working until he can party all over again. I overhear her tell him to at least try saying hello to me for a change. I sneak into their room to tell them I'm gonna be late. My dad pulls my hat off my head to kiss me and grimaces. He didn't know my skin was so bad."

I told Karl I felt rejected, rejected like I felt when Jasper wouldn't pay for dinner or make love when I wanted to, like when Jasper left me and refused to speak to me for no reason at all, rejected like when my mom accidentally told me she didn't want kids in this lifetime, like when my father stayed away too long or didn't make time for me. Like when he died too soon, too fucking soon.

Karl said things like I should focus on me, on my career, on my boundaries. That he thought it would be great for me to stay open to dating so I could practice being a girl and allow myself to be nurtured. I was to let the man pay for dinner no matter how uncomfortable it made me, accustomed as I was to going dutch, or picking up the tab entirely.

And so it went. Week after week little salty pools formed in my ear canals. No matter what I confessed—dropping out of school and not going to college like I wanted, sneaking food, lesbian orgasm dreams—he was always supportive, ending every session by saying "All right now." Then I'd leave, clutching a Kleenex at my leaking face, feeling like a slightly lighter wreck than the week before as new concepts began to fall into place like a train station schedule board.

Back in my car, I'd feel defeated. I'd start the engine up and tell myself, Just hang in there, Mer, someday you won't feel anything for Jasper at all.

By the time I got home it would hit me. I'd rest my head on the steering wheel saying: I am alone and this is my life.

●　　　●　　　●

"Mer Mer Mer? Are you there? Pick up the phone, Mer, I gotta talk to you! Mer Mer Mer?"

I dropped my purse and ran for the phone. "What? Sadie, what is it." Tulie took this as a cue for playtime. She ran and grabbed her tennis ball, held it in her mouth, nudged it at my kneecaps.

"The girl at the restaurant with Jym?"

"Huh? Oh, yeah?" Tulie dropped the ball at my feet, looked up at me. "Off, Tulie! Off!" I whispered. She scooped the ball up in her wide mouth and skulked off to her little bed to suckle her ball.

"The model Jym was with?"

"Yeah?" I said with mounting impatience.

"It's his ex."

"So!" I snapped angrily.

"So? So we have a deal."

"Sadie, he's fucking his ex-model girlfriend. Why are you calling me?"

"Wife. It's his ex-wife."

"Whatever." I rolled my eyes, began to look through some mail I had left lying on the kitchen counter. Bills, bills, coupons, missing children, and a postcard from my old friend Michael with a Rumi poem and a stamp postmarked Tunisia.

"Apparently he dated *Rose* in college."

"Wait, what? His ex-wife's name is ROSE?" A rush of adrenaline flooded my system. I screamed.

"I know, I know! He's-in-New-York-for-a-week-but-then-he's-coming-back-and-I-gave-him-your-number-and-I-hope-that's-all-right!" I screamed again.

"Sadie, what if he calls me?"

"He's probably gonna."

"What if he's my soulmate? What if he's my husband? What if the reason Jasper dumped me was so I could meet—" My phone clicked. "Hold on, Sade." I clicked over. "Hello?"

"Hello? America? This is Jym Court calling. Your friend Sadie gave me your number."

"Oh my God."

"Is this a bad time?"

"No! *No!* I mean, I'm just on another call right now." The phone crackled and echoed with fancy hotel long distance.

"Oh, well, I can phone you back if . . ."

"No!" I shrieked maniacally. "Hold on." I clicked back over to Sadie. "Jesus, it's *HIM!*"

"Oh my God. Oh my God!"

"What should I do?"

"Talk to him!"

"Now?"

"Yes!"

"What should I say!"

Lightning fast she said, "Just be yourself. Just be normal. Then call me right back!" She hung up.

I clicked back over. Calmly I said, "Hello Jym, it's good to hear from you." What was wrong with me? I sounded like I was wearing a skirt suit.

"Uh, well, the reason why I'm calling is I was wondering if you might be interested in joining me for some supper." Some supper! *Supper?* How positively civilized! I held the phone to my heart, then put it back to my ear. ". . . I mean if you're available then," he said.

"Oh my God, I'm so sorry. When?"

"Or, another night if that one's bad."

"No, it's probably fine. I just need to know when you mean, exactly."

"Well, I meant this Saturday, but it could be next Saturday if you'd prefer . . ." And risk him getting a girlfriend by then?

"*NO!* This Saturday's great!" My eyes went big as saucers. Jesus God, I don't believe it, a date with two days' notice, like a gentleman, like in the olden days, like out of a fairy tale, like

166

out of a movie! Holy Christ! Calm down and breathe, Mer! I lowered my voice. "Well, great. See you then, Jym. Good-bye."

"Wait! Where shall we meet?"

"Oh my God, I'm sorry, I'm in the middle of eight million things . . ." I smacked myself in the head. Idiot.

"I could pick you up if you like?"

"Fine!"

"Great! Well, I'll call you Saturday morning to sort out the details. Are you a morning person?"

I bit my finger. "Oh, yeah, totally!" Tulie looked up at me from her little daybed, then put her head back down.

"Saturday, then!"

"Saturday it is!" When I put the phone down I screamed again and ran over to give Tulie a little squeeze. She hopped up on her hind legs and we danced around like a couple of maniacs. Then I flopped down across my bed without crawling under the covers and went over the call blow by glorious blow. I'd call Sadie soon enough, but right now the moment belonged to me! Jym Court called me. Jym Court called ME! From NEW YORK! Jasper never would have done that.

Or if he did, I'd be worried the whole time that he was spending a fortune calling me from a hotel. Of course, if it were Jasper he would have told me to call him back and pay so he could save his money. Not Jym.

I wanted to call Jasper and tell him everything, but I knew he was not a friend to me. Not anymore. I could be consumed with thoughts of Jasper no longer, not when I had Jym to think about. Suddenly I didn't feel like staying home.

I picked up my journal and took a drive. My plan was to find a coffee place and just WRITE. I was so spaced out and drove for so long I ended up all the way downtown, so I decided to go to the Mom & Pop Kaffeehaus.

•   •   •

167

It wasn't until I walked through the door that I remembered I had stolen a cup the last time I had been in there. I wanted to turn and leave, but before I could the guy behind the counter recognized me and shouted, "Hey I remember you! Hazelnut latte, no foam. You stole a mug last time you were in here!"

They had changed all the art around since my last visit. Now it was all portraits of puppies, bunnies, kittens, and a baby monkey with a cast on his tiny arm. The show was called *Fluffy Things*.

"Wow!" I blushed. "Ohmygod, I'm so sorry, I completely forgot. How much is it?" I reached for my wallet.

"Don't worry about it, it's on me."

"No no, really, I'm not like that!" Then I thought about Karl's orders to receive and ordered an Earl Grey and said thank you instead.

While he separated the leaves from the tea with a white plastic and mesh strainer, he said, "Yunno, I'm reading this really interesting article on the lotus blossom and all its uses and about how scientists are studying its surface to learn how to make a better house paint because nothing sticks to their petals. That's why they were selected, for their spiritual significance. Did you know that?" He smiled and put the tea on the counter. I smiled back when I noticed he had poured it into a paper cup. "Milk and sugar?"

"Half and half."

"It's really cool." He put a metal thermos full of half&half in front of me.

"Huh?"

"The article."

"Oh."

He watched as I poured in threeish sugars from a free-flowing sugar dispenser and stirred my tea. "So, how's it hanging."

I thought about Karl and his instruction for me to practice

boundaries. "I don't mean to be rude but I don't really feel like company right now." Karl would be proud.

"That's cool."

I scooped up my cup, walking in time to Shelby Lynne on the jukebox, and plopping down at a small table, began writing in my journal:

America Court. America Court.

I practiced doodling my name with his last as my own.

Jym and America Court.

It looked kind of awful but who cared.
I worked on a hyphenated version instead.

America Throne-Court.

While Bob Marley belted out "Redemption," I perfected the transition from the capital *J* to the lowercase *y*. I didn't put a tip in the jar when I left or even say good-bye. When I got home I found out I had booked another voice-over. I thought, Rewarded. For all my good growth.

•   •   •

Later that night, lying in bed, I thought, Jym with a *y*. Jym with a why the fuck not! Then I thought about the lotus blossom, and about my parents' hippie friends who ditched their last names and took a whole new last name entirely. Jym and America Lotus, because nothing sticks to them, because they are untainted, like us.

EIGHTEEN
OWLS

"Talk talk talk yeah, birds talk to me."
—Crowded House

At 11:47 A.M. Jym called to square the pickup time. I almost burst into tears when he asked, with real interest, how I was doing. To know that I was talking with a man who I was not paying who still wanted to know about my feelings.

For the rest of the day that followed our nearly twelve-minute call—when I wasn't busy daydreaming about what our children would look like or wondering whether he'd make a good father (this I vowed to find out at dinner)—I noticed how amazing plants and animals and the sky and birds were.

But by 7:22 P.M. it had all worn off and I was becoming more and more socially unstable with every revolution of the second hand.

Wholly unsure of how to behave or fill the remainder of time without my head exploding off my body, I realized that my entire life hung in the balance, that if things went well with Jym, it meant I was indeed moving on and away from The J.H.I., *but* if things went lousy, I was destined to be alone and miserable for the rest of my life. Sadie gave me implicit orders to wear something sexy or she would personally off me.

A few things make me feel sexy: tights, not pantyhose, but tights. I love how they made my whole lower half one stream-lined package. (I feel taller, skinnier, and sexier.) A G-string under a flowy skirt also does the trick. Big balloony dresses with

thick men's socks to the calf and clunky shoes, preferably platform, work, too, as do overalls and really well-worn T-shirts. All
of these things were in a large discard pile on my bed.

Finally, I put on a saffron-colored blouse, hoop earrings, a
favorite pair of bell bottoms with a sixty-nine patch on the
back pocket, and a pair of motorcycle boots and looked at
myself in the mirror. Jasper always seemed to think this outfit
was attractive, so maybe Jym would, too. Then again, maybe
Jasper didn't really like my clothes at all and that's why he
dumped me. Maybe at thirty I just wasn't sexy anymore.

I quickly changed my shoes, put on a pair of sexy strappy
heels. They looked awful with the pants. I changed back into
the boots. In the end I opted for a black silk slip, a black
drapey shawl, and ballerina flats.

7:52. Shit shit *shit,* Magruder!

He'd be at the door in eight minutes.

Fuck the producer guy. If he didn't like me for me, what
was the use of him.

I decided to appoint the remaining minutes of my meltdown
to wrestling up a decent hairdo out of the ether. I couldn't
decide up, down, low ponytail, high ponytail, braids, wavy or
straight, sloppily swept up, sleek, or loose. His ex had worn
hers down in a wild mane. I could not deduce psychically or
logically, though I tried, whether Jym preferred to stay with
what he knew hairwise, or deviate from the norm. When the
doorbell rang I decided on down, with a sparkly blue barrette.

In a frenzy I checked myself in the hall mirror for stray
threads, things in my teeth, deodorant balls, and sweat stains.
Finding none, I opened the door.

There he stood, freshly showered and cologned, in a light
brown cashmere sweater, black tailored trousers, and funky
black boots with silver buckles across the toe. I leaned against

the door to steady my balance. He was more handsome than I remembered.

We stood in the doorway smiling goonishly at each other while I pulled on the ends of my hair like a nervous schoolgirl. "Are you going to invite me in?" he said. For a second, I thought about vampires and how they can't hurt you unless they are invited in, but he smelled so good I wondered if it was too soon to move to France.

"Of course!" I blurted. "I have zero manners, I'm so sorry. I'm so nervous I feel like I'm getting diarrhea." Jesus, Mer, what is wrong with you? I blushed and bit my fingernail nervously to keep from saying anything else idiotic, but he just started laughing.

"I'm nervous, too. Maybe we could just hug for a while." I could not believe my ears. "Yes!" I announced, utterly relieved that (a) we had feeling ill in common and (b) Jym, unlike Jasper Husch, was a problem solver.

In my arms he felt vulnerable and manly at the same time, maybe because I knew he had been loved and divorced. His body seemed to have absorbed the experience and was whispering it to me in soft wool and vetiver.

We stood like that and held each other until only the sound of our breath and our heartbeats and rushing blood mattered. I heard Tallulah's nails click click clicking against my hardwood floors. I could feel her at my ankle sniffing Jym's leg. I pressed my nose hard into his cashmered arm and deeply inhaled.

He let go first, stepped back and looked at me. "You look really beautiful. I really like your hair that way."

"My hair? Oh God, it was driving me Brazil nuts about thirty seconds ago!" Brazil nuts? Jesus, Mer, who talks like that? I died all over again, fearing maybe now he knew what a complete moron I was and was only waiting for the right moment to unapologetically do an about-face.

But he took my hand and asked, "How 'bout a tour?"

•   •   •

As Jym opened the door of his white convertible Jag and I slid into the cream-colored leather seats, I learned an ugly truth about myself, that, in a heartbeat I had become one of the girls that Sadie and I hated most. The ones with the boyfriends that took them to fancy restaurants and bought them expensive presents and took them on all-expenses-paid vacations. I always thought Jasper made me stronger but now I realized that he just made me feel unloved. I mean, I couldn't get Jasper to fold my laundry.

When the seat belt form-fitted itself snugly around me and Jym flipped the switch that made my seat heat up, I decided that no matter the outcome of my alliance with Jym, I was over struggling-poverty-art-boys entirely.

At the hidden restaurant in Malibu with Sol in the name, people could not help but stare at the attractive glowing chemistry factory seated at table four courtesy of a twenty dollar bill slipped discreetly into a bloated maitre d's hand. Jym ordered for me and kept calling me Dollface and I felt like one instead of like an every-man-for-your selfer, like when I was with you-know-who.

Over the weird French appetizer with the tiny sweet pickles, boiled potatoes, and hot, smelly cheese, I discovered Jym, unlike Jasper, had a real job making real money. Jym worked for a company that made TV shows and low-budget top-grossing teen horror flicks. Jym was in Development. His dream was to blend the teen format with adult content and make his mark giving the game show world the legitimacy it deserved. Jym went to college. Jym graduated.

Jym didn't believe in astrology, even though he knew he was on the cusp of Virgo/Libra with a Scorpio ascendant and a Pisces moon. He actually had an office and a phone and an expense account and a personal assistant and an apartment with its own parking space. Jym, unlike Jasper, drank non-decaffeinated things and had been to therapy. Jym thought therapy was *important*. Jym had two cats, but loved dogs, too. Jym liked sex. Jym, unlike Jasper, was a real grown-up looking to be in a real monogamous committed relationship. When the shaved white radish and frisée salad with truffle oil and mango dressing arrived and Jym said he hoped to get *married* again someday, I almost choked on my own saliva.

I thanked God for my body's amazing autopilot control system in charge of things like swallowing and breathing and beating my heart because everything I wanted was seated directly across from me.

When the rabbit stew in the individual clay pots arrived, I wanted to tell Jym everything: That I was afraid all the time, that I wanted him to hold me all night long, and tomorrow night and for the rest of my life, because he was a *man* and a man is what I needed, because he made me feel like a woman. I wanted to tell him I needed him, and how much I had lost, but that it was all worth it now because he existed. Instead, I said, "The key lime pie sounds good." But Jym ordered coconut crème caramel and apple pear tarte tatin with caramel sauce for dessert anyway. "*Trust me.*"

When it arrived, he rocked in his chair like a big kid and smacked his lips and said "Scrumdidliumptious!" I really admired how totally unafraid he was to express his childlike wonder and dorkiness over little things like smell and taste and texture! I just smiled and smiled and beamed him love.

When the waiter brought the check I repeated my therapy mantra. "I am the lady, not the caretaker, not the eldest child, not the mom." But I didn't have to worry because Jym was Catholic and from Illinois so, unlike Jasper, he reached for his wallet and paid with a shiny new corporate credit card.

"You little tax-write-off!" he said decadently, while the little candles on all the tables flickered their Morse code message, *he's the one, he's the one.*

I looked up at the ceiling and saw a big mural of a blazing sun. How many times had I cried over Jasper when now it all seemed like a funny dream? What was I ever so upset about? That's when I figured out that *sol* means sun. Sun. Sol. Soul. True love is what was allowing me to see the sun as soul. Sol. Sol mate. To be love itself, an ever-shining sun.

As he sensually sucked back the last warm caramel-coated apples and flaky crust crumbs and waited for the waiter to return with his receipt, I couldn't help but wish it was me in his mouth. No, Mer, you mustn't rush things, I told myself. You are going to let things take their natural course.

So, on the drive home, I asked him, "Do you have any venereal diseases? Because I think we should get AIDS tests together because even though we would definitely be using condoms for the first six months, I really think we should get tested."

He kept his left hand low on the steering wheel, giving it additional support with his thigh, and then looked at me for a poignantly long time, considering we were in a moving vehicle. Then, with his right hand, he brushed a few strands of my hair out of my face saying, "You're reading my mind." Then he hit the accelerator and we overtook a beige Plymouth trying to get in our lane without any effort or remorse.

We sped past a big moon shimmering on a certain Pacific Ocean with top down and the heat on, Cat Stevens blaring on the CD player, and I felt so happy I felt drunk—both hyper-alert and giddily anesthetized. You could have performed surgery on me that minute and I would have felt zero pain. I wondered if I had always chosen love over money because I had grown up with excess, and rebelled by choosing poverty. Or maybe if I mistook poverty for grounded reality because I had never found the two available in one package. Or maybe I chose love over money because my mother did, because when my parents splurged on us it meant my father was fucking someone else.

All I knew was one night of being treated so well by someone who was interested in *me* made me think I had come a long way in a few short months of heartbreak and therapy.

I thought, If I die on the way back from the five-star restaurant *he* chose, I'll die a happy woman.

Jym walked me to my door and asked me if he could see me on the weekend. A moth circled the overhead light. I swept the wooden deck with my left foot. It made a sweeping sound. Shuffle step kick, shuffle step kick. I accidentally kicked the welcome mat out of place. A big black spider ran toward my foot. I jumped back. I shrieked. Tulie watched us in the window.

"So is that a yes?"

"Um, yeah, OK, I . . . sure, yes, I'd love to."

"Saturday then?"

"Sure! Yes!"

He leaned in and kissed me softly on the cheek, like a gentleman. "Goodnight."

I had to giggle. "Goodnight," I said, all swoony, and slipped inside, closing the door behind me quietly. I pressed my back into the wood and smelled the dark, with its damp earthiness and magical unknown. "Thank you, God, thank you, God. I have met the man I am going to marry, I am sure of it." Then I scrambled into bed and dialed Sadie's number.

"Sadie," I said, kicking my feet free from the too-tucked-in sheets, "pick up the phone. He said he wants to get married and everything!"

She groaned slightly when she picked up. "What's wrong with him?"

"Nothing's wrong with him!"

"Something's wrong. He probably has a small cock. No man with a big cock wants to get married."

I giggled. "I don't think it's small."

"You slut!"

"No! I sort of felt it when he hugged me."

"Listen up, girlie, you are not allowed to have sex with him until you have seen his apartment, to be sure there are no *Star Wars* action figures in their boxes on display. To make sure he is a grown-up. Do you understand me?"

I bit my lip. "I think he's the one."

"The one what?"

"The one one."

"Are you saying you'd stay with him if he was paralyzed from the waist down?"

"I think I am."

"Are you saying you'd stay with him if he was HIV?"

"Sadie!"

"Well?"

"I think I would."

Long pause. "Are you telling me you could eat his ass?"

I broke into peals of hysterical laughter. "Yessss!!!"

"Oh. My. God." I heard her take in the seriousness of what I had just said. After some time she managed, "Well, I'm not paying for my bridesmaid dress. And it better not be ballerina pink." There was panic in Sadie's voice, perhaps the fear of no more girlie slumber parties and crushes on boys in coffeehouses, or the fear that I could be moving on without her before we even got to be single together.

"Come on, be happy for me! You're the one who set us up."

"To *date*, not to marry, to DATE." I bit the edge of my

duvet. "And it's our generation's job to keep the population explosion down, so no kids, ya hear me?"

"Not right away anyway."

"Jesus," she said utterly disgusted. "Goodnight, Mer."

I hung up the phone and pulled my covers over my head. They smelled all baby powdery clean. The light shone pink through the hand-sewn flowers. Tulie made her licking sound and I didn't even mind. I reached my arm out from under the blanket and turned off the light.

Just then I heard that owl in the big old pine tree in front of my house and I remembered that my mother had told me owls mean wisdom because they have full sight even in darkness, so I took this moment as a great blessing from the Creator. I sat up on my knees, and rested my elbows on the window ledge, straining to catch a glimpse of him in the moonlight.

I had never noticed just how tall that tree was.

NINETEEN
HOPE—A TRIBUTE TO THE COLOR BROWN

"Jolene heard the singing in the forest,
she opened the door quietly and
stepped into the night."

—Cake

The next morning the biggest bouquet of white lilies arrived at my door in a brown vase with a note: *From your not so secret admirer. Love, Jym.* I hummed the "Wedding March" while I put them in water.

Jasper who?

TWENTY
BELLY BUTTON

"God have mercy on the man
who doubts what he's sure of."
—Bruce Springsteen

"Welcome to my padarooski!" Jym announced the following
Saturday night as he opened the door to his highly Ikea-ed two-
bedroom apartment, done in creams, white, and light woods.
"Come on in and meet the freaks!" Two cats nearly immobilized
by fat meowed and meowed in steady unison on a well-worn
braided rug. "Freaks, Dollface. Dollface, freaks. The fat one is
Messy and the fatter one is Bessy." The larger of the two had an
inspired Freddie Mercury-esque overbite. Jym knelt down to pet
their bellies. I melted.

"How did they get their names?"

He coughed. "Uh, my ex named them. Messy because her
hair always mats up and Bessy because of Bessy Buckley. From
the musical *Cats.*"

My face went hot. "You mean Betty Buckley? The mom
from *Eight Is Enough*? It's Betty Buckley."

"Yeah, she loved that show."

"But..."

"Yeah, I know." He closed his eyes. He tried to shrug their
history off by rubbing the smaller, shaggier cat with the clumpy
dreads. She tried to scratch him but her reflexes were too
slow. He stood quickly and moved toward the kitchen. I followed him.

Jym had a railroad apartment: you moved from the living room through a spare bedroom he converted into an office, through the kitchen, then presumably into a dining room behind a swinging door, and beyond that probably a master bedroom of some sort, from what I could make out anyway. Thus far, not a *Star Wars* action figure in sight. "Do you want some water or beer or wine?" he said, as he pulled two glasses from a cupboard.

"Sure, water would be fine," I said, as he poured a glass of '94 Merlot. He handed it to me and touched my hip.

I smiled shyly, giggled, "No, thank you."

"You don't drink?"

"Actually, I'm allergic."

"Oh? What happens when you drink?"

A wave of feral heat burned in my belly, butterflies on fire. "Um," I said, blushing. "For one thing, I get a little bit sexual."

"Really," he said, swirling the wine around in my reject glass. He smelled it. "That doesn't sound too bad."

"A lot bit sexual, actually."

He handed me back my glass, then leaned against the door frame, saying, "Don't worry, I don't bite."

"Don't worry, I don't bite." I blushed, then took the smallest sip. Behind him, on his fridge, I noticed a postcard of four monks standing on a hill, arms raised to the sky, praying to a big fake gold sun. It was held in place by a pepperoni pizza refrigerator magnet. "Hey," I said, "that's my father's painting!"

He took another sip of his wine. "Isn't that a coincidence?" he said, staring me down like a cheetah. Then he pushed open the swinging door and I saw *it*, a chandelier! A grown man who wasn't gay with a chandelier! Below the big droopy crystals, an orange-and-white checkered tablecloth on the floor with about three dozen blazing tea lights. The candles made the chandelier cast starry rainbow streaks on the walls. Cartoon hearts and flowers shot out of my eyes like that cartoon skunk floating around that amazing two-bedroom apartment within walking distance of at least four Starbucks.

I thought, See you at the altar.

We ate take-out Italian with real silverware and listened to classical music with a few too many crashing cymbals in my opinion and then talked about his favorite movies and magazines. He subscribed to everything: "I have to, to stay on top of things. Yunno, for work."

"You obviously get the home magazines." Stupid, stupid. "I mean, because this place is so beautiful."

"Yeah." He looked around, took in his gift. "I thought about getting it submitted to *Metropolitan,* or *Home and Garden* or *MS Living,* but . . ." He trailed off, looking at the floor. "I just rent, so . . ." He topped off the final sip in his glass, stared at me. "You look really beautiful in this light." Jym touched my cheek. His hand felt moisturized, save one stray hangnail that dragged a little. I didn't say anything. It was a good thing because just then he leaned in to kiss me. It was soft and a little wetter than I imagined. Fire-coated winged creatures danced in my belly. I panicked.

"I should probably get going," I said suddenly.

"OK," he responded too quickly right back. As we gathered up the dishes, I wished I could take back what I said so Jym could unsay OK. It made me think he didn't like me anymore. But then he touched my hip and walked me outside and said, "Goodnight, Dollface," lightly stroking my hair.

"Goodnight," I said like some mute, lobotomized Juliet. I turned to go, followed a little brick path that led to the street.

"Hey, Mer?"

I turned back. "Yeah?"

"Do you want to stay the night? I promise I won't try anything." He crossed his heart as proof. Adorable!

Mer, be strong, I thought, don't blow it, don't rush. I could hear Karl's voice in my head, like Obi-Wan, "Wait, Luke, wait."

"I just thought it would be nice if we just . . . held each other tonight," said Jym as he slunk toward me, softly rubbing his soul patch.

Mer, be strong, pace yourself, pace yourself . . . Besides, there's no one to let Tallulah out. I blurted, "Sure, I'd love to!" Jesus, Mer, what an idiot. I heard submarine attack sirens in my head. ". . . But I don't have a toothbrush." Good girl.

"I have a spare."

"What?"

"Toothbrush. I have a spare toothbrush."

"Of course you do, you have all those teeth." I practically skipped back into his padarooski.

He let me wear his big flannel jammies to bed while he wore a T-shirt and some Abercrombie & Fitch boxers. Of course, he left his calf-length socks on. He squeezed some blue gel toothpaste on my fresh new-out-of-the-box red toothbrush and we brushed our teeth side by side, like a couple.

As I bent forward to spit, I caught our reflection in the mirror. I thought, We look good together.

In his big asthma-proofed bed with the hypoallergenic comforter and matching pillows he stroked my cheeks and hair while I tickled his back underneath his T-shirt. "I'm really glad you're here."

"Me, too."

"I know we aren't in charge of life's little gifts, but I want you to know I am open to receiving them."

"Me, too."

Suddenly his breath was on me. It smelled like those creamy pastel after-dinner mints. He tenderly kissed me goodnight and we hugged, pressing our pajamaed bodies close. Nose to nose now, he said, "Goodnight, Dollface."

"Goodnight, Giraffe," I said, just like that. I nicknamed him back, just like that. It just came right out. Dollface and Giraffe. It took me and Jasper ages to come up with Guava. It took us so long that we didn't have the energy to come up with another name, so we were both Guava.

I thought, Holy shit, maybe my life is going to work out after all.

Even in the dark, I could see he was looking at me and smiling and I was flooded with the alarm one feels when one glimpses the entire rest of one's life . . . and likes it.

"Goodnight," he said again.

"Goodnight," I said. Then Jym just held me until we fell asleep like monkeys, a tangle of arms and legs and my hair.

In the morning, Jym microwaved me some chai tea, bachelor style, but poured it into a big beautiful aesthetically pleasing cup, like a grown-up. Why does everything taste better when someone else makes it? Jasper never made me a cup of micro-waved chai. Then again, Jasper didn't own a microwave.

After Jym showered, he told me if I ever wanted to leave things at his place he would empty out a drawer for me in the bathroom. If I ever? I drove home in a moonwalking state of shock.

There I found two puddles of urine and one steamer.

It was worth it.

"Does this mean he's my boyfriend? Do you think, Sadie, do you?" I said as I damp mopped.

"Not if you only dry-humped. Dollface and Giraffe? Jesus, Mer, my stomach. You are making me physically ill. What about Jasper?"

"I'm totally over him. It's just like his fax said, 'people grow and move on.' He's on a path and I'm on a path and that's just the beauty of life."

"Euch."

"Sadie, why can't you be happy for me."

"Because you're nuts. You haven't even had sex with him yet and you think he's your boyfriend. What if you hate him in bed? What if he makes porn face when he cums? What if he's a premature ejaculator?"

"Sadie!" Tallulah came traipsing in and nudged a rope chew toy in my lap. I was feeling generous so I wedged the phone between my shoulder and my ear and tossed it, even though it was wet with her stinking saliva. It skidded across the kitchen floor and made a friction sound as it disappeared under the stove.

"I'm just worried about you is all. You complain nonstop about Jasper and then miraculously overnight you are planning your future with a guy who sounds like a high school basketball PE coach. Can you say *rebounding?*" Tallulah reappeared with the toy. I bent down and tossed the damp horror east.

"You're the one who fixed us up!"

"To *date,* not to fall in love with. To be honest I really didn't think it would go anywhere . . ."

Tallulah reappeared enthusiastically with the wet ropy chew toy, then dropped it and sat panting, waiting for the next toss. I teased her by holding it over her head and lowering it every now and again. "We know that Auntie Sadie is just a little jealous, don't we, Tulie? You understand that I am not in charge of life's little gifts, I am merely open to receiving them."

"Auntie Sadie is just gonna go throw up now. Bye, Mer."

Tulie nipped at my hand. I swatted her down, put the chew toy on top of the fridge where she couldn't reach it. "Bye, Sadie," I said, utterly fascinated with the communication device in my hand.

I thought, Aren't phones amazing?

I knew I was *in love* because when my French neighbor started up his uncommonly loud leaf blower and beat his car senseless, I didn't care. When Spoonie called to tell me he and Lila ran into Jasper at a photo exhibit in Silverlake, I didn't care. When my mother called to tell me she was thinking about selling the home I grew up in, I didn't care. I only thought, If Jasper was a cosmic joke so that Jym Court could be the stellar punch line, I am laughing with the Almighty this minute!

On Thursday I saw Karl. He didn't even have to prod me or ask me how I was or anything. I just blurted out a monologue of unbridled joy. "He can't stop buying me gifts. Sweaters, socks, bath products, soaps . . . He calls me Dollface and e-mails me from work nonstop, and when I call his office, even the receptionist seems happy for us. She always puts me right through, even when he is in the middle of an important meeting. He says adorable things like 'scrumdidliumptious' and 'what's cooking' and 'nada piñata.' He's funny and playful and masculine and smart and has an important job, and that makes me feel important. I mean, miraculously, I am beginning to feel more like myself again. Only, I'm a me I have not known before! And the more I like myself, the less sense it makes that Jasper didn't want me, that my father didn't want me, when I'm great, only now I don't care because Jym wants me and he's great and, and, and . . ."

"What is it, America?"

"I'm just really happy," I said, only then really seeing Karl for the first time. I saw clearly that Karl had been re-parenting me all along, teaching me *by example* for the last few weeks that I deserved more, because Karl gave me more. Karl cared about me. Karl listened to me. As a result, I had attracted someone else who cared as much as Karl did. Now I knew it was time to quit therapy.

"Did you have sex with Tim?"

"No!" I blushed. "His name is Jym."

He nodded. "Good, because the courtship phase is extremely important. Remember, you can't roast marshmallows in the power struggle phase if you haven't built a fire in the courtship phase! That way, if you *wait* until you know who you are dealing with, you can enjoy *s'more* of him later on!"

"I'll wait! I'll wait!" I giggled. It made me miss my dad, to be scolded like that.

He winked at me. "All right now, our time's up for today. Next week same time?"

I nodded my head. I didn't think Karl was ready to hear the truth. So on the drive home I phoned him from my car, thanked him for all his help, and canceled next week's appointment.

Later that night I saw Jym's pubic hair for the first time.

We kissed and dry-humped for a hot while and I could feel him hardening. As he pulled at my shirt, trying to get it over my head, I thought, Oh God he's going to feel my adult acne! Fine. Better to get it over with. He should know this about me. If he is anything other than understanding, it's his problem. I would still accept him if he had a few zits. He said nothing, just continued to kiss me so deeply and so sweetly that all I could do was relax. Then he stuck his hand in my jeans and, checking for wetness, began to finger me.

I unzipped his trousers. He wasn't wearing underwear. I thought, How sixties of him. His cock flopped out like a lazy showgirl. Jesus, I thought, he's huge! I began to suck on him a little with his trousers still on. He fully stiffened. I tugged at his pants and he lifted his hips so I could pull them all the way down.

That's when I saw his pubic hair. It was shaved. He had almost no pubes, only razor stubble. Like Don Johnson in *Miami Vice*. He really should have warned me, although I couldn't imagine how it might have come up . . .

Try to maintain, I told myself, this is the same nit-picking that tore Jasper and me apart. Just try to accept him for who he is. So what if he has a few kinks, you get kinks with everybody. It's just a matter of finding the ones you can live with. I didn't want to break the mood so I did a kind of blow dryer technique on his stubbly balls to make the negative energy vanish.

He was moaning and gyrating then. Thrusting his exceedingly large cock in and out of my mouth. It whacked the roof of my mouth with the force of the end of an industrial flashlight. He was a gentleman, however, and pushed my mouth away before he came, and it mostly all landed in his exceedingly large belly button, and my hair.

Turned out he was a screamer—also a bit shocking—but then these are the things that one can only find out by jumping in.

We lay there for a little while in his afterglow, me on his buttery chest, him tugging on the ends of my crispy hair. Then, suddenly, Jym sat up and started to cry. "There is something I have to tell you that you might freak out about." My mind raced. What could it be? Herpes, AIDS, cancer? We already talked about that stuff. Did he lie? Is he a sociopath? Did he kill someone? Is he still *married?*

"This is really hard for me, but, I think I'm falling in love with you." He nuzzled into my tiny bare breasts. "I just feel so selfish for coming first. I wanted to stop, but your mouth felt too good. I'm sorry." I patted him on the back then thought, Wait, am I consoling him or mothering him? Either way, *TURNOFF!* "It's just that it takes a really long time for my penis to get an erection again." Penis? Erection? Was I dating an anatomy book? He leaned up and kissed my cheek.

I thought, You know something, it would have been nice if you had given me an orgasm first. Or at all. Or, say, *now*. I guess he kind *of* tried, or is he just a lazy pig? I was angry now.

"Oh, baby, I'll make it up to you. Come here, Princess. Whattsamatter baby. Whattsamatter?" he kept repeating. Whattsamatter was my face was smushed under his sweaty pit, only I didn't say anything because he was just crying and already felt like a big fuckup. "Please forgive me."

"Of course I forgive you," I said, even though I didn't.

I thought, Why can't he just get over it and seduce me now? If he wanted to give me an orgasm so badly why didn't he just do it? Why doesn't he just give me head right now? Or, at the very least, finger me. Anything, just do it now now NOW. Or is this some twisted manipulation so he gets out of it altogether? And how come I can't say any of this? Now I feel like I'm a freak for even wanting him to and now he has kind of totally gotten away with it. And now it's too late to even ask and, anyway, why should I even have to ask, and now there is just too much pressure!

"Let's just hold each other," he said.

We leaned back and he draped the blanket across us. I lay against his wide, flat chest listening to a revving engine nag and stall. I thought, At least he's falling in love with me.

After a little while, he grabbed my hand and let me feel him hardening. "Stroke me," he whispered. I did. I was still a little crabby from before, but his passion for me dissolved my irritation, and before I knew it, gold foil was coming off an extra-large condom. Miraculously we managed to climax at the same moment. I started crying. Jasper was truly behind me now.

"Come here," he cooed and held me close.

First-time sex is so weird.

•　　　　•　　　　•

It began to rain as we lay in each other's arms. We listened until I felt Jym twitch himself to sleep. Overall, not the greatest, but I knew I would sleep like a baby, certain that there would be many many more opportunities to perfect our lovemaking.

In the morning I heard him get up and shower. I listened carefully to his bathroom sounds—wet feet on linoleum, the brushing of perfect teeth, the coughing up of phlegm, rinsing of the sink, tapping of the toothbrush. Soon I would have to move my car, which was blocking him in.

I thought, I can live with this. I mean I think I can live with this.

TWENTY-ONE
HIT TV

"Why?"

—Annie Lennox

That first couple of weeks it was all faxes and phone calls and e-mails. Jym was literally healing me with his adorableness:

Dollface,
Recipe for Happiness:
Seeing your face
Smelling you
Hearing you laugh
Hearing you cum
Holding you close
And 4 T. vanilla
Love always,
Jym the Jyraffe

(I liked how he did the clever thing with the tablespoons and the *Jy* in Jyraffe.)

And this one:

Baby, Sweetness, Honey, Love, Dearest, Angel, Peaches, Darling, Gorgeous, Sexy Pudding Pants, I want to chew your clothes off and make you squeal like, well, something that squeals!
Jym "Barry White" Court

And this one:

> Roses are red violets are blue I'm fully hard and want to come
> over there and make sweet pumpkin love to you.

(pumpkin love because for Halloween we got a little naughty
in the middle of carving a pumpkin together!)

Then one day, out of the blue, he just said, "I just think you
should have this" and handed me a key to his swanky high-
tech apartment *avec* chandelier.

The best part of any relationship, the only noble cause worth
aiming for, is the settling in. I despised the courtship phase, the
"Steely Dan" time of the relationship when you swear up and
down that you have the same taste in music, the calculated dis-
pensing of half-truths that eventually break down and give way
to what is real. It is only when one is truly brave, like me and
Jym, that one is able to let all the disguises fall away and
be granted entry into the glorious land of We. Jasper and I
couldn't even find our keys to the car in the parking lot near the
entrance of such a place.

What I loved most was the regularity with Jym, the monot-
ony, the routine of simply being. The discovery of when we both
wanted sex or dinner or time to ourselves and the careful
negotiating of it all without killing each other.

I already knew the mornings by heart. First, Jym would
shower and dress, then he would heat us up some chai tea from
Trader Joe's (bringing mine to me *in bed*), toast me, take a sip
of his, smack his lips and say, "Scrumdidliumptious." Then, one
of the cats would either spit something up or meow too long,
causing Jym to yell at them both. Now I'd have to get out of bed
to move my car, which was blocking him in.

In the evenings Jym would get home around 8:30 P.M., and since I didn't like to eat late and Jym didn't cook, we'd usually just order fancy oil, cream, and butter-drenched takeout, and watch TV. I was careful not to cook for Jym because I didn't want to turn into his little *hausfrau* like I was for Jasper. I was hyper-careful not to repeat old destructive patterns that turned me into a mother or resentful lover. Then, after I watched Jym watch his game show, sitcom, or teen horror competition duke it out on the boob, we had sex.

On weekends the sex times varied in between watching Jym play street hockey with the guys from work, watching Jym get a manicure for work, walking my dog, seeing movies, and watching Jym snack on lunch meats. I would watch him roll up the sleeves of his pin-striped monogrammed shirts and tear the pink processed meat away from its neat stack, dip the wiggly square with the rounded edges directly into the mayo jar itself, getting dollops of white goo directly onto his elbows, wrists, and hands. I feared for Jym's cholesterol level but praised him for having the courage to do it in front of me as, in my opinion, this was the type of thing one did on one's own time behind a locked door.

Jym astounded me, he was unafraid to pick blackheads, fart, and listen to his flirtatious female messages in front of me. This was the beauty of Jym. Largely, it was through my acceptance of his little quirks that I was beginning to realize how I was partly to blame in the demise of my relationship with Jasper.

I never really let Jasper be Jasper. I was too busy hating everything he did that was not related to me because I felt threatened that Jasper's choices took him away from *us*, like his love of porn, or his affection for seeing movies in the gayest hardcore neighborhoods of San Francisco, when there were plenty of other theaters within walking distance for seeing those same movies. While I always thought he was stupid and

secretly gay, now I saw he was just a sensual, life-loving inno-
vator. With Jym, I was willing to watch him eat processed
meat and saturated fats and not even mind so much because a
happy *him* meant a happy *us*.

For the first time I felt I was in a real grown-up relationship;
mainly, for the first time in my life I felt motivated to work out
(partly because Jym didn't and partly because Jym was around
models and actresses all day long). Plus, by the time he'd get
home late at night, I'd have missed him a whole day's worth
and actually *wanted* to see him again whereas Jasper worked at
home and we were always in each other's hair and space,
never taking time apart, unless I was in LA for a couple of
weeks trying to book a voice-over job. Doing stomach
crunches on Jym's sisal rugs I could not believe I was ever even
depressed.

Later that night, entwined on Jym's sofa, he asked me why
we hadn't made love in my bed yet, asked if it was because of
Jasper. I told him maybe I was still holding on to a small part of
him. I was so grateful to be busted, I had to have him that very
minute, so we got in the car, drove to my place, and did it,
slow and missionary. Then it was official: Jym and I were for
real for real.

Thanksgiving came and went without incident, even though
it was the day before the anniversary of my sister's death and
Jym and I couldn't be together. His family had been expecting
him home in Illinois and he'd already bought the ticket before
he'd even met me. And besides, he promised we'd spend
Christmas together, and that was by far the more important
holiday of the season, so, no big.

My mother didn't bother me once the whole day, even
though she talked at length about exciting upcoming events
that were planned around my father: a retrospective in Prague,

a nine-page spread in *Art in America,* a cover story in the *New York Times Magazine,* and a touring slide show in elementary schools across the country. She made the gravy and her world famous (in her mind) cornbread, ginger, and chestnut stuffing. I felt happy. I even helped make pie crusts because I actually had something to be thankful for.

I even had a terrific chat with Lila. Spoonie talked about maybe going away to a spa for a long weekend as a foursome! Though I will admit I did get a little peeved when Lila said, "It's so great that Jym's finally calmed down, yunno, because of his reputation for being such a player and all." I just had another helping of turkey and all was forgiven.

Of course, it helped that Jym faxed me romantic mushy stuff about 179 times that day.

The next day, however, I was feeling particularly bloated and we had our first fight. I managed to get him on his cell phone and made the mistake of telling him I felt lonely and a little bit fat. Jym told me bluntly he didn't believe in feeling sorry for one's self, to which I replied I didn't feel sorry for myself; I was just feeling sad. (I also made the mistake of mentioning that I was envious of his work because he was gone so much.) He said I was just like his ex-wife and why didn't I just get a job, any job, and focus on problems I could actually solve. "I mean, what do you even do for a living? All I see you doing is getting an allowance like a thirty-year-old child, while the rest of the world works for a living." And I said "You're just jealous." And he said "of what," and I said "not having free time" and he said "To do what? Sit around and get fat?" Then I said "You should talk, what about your bagged meat obsession?" and he said "At least I buy it with my own money" and I said "Yeah, and you'll pay for your hospital bills with your own money, too!" So he said "At least I have health insurance!" That shut me up, because I wasn't sure if I was on a co-pay because I didn't even know what a co-pay was.

Then he hung up on me and didn't call me for two days, even though I had to go to his apartment twice a day to feed his cats. Apparently he felt perfectly justified not apologizing.

I wanted to call Sadie, but she was still mad that Jym and I had progressed past the one-night stand she had hoped for and I didn't want to give her a reason to celebrate. I thought about calling Karl.

Instead, I went and picked up Kitty Litter and wet food for Jym's cats. At Dog Slave on La Brea I ran into the coffee guy. I apologized for being such a bitch the last time I saw him. He just said, "No worries, mate," in a fake Australian accent and asked how I was doing. I made the mistake of serving up a nice batch of my dumb relationship problems, to which he said, "Without knowing you, I would say you're looking for ways to push a nice guy away. I'd just blow the whole thing off." He was standing near the catnip mice, wearing a "Jesus Saves, Gretzky Gets the Rebound and Scores" T-shirt, which made me feel kinda sorry for him, so I thanked him, paid for the goods, and got the hell out of Dodge.

On the drive home I called Jym and apologized and we "agreed to disagree." Jym made me promise to get a day job and/or not feel sorry for myself. By the end of the call, he could tell I was still a little upset, so he told me that we could get a spare crate for Tulie and leave it at his place, so the animals could start getting used to one another. I felt a lot better. Then he regaled me with stories about pre-Xmas shopping with the family and first snowfalls and icicles and fireplaces and cider and drunken aunts and being snowed in. All in all, I counted only seventeen Scrumdidliumptiouses.

When I got back to his place, there was a giant puddle of hairball stew. Scrubbing the floors with soap and lemon-scented ammonia, I sat back on my heels, pushed my hair back with a black industrial strength rubber glove, and (smiling) thought, Maybe I should have a baby.

Then I drove home, curled up with Tulie, listened to the rain falling on my roof, ate an entire bag of Oreos, and fell asleep.

Two weeks before Christmas, Jym and I went out for dinner and he broke the news to me over oysters on the half shell that, unfortunately, he would be away in New York. For Christmas.

"It's business, Dollface," he said matter-of-factly as he sucked back another hot sauce–infested piece of sea slime. Some translucent liquid dribbled out of his mouth. "Scrum-didliumptious!" he announced when his head recoiled. I frowned.

"But . . . you promised!" He handed me an oyster he'd prepared for me. I cupped the shell and its jiggling contents in my palm, touched the hot sauce with my tongue, then put it back on ice. I took a large gulp of water.

"Look, Dollface, we are courting these hotshot puppeteers and—"

"Hotshot puppeteers?" People put their forks down and stared. Calmly Jym wiped his face with his napkin and said evenly, "I'm trying to make Hit TV here, Dollface, but I promise we will have New Year's together."

I started hysterically laughing. He signaled the waiter for the check. "Hotshot puppeteers" and "Hit TV" repeated in my head along with a phony laugh track. Jym looked around the restaurant nervously.

"Why didn't you ask me to go with you?"

"Is *that* what this is about?" Jym said, patting my hand. "I just assumed you'd want to spend the holidays with your family. It won't be much fun, Dollface." He held my chin in his hand, made a boo-boo face. "Besides we have two whole weekends before I leave, for just the two of us." I softened, leaned in to kiss him. He kissed my forehead, wiped his mouth on his napkin and folded it in his lap. "Also, I need someone to watch the cats."

We drove home in silence.

Since Jym was going to be away, he wanted to sleep at his place for the remainder of the month so his cats knew how much he loved them. To appease me, he went out the next day and surprised me by buying Tallulah a little bed and setting it up for her in his living room.

That first weekend dedicated to just us, we went shopping at the Beverly Center and I helped him buy presents for all the people he worked with and for some people he hardly knew. Whoop-dee-doo. The whole time he complained about how much money he had to spend, and how people were constantly taking advantage of him and his hard-earned money, so I ended up feeling guilty when he asked me if I wanted him to pay for a sweater I'd already added to his gift pile. I was so shocked that he had put me in the position of deciding whether or not he should buy it for me that I said no thank you, even though he would and did spend almost $700 on thoughtful gifts for people he was *not* fucking. Worse, Jym seemed genuinely *grateful* that I was not taking advantage of him the way they were.

My face burned with resentment and feelings of abandonment. I thought to myself as the salesperson rang up the unflattering orange sweater I would hate forever and come to associate with the pain of this moment, He likes the people he hates more than he likes me.

In the evening, he broke dinner plans with me because he was busy doing prep work on the sock puppet phenomenon. His exact words? "Dollface, I gotta stay here and make U.V. for the Flyover."

"What's 'U.V.,'" I naively asked.

"*Über*-viewing."

"Oh. What's 'the Flyover'?"

Jym looked annoyed. "Yunno, the people between NY and LA."

At first I thought he was joking when he said that he was blowing me off for the flyover; then I realized he wasn't, and that I was dating a mutant with a get-famous complex who works with socks.

My unstated fury turned to uncontrollable, borderline-violent, laughter.

"What?" he said.

"Nothing."

That night I slept at my own house, in my own bed, feeling more alone IN a relationship than out of one. Then I called him an *Über*-asshole in my head and made myself laugh out loud.

The following Saturday before Jym left for the Big Apple, he took me to buy a small tree which we decorated with tiny purple lights, handmade ornaments I had collected over the years, and tinsel galore. I accidentally broke a beautiful silver glass ornament Jym had given me and he yelled, but then apologized. I felt terrible. More than that, it felt mysteriously symbolic somehow (even though it came from Banana Republic and they still had about a million more left). I put dried rose petals I'd been saving in the shiny fractured half sphere and we hung it up anyway. Though fragile and useless, I thought it still retained something in its jagged beauty.

Later we made love before we went to sleep and he had an orgasm, but I didn't.

In the morning, Jym screamed at Tallulah and then at me, because overnight she had gifted him with a nice steaming pile of my disowned rage on his pristine hardwood floors. As he droned on and on at earsplitting volume about how it would leave a stain and how now he probably wouldn't be able to get his deposit back, I thought, My, he is really quite the little rage-a-holic.

Mom much?

I told him that I was convinced the only reason I had a key to his place was because he wanted me to water his plants and feed his cats while he was away. By now he was screaming loud enough for the neighbors to threaten to call the police through the cracking plaster walls while he intermittently paced and packed fancy ironed pin-striped shirts into a black Tumi hanging garment bag, while I ammonia-mopped his precious floors down on all fours.

That's when he announced, "You don't respect what I do!" out of the wild blue. I assured him that I did and he blurted, "I bet no one ever stood up to you before and told you you're wrong. I bet you always got your way. I bet no one has ever told you no." Like it was his personal duty to be confrontational with me.

"BLAAAAAAAAA!" I shouted up at him, like a juvenile delinquent. He just stared at me. I started laughing and went to kiss him, and even though he let me, neither one of us felt resolved.

Later, when I drove home from taking him to the airport, I couldn't help but think how remarkably similar this felt to the last time I took Jasper to the airport. I shuddered.

Tallulah hopped into my lap as we drove up La Brea, past rows and rows of houses with sleeping trees or wreaths in their windows. Stopped at a red light, Tulie's funny face made some leathery-faced men in a beat-up pickup with a dancing hula girl on the dash laugh.

I just smiled and drove on.

TWENTY-TWO
MERRY XMAS

"Step right up march push crawl
right up on your knees."

—Nine Inch Nails

My mother cooks only one truly amazing meal a year and that's Christmas. We have this great tradition of taking in strays who don't have families or can't make it home, but there is a price—we eat turkey and all the fixins, like a normal family, but for some reason my mother insists on making dozens of tiny individual meat pies for the baby Christ's birthday.

Since our oven is too small, she can only bake a few at a time, so she tortures everyone by making us take numbers and forcing the guests to eat in a round-robin row-row-row your boat sort of way. Some sit while others of us wait, smelling curried chicken, mincemeat, stewed fruits, and vegetable medley for the vegetarians (that may or may not still be available by the time they are called to the table). In the meantime, everyone has access to an enormous pot of mashed potatoes and mulled wine.

Spoonie and I have tried to talk her out of the madness but she seems to think this allows people to mingle, be freethinking, and casual. Thanks to therapy, I secretly think the reason why she likes it is because it prevents any real intimacy from taking place.

Since my father's passing, we begin festivities around 3:30 in the afternoon (although the meal never actually gets under way until *well* after eight or nine), but it can take as long as six hours to make sure everyone is fed. Usually by this time, they are hungry again for seconds.

I had spent all day making small talk and pie crusts galore, letting them rest empty near a mirrored disco ball Buddha that the feng shui people had talked my mother into buying to attract money, while intermittently checking my messages to see if Jym had called (he hadn't yet), anything to avoid watching Spoonie and Lila fall deeper and deeper in love. I called Sadie in Idaho, where she was visiting family, to wish her a Happy Merry but she was out sledding with her tiny cousins.

I missed not seeing my dad grouchily crouched in his favorite chair in front of the overly tinseled fire hazard of a tree. And tonight, in walking through the two-story craftsman house, outside and up the wooden spiral staircase that led to the modern addition in the back, I felt the smoothness of the wooden banister where my father rested his hand on nightly pilgrimages to his art sanctuary, and didn't push the feelings away.

I felt in the dark for the sconce Spoonie had painted monsters on as a Father's Day present when he was five, and flicked a light on. Paintbrushes in old tea tins; acrylics, oils, gouache arranged by color from lightest to darkest; charcoal, gesso, scissors, palette knives, colored pencils, glitter, glue, along with stacks and stacks of pressed paper and thin strips of metal, all on homemade shelves. Everything was just as he left it, even his full-to-brimming ashtrays, just as my mother had preserved it for him, like the next museum tour would start in five minutes. Like he was going to come back and knock off a masterpiece any minute now.

A painting of Cupid rested on an easel, a favorite painting of my mother's from B. Throne's satirical *Archetype* series: Dan Quayle as Mickey Mouse, Fidel Castro as a bloated Six

Million Dollar Man, Angelyne as Cupid, and Bowzer from Sha Na Na as Jesus. I studied the airbrushed cherub hovering over a moon-base Los Angeles where a lonely-looking woman in a floppy hat and sunglasses lounged poolside waiting for her dreams to come true. It seemed the more Jym and I settled in, the more I saw that my old restlessness and depression weren't going away; it was only playing peek-a-boo while I was distracted by Cupid's fucking arrow in my ass.

I missed watching my father paint, missed watching creases form along his brow as he concentrated deeply on the task at hand. I liked his little rituals, how he'd always light a candle before he began, or midway through a session, how he'd take several breaks, stopping to smoke and pace, or the way he looked when he'd completed a painting; he'd hook his long fingers under his nose and lean in close, examining it with soft eyes, like a lover.

I grabbed a small tube of paint, recalled my fondness for thievery—how I loved to steal my father's nearly finished tubes of gouache in the hopes of delaying him slightly, though never taking anything he'd miss too terribly. If he was in a good mood he would say "Camilla, a little squirrel got into my things again," and she would say "It's probably a poltergeist," and I would squeal with delight hoping to be caught and hugged.

I placed the battered tube next to a nearly empty box of my father's favorite cigarettes. The vague smell of turpentine reminded me of cleaning my father's brushes in the laundry room sink with my mom. I loved that.

One of my favorite Boris Thrones is a large oil-on-canvas with a very small camel and a bouquet of watering cans in dark and murky depths. When I was nine I had tried to imitate him and this painting, working with crayon, ink, and paper. I held it up and he said it was good but would be better in oil.

In the corner of the room stood a textured light fixture of an enormous copper dragon my father had made. Someone offered him $500,000 for it. My mother went pale and begged him not to sell it even though we needed the money.

Reams of dust-covered canvases lay alongside that eyesore, and nearby a tilted maple and metal drafting table held a light box. I moved toward it. On its milky surface, three slides—photographs of my father that he had selected for a book about what ended up being his last works. I looked at him through a loupe, up close. They had been taken a few weeks before he died.

My father hated Christmas. We would wake him moments after he had gone to bed after an all-nighter, and he would resentfully sit in his papabear chair while we tore through countless presents my mother had spent weeks accumulating and wrapping. It must have brought him some joy to see us so happy over piles and piles of useless stuff, but he never let on. Maybe he was embarrassed because my mother picked everything out and he just put his name on the card. One year I got a particularly disturbing black lace and leather vest. It looked like something a gay dominatrix card dealer might have worn during cowboy times. That was the same year he was thinking about divorcing my mother. And the same year he made me a present for no reason.

In some airport overseas, he stuck a coin in a machine and made me a lightweight, silver dollar–size coin that said "I love you" or "I miss you" or something. It was supposed to bring you luck but I lost it. In some ways, I didn't mind because he was visiting some dancer lady at the time, but I was still sad because he made it himself without any prodding from my mother.

Downstairs, in the living room, I could hear a blend of acoustic guitars and laughter drifting up through the floorboards. I picked Spoonie's out of the din and savored it like a ripe berry. Then I turned off the lights and went back inside.

•　　　•　　　•

"Give me a hand with this," my mother squawked, wrestling a shiny brown bird onto a large serving tray. I moved through the kitchen to arrange the garnish and preserve the drippings for gravy. At the sink, my mother strained boiled potatoes for mashing, the steam rising up above her like starchy apparitions.

With her back to me like this, her pale white neck peeked through a tangled mess of hair. Soft, smooth. She used to cook barefoot, wearing her hair tied up with toothbrushes, pencils, or my father's discarded paintbrushes.

"Let's eat!" she announced, and we did.

Later, watching the lovers exchange gifts, my heart melted. Spoonie gave Lila a red G-Shock watch and Lila gave him a matching one in yellow. "Thanks, Honey Boy!" "Thanks, Money Girl!" they said in hushed tones of tenderness and surprise. Then they gave each other matching turtleneck sweaters, board games, journals, sheets, books, mugs, robes, slippers, facial scrubs, bubble bath, socks, boxers, and an enormous box of chocolates which they donated to me because I was eyeing it.

Even though I was so full it hurt to lie down, I raced to squeeze or bite every chocolate to see if I was interested in it. Anything caramel and almondy, butter creamy and mocha-esque I got. Fruits, liqueurs, coconut, and nutty brittles I left up for grabs. Then I vowed to work out and maybe even fast for a day so I could button my pants before Jym came home.

When I got back to Jym's place to feed his fatcats, there was no message from him, only a narrow inlet of otherworldly cat throw up. I was just heading for the ammonia when I heard Jym's voice on the machine then, and, reaching for the phone, I slipped in the vomit, banged my head on his chandelier, *and* managed to break a clear hanging crystal teardrop. Merry fucking Xmas.

•   •   •

I picked Jym up from LAX. He was so handsome in a new cash-mere Dr. Huxtable–style sweater and Santa hat, that I forgot to stay mad at him. The plan was to head straight back to his house, have our own belated Xmas together, and sex sex sex. "Scrumdidliumptious!" he shouted, leaning out the window as I paid the three dollars at the airport parking kiosk.

We took Century Boulevard to Aviation, turned left, and got as far as Manchester when my little Audi lurched forward and made an awful popping sound. An even crueler hissing and a final lean to the right added up to a blown front right tire. "I have a spare in the trunk," I said, "I just don't know how to put it on." Jym shook his head and angrily got out to survey the damage, then climbed back in the car and said we'd better call AAA.

While we waited for the tow truck guy, Jym said, "I never noticed you had a mustache before." I caught my reflection in the rearview and, in the winter light, the hair above my lip *did* seem a bit darker than usual.

When the skinny sweaty guy in the red-and-white baseball cap and matching shirt showed up almost an hour later, he asked Jym why he hadn't put the spare on himself.

When we finally turned onto Jym's car-lined road, Jym said, "Dollface, I'm tired."

The tire episode was certainly a buzz kill but once inside I gave Jym his gift anyway. An antique robot that shot real sparks from his tiny raygun. It turned out he had no gift for me because he was so stressed about the puppet show that he'd gotten no shopping done. Then he said he didn't really have time to buy anything anyway. Then he said he didn't see anything he liked. Then he said, what do you give the girl who has everything; then he said he really just wanted to wait until he had more time to find just the right thing.

I would have preferred just, Sorry.

Later, in the middle of a great dream I was having about

being a long-distance runner, Jym mounted me. I didn't open my legs fully or climax because I was too freaked about my mustache and the whole present thing. But not Jym. I just kept my hand to my lip and stared at the ceiling until he was done.

In the morning Jym announced that it had completely slipped his mind to tell me that today was the day he had scheduled to have his house de-fleaed. He told me the exterminator said it wasn't safe for me to be there while they debugged the place, and that it would also be wise if I took all of my clothes and belongings home, anything that I didn't want contaminated with the toxic foam. Jym brought me a box from the hall closet and watched me pack up, sweetly assisting by putting Tulie's crate and toys in the car. When I came back in the house to help him with his stuff, I saw that he had packed a box full of my bath stuff. I laughed. "At this rate I'll practically be taking everything!" He just smiled at me as he zipped some of his suits up in a Gucci garment bag, saying, "I'll just dry-clean the rest."

At 11:17 A.M., in the middle of bleaching my mustache (and while I was at it, bikini line), my phone rang. "I have to tell you something I'm afraid you won't be able to love me for." It was Jym calling from his office. I was sitting in a floral bikini top straddle-legged on the living room floor, organizing receipts by month, cash or credit, personal or business (just one of the many perks of dating someone who was so organized), while I waited for the white cream on my upper lip and bikini region to take. "Do you have a minute?" I sat up a little straighter, furrowed my brow.

"OK . . ."

"I told you a little lie. There was no exterminator. Actually, I called a locksmith."

"Huh?" The bleach was starting to burn.

"I want you to know I respect you but I am really not ready for a relationship right now. I thought I was, but now I realize

I was just rebounding and I just want to get to know myself since I have never really taken any time off for just me and it all happened so fast, plus we don't really get along."

The bleach was really burning now. I waved my hand in front of my face to cool my upper lip. "I'm sorry, are you breaking up with me?"

"I guess I am."

"On the *phone?*" At least this was progress. "Can we at least talk about this, say, later, *in person?*"

"I wouldn't be comfortable with that."

"WHAT?" I blew air at my crotch to cool the tender skin.

"I just feel that we don't . . . get along," he snapped with a grotesque finality.

"I think we do," I said defensively, eyes watering from the bleach smell.

"We don't."

"Well, I think we do!" I was standing now, pointing at the receipts.

"Look, Dollface, I don't want to argue anymore. This isn't about you, it's about me. I gotta run."

"But I didn't do anything wrong!" I was laughing now. "You pursued ME!!!!"

"It's just, I'm not done grieving my last relationship and this all happened so fast. I was hoping for a friendship that slowly built into something . . ."

I hopped from one leg to the other. The burning irritation had really intensified. "OK, Jym, fine. Let's just take things a little slower . . ."

"I don't think you understand, it would just be too painful for me. I should really go."

"But . . . but . . . but you work with socks for Godsakes!" He hung up on me. I called him right back to ask him if he was bipolar but he wouldn't accept the call. I stared at the phone, then made a dash for the bathroom.

I ran cold water over a well-worn rose-colored washcloth. While I rinsed my skin down with the cool cloth, I thought, Back to Jail, do *not* pass Go, do *not* collect $200. Thanks for nothing, Jym with a WHY. I felt like one of Jym's sock puppets. Like a hollowed-out sac of flesh with God's hand up my fucking puppet ass.

I was about to go into old me, leaving hostile messages on every one of Jym's numbers—home, car, office, voice mail, e-mail, *and* pager—telling him he was a fake human, a nonperson, a cyborg, but something happened. I realized, if he was freaky enough to organize a lockout, he was freaky enough to be all wrong for me. Just like Jasper.

I heard a plane fly overhead, thought, They seem to be sailing overhead with increasing regularity. They must have changed their flight path.

Truth be told? I felt nothing, just like Karl said I would.

TWENTY-THREE
NOT SEE PARTY

"You are witnessing a start, a new life
you are witnessing the start of my fabulous life."
—Katell Keineg

"Ben Affleck is going to be there!" Sadie meant the big New Year's's Eve shindig Lila had gotten us all invited to. Even my mother was asked to come. Lila also organized for Spoonie's band to be the entertainment. It was a kickoff for a new magazine called *Launch,* and the theme for the party was, surprise, OUTER SPACE! Lila had gained us entry because she had secured the much-coveted premiere cover. It was a photo of her in a silver bikini straddling a bullet-shaped rocket that said "Uranus or Bust."

I didn't want to go for the following four reasons:

(a) it was a party,

(b) it was on New Year's Eve,

(c) my mother would be there, and

(d) Spoonie and his steady girlfriend would be positively adorable together the entire night.

I mean, you don't put an orphan in a room full of happy families, do you?

When Sadie picked me up at nine she announced, "You are not going out like that." I had assembled a man-get-thee-back sort of costume for the occasion, featuring a grannyish, yellow-and-lime-green floral-patterned muumuu housecoat type

215

deal, black-and-white argyle socks, and purple clogs. "Why not?" I had said in mock defiance.

Sadie rolled her eyes. "Because nobody wears clogs in space. They are bad enough on earth." This from a woman in silver jodhpurs and a pink fluffy tube top. (Not to mention her silver strappy platforms that showed off her hand-painted silver-and-pink daisy toenails.) She was back to her old self, all right, now that I was single again.

"I need tenderness!" I crossed my arms and pouted. "Anyway, who am I gonna meet at a *party*?"

Sadie rolled her eyes and jumped up. "Exactly no one so long as you're dressed like that. Or worse, you'll meet the type of person who would be drawn to you in that outfit and trust me, you don't want that. Besides you know the rules, A-B-C, 1-2-3." Smugly she pushed me toward my closet and began to rummage through my tissue-thin summer dresses like a Valleyite at a Barney's sale.

"Thank you, but I have no interest in men. I am through with them." Sadie held up a sheer lilac-colored slip. "You do realize it's the middle of winter." She put it back in exchange for a plaid skirt and baby-T combo.

"I'm tellin' ya, A-B-C, 1-2-3. Pose, counterpose," she said again, making crisscrossing karate chop hand gestures. "If Jym doesn't call, work out so your ass attracts someone who will. If Jasper's career flourishes, date his boss. If his boss doesn't want you, fly to Europe and have a fling with someone who does, like an emperor or something. Now, tonight you are going to look pretty and have fun if it kills you."

"A European emperor? Hello! Bad listener alert!" She began to physically pull the balloon dress over my head. "Sadie," I said, trying to untangle my hair that had got caught on a button, "what I need is to get over Jasper and *men* completely."

"You're the one who said you were *over* Jasper, that he's on a path and you're on a path . . ." She pulled harder. I was thrashing like a drunk in a straitjacket now.

"That was before Jym decided to dump me. It's his fault I'm thinking about Jasper. I just can't believe people think it's acceptable to love you one day and run out on you with zero answers so that you're left holding the bag, again. Jasper is probably with someone else in a loving committed relationship this minute."

"Please. What makes you think either one of them has any skills to actually be with *anyone?* You are going to have a good life, missy, so let's hit it." She chose black patent leather high-heeled tennis shoe boots, then coiled my hair in big loops about my ears, blew silver glitter on my eyes, and spun me around to face my reflection in the floor-length bedroom mirror.

"That's a lot better," I said, bored to my core.

"And don't think you are going to ever get any answers out of Jasper or anybody that would ever satisfy you anyway," she said as we flew across Mulholland in her black Ford Explorer. "I mean, the guy has the personality of a fucking radish, and no one likes radishes."

"Rabbits do," I said, squinting my eyes, and stared out at all the city lights. They made rainbow tracers as we sped past.

We stood in a dangerously long line, hoping to get past the red velvet ropes just so we could be assessed by five ripped doormen as to hipness of space agey costume and general validity of the statement "I am on the list." I thought out loud, "Who invites people to a party and makes them wait to see if they are allowed to come in?"

"Apparently Condé Nast," Sadie said, wryly.

I had almost talked Sadie into leaving when the coffee guy recognized me by my hair and pulled Sadie and me by the arm past the others who would spend at least forty-five more minutes shivering in the cold. He knew the doorman. I silently apologized to each and every Martian, astronaut, and Venusian Goddess as we slinked past—I know, I hate me, too.

"How's it goin'?" asked our grinning savior in the baby blue fleece blanket, draped across his shoulder like a toga. We were now safely inside the all-silver rotating room forty stories high. For some reason I was excited to see him, particularly his white skin and black chest hair hypnotizing me with their crop circle patterns. I racked my brain trying to remember if we had ever exchanged names. Then I noticed the thing he was attached to—an all-legs blonde drop-deader in Eskimo boots, headdress, and fake fur bikini. This set against bedroomy cat eyes and dark eyebrows. She looked like a Siberian husky only taller.

It didn't matter.

"There's Ben Affleck!" Sadie announced suddenly and pulled me toward the bar with arm-dislocating force.

"Well, bye!" I said to the coffee guy. "Oh, and thanks!" He did the "Catch you later" jerk of his head, disappearing beyond an enormous ice statue of a bald eagle in an astronaut's helmet, clutching the earth in its talons.

Sadie put her hands on her hips. "Shit, we lost him!"

"I was talking to that guy, you know."

"Who, future Caesar? Please. He looks like a poor man's Tom Hanks."

I thought, He really does look like Tom, then barked, "Why is it fine for you to chase someone but I can't have one simple conversation."

"That's because you try to make one simple conversation your new boyfriend. Fun *only*, missy!" She chewed on her index finger and scanned the crowd. "There he goes! Ben at six o'clock!" She tore off into a cluster of Spocks, leaving me standing stranded to survey the futuristic onslaught. People roamed around like zombies, only shinier, with free, colored vodka drinks in tall glasses.

My jaw ached from fake smiling at people I had auditioned for, or with, on jobs I had not gotten over the years in various offices around town. I felt queasy with loserishness as the bar made a new rotation around another voice-over enemy.

By the stage in the center of the room where Spoonie would be performing in less than an hour, I overheard a freaky girl I lost a foot deodorizer ad to brag about dreaming the cover of *The Dancing Wu Li Masters* when she was only eight, *before* she ever saw the book. "It totally rewired my matrix." She was hitting on a smooth-faced agent from my agency with a greying ponytail held in place by Buddhist beads. He wore a yellow plastic lifesaver around his paunch and T-shirt that said Jewpiter. She'd have her own sitcom by sunrise.

Standing by a giant glass window, I realized I had a perfect view of hell. I suddenly ducked behind a fake ficus to avoid my mother, who was now arm in arm with Quentin Tarantino. I did not even want to know what that could possibly be about.

That's when Baby accosted me instead. Everybody called her Baby because she had a head too big for her body, zero attention span, and, moreover, because that's what she called everyone else. Baby was in Publicity. My father worked with her for a stretch. Betty Boop on drugs, my mother would say. Girls like her made me want to eat more, even when I wasn't hungry, just to punish them.

"Baby!" she said when she saw me. I tried to pretend I didn't see her, that I was interested in a fake plastic leaf, instead. "Baby!" she said again, kissing the air beside my cheeks. "You just don't meet real men out here! Come visit me in New York where you'll be a star on the bar scene!" Then she introduced me to a brooding twenty-something actor she'd end up fucking on a motorcycle in an alley in about an hour (another reputation she didn't seem to mind). "This is my friend Craigles," she said, pulling on some silver-beaded elastic bracelets on her wrists.

James Dean raised a beer. Baby wanted me to go to Bar Marmont with her and her thug escort for drinks.

"I can't because I'm here with someone."

"Oh, is he here?" Baby asked, craning her neck and puckering her collagen-injected lips. "Is he a celebrity, too? Spoonie sure got a good one. Did you see the piece in *In Style*?" Craigles looked around, too. It was like he was on a time delay.

"HE is a she. And no, she's behind the scenes." Did I just sound lesbian? Does a PR lady think I'm lesbian?

"Oh." She looked confused. "I don't remember, help me out here, are you gay?" said Baby, eyebrow cocked. Craigles stared, too. Suddenly her bracelet flew apart and beads scattered in a million different directions. Baby started to bend down, then thought better of it. Craigles took his cue to be a gentleman and bent down. Baby grabbed him by the arm, pulling him back, and said, "Never mind, you can just buy me another one when you're a star!"

"No, I only meant my best friend, who's a girl."

"Pity," Baby said sadly. "We were kind of hoping for a three-way." Craigles winked at me and they walked away.

I scanned the crowd for any sign of Sadie so we could make our escape. The bar made another rotation and I passed the coffee guy again. He held an invisible phone to his ear and mouthed "Call me." I laughed and gave him the Fonzie because he was such a giant dork.

In line at the restroom, I found Sadie. "Cosmopolitan?" She tried to hand me the pink drink.

"No, thank you. Where have you been? I want to leave!"

She swallowed her drink in a single gulp. "Ben-land. Too skinny." Once she broke up with a guy because he lost so much weight that he actually shrank to a woman's size four. If you mention his name Sadie will convulse as if recalling severe food poisoning.

As a tray of multicolored Rice Krispie treats went past on a silver tray, Sadie went with them calling, "It's not even midnight!"

Alone again, I made my way to a nearby table where a set of twins in matching puce jumpsuits, accessories, and headgear sat staring at the empty stage, as though a show were already in progress.

"Hey, you look like Princess Leia!" said the shadow that loomed above me now. I looked up in time to see the most angelic human I'd ever beheld—olive skin and green eyes and long black hair tied up about his ears in two loopy coils.

"Hey, so do you." It was true. To top it off he was wearing a pair of plaid pants, an olive green T-shirt that exposed his pierced navel, and a pair of silver *clogs*.

"You looked so glum, I thought I'd come over here and cheer you up. Charlie Mate!" said Charlie like we were old chums. He sounded like Tom Waits. He gave me an elbow to shake as his large manly hands were in the middle of attempting to peel an orange in one perfect tear. His knuckles looked like the knots in a hundred-year-old tree.

"America," I said.

"That's a cool name," said Charlie. "Were your parents hippies?"

Whenever I have a conversation with an intimidating guy, it always feels like that scene in *Ordinary People* where Timothy Hutton runs into the crazy girl who tells him everything is going great in her life. The next time he hears about her, however, she has committed suicide. I wonder if he can tell that he is saving my life by having eyes that green.

"My dad was an artist," I said reluctantly.

"Your last name's not Throne by any wild chance?"

Uh-oh. "Actually it is."

"Your dad was deep." He hit his chest with the flat of his palm and nodded his head solemnly, then smiled, so I smiled, too.

"Thanks."

"Yeah, I mean, I figured there can't be too many Americas running around. Voila!" he said, and handed me half of the orange prize with his sticky citrus-scented paw. He reminded me of a cross between Winnie the Pooh and a golden retriever. I was so relieved he knew who my father was but didn't make a big deal out of it I wanted to cry.

Suddenly an old guy in a gold Speedo and gold roller skates offered us kimchee Caesar salads in paper cones which we ate with our fingers and ended up burping throughout the entire rest of our conversation because the dressing was made with rancid oil. At first I was embarrassed by the continual belching, but Charlie turned it into a game. Points for loudness, duration, smell, and frequency. After discussing our favorite books, music, artists, and places to hike, along with therapy and yoga (we both go to Golden Bridge!), Charlie asked me, "Do you ever just feel *done?*"

"Well, actually, yes."

"'Cause I sure do. Excuse my French but no more bullshit, yunno? That's what I'm about."

"I hear ya. I am beyond done with about seventy-three things, including men, dating men, dealing with men, not dealing with men, oh, and did I mention men?" It felt so good to not care if I was impressing him or not.

"Taking care of other people's feelings is pretty overrated. My motto in life is just make *yourself* happy," he said. Then added, "Hey, you have something in your teeth."

"Do I?" I said, utterly smitten.

"Check out my ice sculpture." He pointed to the giant frozen bird.

"You did that?"

"Mm-hm."

"You're an ice sculptor? In *California?*"

"I'm a real rebel."

Just then Lila appeared behind us. "God, please tell me you two know each other and planned these outfits because you practically look like twins!" Then Lila turned toward the stage. "Spoonie's on in like three minutes." She pointed to her red G-Shock. "See you next year!" Then she darted off but not before mouthing, "He's cute!" when Charlie wasn't looking.

The lights dimmed, but not enough for me to miss a glimpse of my mother positioning herself next to Denzel Washington at the foot of the stage. Then the crowd began to throb like a giant amoeba, in time with the industrial guitar, drums, and electric bagpipe. I spotted my mother going in for the kill, by nudging Denzel to clap, which he halfheartedly did for a measure, before moving two people over. I smiled at Charlie. He smiled back.

At ten seconds to midnight Spoonie stopped the music and for a moment everything was perfect. Then we all counted down: Ten! I looked at Charlie. Nine! He wouldn't try to kiss me, would he? Eight! Charlie looked at me with a devilish grin. Seven! In the corner I caught a gander of Sadie making out with a fat Spock. Six! I looked back at Charlie, smiled and blushed. Five! Maybe he had a girlfriend. Four! Maybe he didn't. Three! Anyway, it's too soon to kiss—I started to perspire. Two! No more guys. I closed my eyes. "ONE!!!!" we all screamed. Just then Charlie reached over and grabbed my hand and licked it.

When I got home there was already a message on my answering machine from Charlie Mate. "Are you around? Are you a square?"

"I say that!" I screamed out loud!

"I just want to say it was really nice meeting you tonight and I hope we can get together when you have some free time."

As I lay down on my bed and swathed myself in cozy layers of white flannel and down, pieces of myself came back to me like iron filings to a magnet.

TWENTY-FOUR

A MONTH OF SUNDAYS

"Close your eyes and try to sleep, close your eyes
and try to dream. We belong to the night, we belong
to each other. We belong, we belong,
we belong together."

—Pat Benatar

Charlie and I met in Santa Monica at the mouth of an old fire road, which wound round a massive mountain to an overlook for a Technicolor view of mountains, sky, and sea. I had called Charlie up that morning and asked him to take a walk in nature with me. It felt good to have a no-pressure outing with a nice guy.

All the same, I chewed three pieces of wintergreen gum. Poor hygiene is just poor manners.

Charlie arrived dressed liked a trendy forest ranger in olive khakis with a vintage Boy Scout shirt with a patch that said 420, mirrored police officer sunglasses, and clunky mustard-colored lace-up boots. I was brave enough to pour myself into a pair of jean shorts and a long-sleeved ribbed purple cotton T-shirt, even though my legs were wintry white and unshaven. I figured I needed to be utterly myself right away; that way I'd find out quick who stuck around.

"This is white sage," he said as we made our way to the first of several plateaus, and then told me its Latin name along with the names of about sixteen other neighboring green items. Of course, he knew about plants. It turned out Charlie had his own little herb garden. Mint and chocolate geranium were his favorites. I was so nervous about my breath and memorizing the plants and their corresponding names that at no time did I notice the ingrown hair on my leg the size of a small dog until we began to dig into our ascent. I panicked. Decided to hug the area closest to the fall so that he wouldn't see the red inflamed boil side of my leg; but Charlie was wily and crisscrossed back and forth in front of me to point out some type of succulent ground cover and tiny yellow wild-flowers. "This is mustard!" He pulled the yellow blossoms off the slender green stalk for me to taste. Mustard, I thought. I had to laugh inwardly because of Spoonie's and my codeword for trouble . . .

"This is licorice and this one is yucca." I stayed low, unable to concentrate on a thing Charlie said because I was sweating so much *and* straining to hide the bump.

I touched IT compulsively now, with every other step. I was all bump and minimal forward motion.

"Are you OK?" he asked suddenly.

"What? Why?"

"Because you're walking kind of funny."

"Oh?" I said, a deer in the headlights.

"You're walking like this." He demonstrated it for me. "Like you have poopie trou or something," he said, grinning. I dropped to the ground and pulled my shirt over my bent knees, buried my face in my hands. "Dude, did I say something wrong?"

"No," I said to my navel, "it's just that you're so honest and I don't know you and . . . and . . ."

He crouched beside me, put a hand on my back. "Just say it."

I pointed to my leg, ran my hand over the fabric that hid it. "Bump!"

"Where?" He pulled at the end of my shirt trying to get a look.

"NOOOOOOOO!"

"Let me look at it." He bent down on all fours and leaned forward. Without lifting my face, I raised the shirt and revealed the lump. "Eeuwwww! It's *huge!* Can I pop it?"

"NOOOOOO!" I screamed again. I pulled my shirt back down and began to rock myself back and forth. "Go away!" I peered at him over my left kneecap. He was smiling devilishly.

"Let me pop it, can I?" His intentions seemed so pure, I let him lift up my shirt once more. Upon closer examination, he decided it wasn't ripe for picking and found some wild lavender, plucked a sprig, crushed the blossom and the stem, and applied it like a salve instead. Then we collected eucalyptus leaves and he told me to boil them with some gauze and apply it like a poultice. I had never heard the word poultice used in real life before, certainly not by a handsome, heterosexual twenty-six-year-old man.

The following Tuesday I asked Charlie if he wanted to hit the museum for the Cubist show that was still running. My dad's stuff had been up for weeks at LACMA and I kept promising myself I'd go. Charlie was dressed like a Salvador Dali painting complete with pocket watch. Before we piled into his giant dented blue flatbed truck with the sticky starter, he climbed my tree. My tree! The one the feng shui people told me prevented me from ever getting a man, that tree. Charlie climbed it. *Climbed* it. Climbed IT. I was so shocked I dropped my purse.

Strolling through the great halls and seeing the look of awe on Charlie's face as we stopped to examine a piece of my father's called *If all else fails choose D, none of the above,* a painting of pure sky, made me recall one of the only things I did like about seeing my father's work on display. I liked it best when the pieces belonged to us, before they had to pack their bags and travel to a gallery overseas: in our living room above the fireplace or propped up against a hall closet or blocking the door to a guest bathroom.

We paused at another from his book called *Barely Mammal*—a Ku Klux Klan guy holding a gun to the head of a black Raggedy Andy doll, and then another, a favorite called *Gargoyle*, which is just a building gargoyle looking after some pigeons with a fountain and a roller-skating street scene in the distance.

Suddenly I'm five, and seven, and thirteen, sitting in my parents' kitchen late at night watching my father heat up a bowl of chili straight from the can. We make color jokes. It's one of my favorite things to do, to have quiet time alone with him like this. While he waits for the lugubrious brown stew to boil, we call out horrifying color combinations and laugh and laugh. I say something like "Apple green and orange plus brown." And he says something like "That's nothing. Beige, mildew, and Washington, D.C." or "Turquoise, leather, and tofu." If I try to argue leather isn't a color he tickles me. Sometimes if we are driving, Spoonie and my mother play, too. Car interiors have us peeing in our pants. Strip mall color schemes send us over the moon. The very *idea* of fabric stores flattens us.

When Charlie and I get to a piece from my father's Cubist period, our feet become cement. The piece is called *From Russia with Glove*. The image is the Statue of Liberty, barefoot in Central Park, wearing a crown of thorns made of splayed Barbie doll legs and an oven mitt. Charlie and I can do nothing except look at each other and know instinctively just how sad it is. The loss of a true humanitarian absurdist.

There was nothing to say.

Then I had an epiphany about Cubism. I had always despised Cubist art, but now I understood that it wanted us all to comprehend the full scope of things, to be able to see and *know* everything from wherever you stood. To see the *back* of the head of those you love and the inside of their heart at the same time as you look them directly in the eye. Inwardly, I thanked Charlie.

When I got home I decided to spruce the place up a little, so I picked wildflowers from all my neighbors' yards and hillsides. Daffodils in an old tea tin in my kitchen window near the sink, iris in a jelly jar by my bed, and a single white camellia in a mint-green-and-white chipped finger bowl by my father's easel.

The next day I was still feeling so inspired from our museum visit that I called Charlie and asked him if he wanted to paint pottery. In the clean little terra cotta–tiled shop on Main Street I was suddenly nervous. I felt the pressure of my father's artistic legacy, and picked out an inconspicuous unfinished soap dish, but Charlie wouldn't have it. He picked out a large white unfinished salad bowl, because he wanted something large he could paint with me. My courage surfaced: I wondered if it would stay at his place or mine or if we should just move in together to avoid an argument.

I let Charlie choose the colors. A girl in a navy apron squirted the paint onto a single square of glazed white tile, orange and ice blue and magenta, dark green and brown, pink and plum. I looked around the room. It was hard not to notice things differently with Charlie around. For example, the relationship between things in pairs: the edge of the table we sat at and the corner of his chair, the bottom of the clock and the door frame overhead, the way the viny plants in the window leaned in toward each other.

"What are you thinking about?" asked Charlie.

"Uh!" I said blushing, twirling my paintbrush in the water, watching it turn a milky blue, "um, things in pairs actually."

Charlie jolted straight up in his seat, turned his side of the bowl around for me to see: a big fat PEAR next to a bunch of dancing bananas with top hats and faces, and a scruffy-looking creature with four legs and antlers that looked like it started out as a dog and then turned into a goat, maybe.

"OK, I know that's a pear, and those are dancing bananas, but what the hell is that?"

He contorted his body to my side of the table to examine it again and then sat up triumphantly. "It's a goatbear!" We erupted into peals of laughter. "What did you make?" He sat straight-spined in his seat now. His whole face softened. "Wow!"

I lightly smacked his arm. "Shut up!"

"I'm serious. It's really nice. Really . . . feminine." I crinkled my nose up. "You're like a real artist. I love the colors."

"Nah." I pulled a face.

"Really." He looked sad now. "Don't close off. See?" He turned the bowl back around for me to see. I looked at what I had done, trying to see it through Charlie's eyes: intertwining vines and roses and two birds and two dancing fairy ladies and some snakes with mosaic multicolored backs.

"Not SO bad," I said, brushing my hair behind my ear. Affectionately he conked me on the head.

Later that night we ended up in a carpeted piano bar at some divey hotel in West Hollywood. Charlie knew that no one was ever there, so we sat and played the piano even though I can't. We ended up singing all the Pat Benatar songs we knew at the top of our lungs to the dead drunk amusement of a few lingering lonelyhearts and some random staffers. Soon the man with the industrial strength vacuum cleaner and the too shiny skin was using the end of his nozzle as a microphone for a duet with Charlie. "Hell Is for Children" never sounded so good.

"Does he have a girlfriend?" Sadie said when I called her from my cozy bed. I had Tulie curled up beside me and I watched her dream with her eyes open.

"I don't know," I said softly, stroking Tulie's pink belly.

"Did he try to kiss you?"

"No."

"Ooh, that's a bad sign."

"Sadie . . ."

"He's either gay or he has a girlfriend."

"Maybe he's just being respectful?"

"You see each other all the time and talk 500 times a day and have all this synchronicity and he hasn't tried to jump you? Something's fishy in Denmark."

"Or maybe he's a grown-up, Sadie, and what's the rush if it's forever?" I said, biting dry skin off from around my index finger. "It's like he lives his life like in The Book! Every day he shows me something else! Every day he has a passion for some *new* thing!"

"He has a girlfriend."

"Sadie!"

"Where's the rose connection? If he's the *one*, where's the rose? Huh?"

I twisted my hair around my index finger. "Maybe she got it all wrong. Maybe that's all superstitious nonsense."

"Just do me a favor and go out with this guy I met in my spinning class. You might like him."

"What guy?"

"He's a math teacher. He's from ROSEville."

"Sadie, my plate is full."

"Well, at least add a side dish for Godsakes, at least find out if he has a girlfriend before you go all gaga on me."

"Goodnight, Mom."

"Goodnight, *Mission: Impossible* to deal with."

On Wednesday night I asked Charlie if he felt like dancing. He suggested that I meet him at The Temple, a dance studio tucked deep in the Valley. Sun Valley far. Ikea far. At a warehouse with a little parking area surrounded by barbed wire. He told me to look for a single red light—that's how I could tell the difference late at night between the dance studio I was looking for and the sheet metal supply house, the wax supply house, the paint warehouses, the marble supply house, and the terra cotta pot and garden outlet.

I was ill-prepared for the calming beauty assault of the large room with wood floors and high airplane hangarish ceilings. A ballet barre ran the length of the room, and in the corner, a bench had been decorated like an altar and lay littered with fragrant magnolias and a row of ligzhted white candles. Industrial music with African and Brazilian samples blared. Barefooted, people of every size, shape, and color had their eyes closed and were just dancing wildly. It looked like a scene out of the *Woodstock* movie, like one of my dad's sittings, only holy.

"Just let your body move the way it wants to. This is like the opposite of yoga. Just totally free your mind. Over there on the altar you can offer up your intention. Tonight I am going to dance the purity of connection along with a little don't-make-me-pay-my-Visa-late-charge on the side." Following Charlie's lead, I slipped off my shoes. He smelled like sandalwood.

He grabbed my hand and pulled me onto the floor. At first I was shy about letting Charlie see the way the music moved me, but when he started hopping around like a Mexican jumping bean, I felt a little more free. After an hour of swaying and jumping and bumping and weaving in and out of sweaty backs and damp pits and fingers outstretched like sea anemone feelers, I was fearless. It actually felt good to be in my own skin. To be myself completely opposite Charlie, who was also himself, and not lose *me*. I felt a radiance in my belly, like we were all walking around with little potbelly stoves full of light, beaming it back and forth at one another. Everyone was just a light being on a path, dancing through life.

I wiped my eyes with the back of my hand for the realization. Maybe this is what Jasper meant in his letter. I looked over at Charlie. His eyes were closed. He was giving himself a long luxurious hug.

Later, over cheap Mexican food in Glendale, I broke down and told Charlie about Jasper and Jym, mainly to get things off my chest, but secretly to initiate a dialogue about our possible future together without scaring him off by talking about myself. I figured he'd just naturally bring up his whole relationship deal if I broke the ice.

When I got to the part about how I didn't understand why all the people I have ever loved never loved me back, including my dad, and that I had never actually seen a relationship that actually worked, it started to sound like a story about a girl I knew once. Charlie must have felt this, too, because in the middle of building his guacamole fortress like that scene in *Close Encounters,* he looked at me and said point blank, "Dude, you didn't do anything wrong. No one did. Relationships are all about flow and finding someone who makes you feel good because they are just flowing right alongside of you doing their own thing. A lot of it just comes down to plain old timing and luck . . ." Even though he said the word "dude," my chest tightened and vibrated like a paper drum, like a revelation was about to blast on through.

Charlie leaned in closer, smelling of onion salsa, dried sweat, and denim, and popped a tortilla drenched in guacamole in my mouth. The candles on the table in clay pots made his face light up like a sun. "When something's right, it's just . . . right. Dude, you're totally great, so don't even sweat it." I felt so seen, I ached.

"I feel so lucky to have met you."

"Me, too," he said, taking my hand. I looked up at him. Tears of joy were in my eyes. He handed me a hankie from his jacket pocket, embroidered with tiny hand-stitched roses. I could not help but laugh. Of course you carry real old-fashioned handkerchiefs with roses on them you miracle.

On my drive home, alone, speeding along Mulholland under a canopy of stars, I thought, Let me get this straight, men *can* do nice things for you? Men can show up when they say they are going to *and* do their own laundry *and* drive *and* let you express your feelings *and* hug you when you cry and give you *good* advice? Is this some kind of a gag?

Then I had a conversation with the moon. When I was little, on the long drive back from picking up my father from his old studio, I would lie in the backseat while my mother drove him home along this very same road. As we wound along, I would alternate between watching my exhausted father's profile while he reclined in the front passenger seat and making sure the moon was still following us. Sometimes it seemed the moon was leading the way, ducking behind great dark pines every now and then, but mostly it seemed like it was making sure we got home safe. Now I'm checking to see if the moon's watching over Charlie tonight. Leaning my head out the window, I was sure her benevolent face was saying yes.

At that moment, Angelyne pulled up beside me in her pink Corvette. She looked spun sugar–fragile, tired. I thought,

Underneath all that hair and makeup and baby doll sexuality is someone just like me, someone who wants love, someone who wants to know who she is and what she does so she can say, "I existed in this moment of time!" and leave her mark on the world for everyone to behold. I wondered what love she had lost, and hoped she had found someone who truly saw her beauty like I saw hers. Like Charlie saw mine. When the light turned green she sped past like a pink human comet. Don't we all want the same things?

When I got home, in my journal I wrote:

> Thank you God. As a result of knowing Charlie Mate these are the things I will not miss about being in a relationship with Jasper Husch and Jym Court:
>
> 1. That panicky feeling that I couldn't be myself.
> 2. That jealous feeling whenever we were apart.
> 3. That anxious feeling when they didn't call.
> 4. That frustrated feeling when we talked things through and neither one of us felt anything had been resolved.
> 5. That lonely feeling when they don't hold me enough or for long enough.
> 6. That painful feeling when we'd have sex and they'd just grind away and only he'd orgasm and I'd feel empty inside and physically uncomfortable if not in actual pain.
> 7. That angry feeling when they didn't care enough to see a couples counselor to work through things even though they said they loved me.
> 8. That less-than feeling when they'd hang out with losers and treat them like they were so much more interesting than me.

Under this, in crayon, I colored a rainbow with pinks and blues and lavenders and reds and then covered over all of it with black crayon, like you do when you're a kid. Then, with the end of a paper clip, I drew a little self-portrait: a girl in a dress of moons and hearts, under a canopy of stars.

As I climbed into bed, inwardly I prayed, If it's not too much to ask, could you make Charlie love me forever and send me a little job so that I don't have to take money from my mother anymore or at least a sign as to my real purpose, just so I know you're real? Thanks.

The rest of the month went like this:

Thursday: Picnic in Griffith Park. Drink virgin sangrias, take pictures with real camera and read poetry aloud in the sun: Rumi, Hafiz, Mary Oliver . . . Discuss importance of classical music. So swoony when I go, accidentally leave wallet in Charlie's truck.

Come home to three annoying messages from my mother, saying she misses me and when can I come help her clean out the office and to remind me she is thinking about selling our childhood home or at least remodel the kitchen (again) and to say the real estate person is coming on Friday so again could I please please please come help her clean out "the office."

Friday: Meet Charlie at Starbucks for wallet and surprise pix. Sit in car and talk for hours. Smell and covet jean jacket he accidentally leaves in back of car. Drive home holding it to face. Get home and post photo of us looking like the Twin Stars on bulletin board above computer I never use.

Saturday: Go on voice-over audition for BBQ sauce wearing lucky jean jacket. Meet at Starbucks to return jacket. Receive gift of old T-shirts and patches Charlie thought I might like.

Spend rest of rainy afternoon alone, whimsically darning socks and jeans with homemade patches and embroidery thread. Have massive crush on Self. Listen to only Bach (Glenn Gould on piano, Heinrich Schiff on cello). Avoid picking up phone when my mother calls again about today being the perfect day to clean out office.

Later, go to Largo with Charlie to see Spoonie open for Repeat Offenders and Squeezeboxx.

Monday: Receive annoying phone call on car phone from my mother about making time to talk to annoying journalist for *Vanity Fair* piece on her to run in conjunction with my father's birthday and retrospective in Frankfurt in the middle of drive to beach with Charlie for guitar sing-along and lesson on how to build fire in sand.

Tuesday: Talk about luck and flow, book commercial for BBQ sauce called Luv'n'Fun. Call Charlie. Make a plan to go to Big Bear to see snow to celebrate. Make perfect cup of Earl Grey tea with half&half and two sugars. Thank God up and down, mostly for getting out of cleaning out office with mother. For first time ever, feel like things are turning around for the better. Think all suffering was meant to lead me to bliss as result of Charlie.

Know beyond a shadow of doubt consummation of Charlie's love for me is only matter of time.

TWENTY-FIVE

BABY'S BREATH

"You keep this love, thing, child, toy.
You keep this love, fist, scar, break.
You keep this love."

—Pantera

You learn a lot about a man from his toothbrush. Charlie had two.

He had finally invited me over to his tiny Silverlake one-bedroom house for a home-cooked dinner. While he checked on the parchment paper salmon and cockle rapini he was cooking in his dishwasher, I snooped around. Out on his tiny wooden deck decorated with small white hanging lights, I met his various herbs in tiny terra cotta pots neatly arranged on a low picnic table bench. Lavender and tarragon and basil, only they had names like Lola and Sweetums and Nettie-Arlene. Near a spotted dish with a generous portion of old scrambled eggs for the neighbor's cat, I spun the tire of a bicycle that hung from a hook under a yellow striped awning and went inside the humble cottage.

Near a large window, there was a small metal card table from the fifties with a white enamel top and three mismatched metal chairs with diamond patterned velvet cushions in sumptuous golds and purples. A patchwork quilt covered one wall while exactly opposite hung an Israeli poster of Sammy Davis Jr. in a pair of sunglasses giving the smokin' guns. Above a foldout futon couch, there were hats with buckles, buttons, plumes, and silk flowers for nearly any occasion. The digs were small, but cozy; magical. It looked as though a secretly rich jester lived there.

While the wild rice steamed, we decorated devil's food cupcakes. We mixed food coloring into little pots of store-bought vanilla frosting, made our own colors. Mauvy brown, orangish-pink, grey. I was as free as a kid again. Charlie put a big swipe of blue frosting on my nose. I let it dry there, almost wishing it were a tattoo.

Then I made the mistake of excusing myself to use his restroom to pee (and secretly see how I looked with blue frosting on my nose) only to excitedly discover we had the same Queen Amidala toothbrush.

When I emerged, waving the toothbrush wildly in my hand, he froze and before he could utter a word his body gave him away. "That's my fiancée's. Mine is the other one, the plain blue one."

"Oh," I said, trying to play it off like I already knew he had a fiancée. "Well, I have the same one as her."

Her sounded funny and separated itself from my sentence, hung suspended in the air like that staticky transmission of Princess Leia when she appears and begs for Obi-Wan's help. Of course he had a fiancée. As I looked around his house now, it became crystal clear.

There were little feminine touches everywhere, China Rain–scented candles, a pink paper lantern in the window, a framed poem written on a stained cookie doily. And a fucking right out in the open goddamned Lilith Fair CD.

At that point Charlie began to pace.

"Her name's Arielle; she's a part-time model who works with the blind, training guide dogs, and she's away right now on a bathing suit assignment in Jamaica but she hates it because the modeling world is so fake and what we really want to do is open up a little restaurant and have a full-service catering business complete with flowers and ice sculptures and hors d'oeuvres and stuff because, I mean, people love parties and with the whole Internet deal I think people are really gonna want to get back to basics like good clean eating and artistry in general, and dinner's almost ready so why don't you take a seat."

I thought about all the men I had ever loved in terms of their toothbrushes. Jasper's had bristles made from hemp and he was obsessed with porn; Jym's was electric and he wasn't so great at head; my first boyfriend used a Water Pik and he never wanted sex. I wondered what horror I was being spared by seeing Charlie's plain blue toothbrush—impotence? infidelity? schizophrenia? *nymphomania?* WAS HE A WOMAN? Suddenly I was furious.

"Did you think we'd have an affair?"

"No," he said sweetly, "I thought we'd become awesome friends."

"Oh, so I'm not good enough, is that it? I'm not attractive enough for you?"

"No . . . I . . ."

I brushed tears away with my fingers. "Why didn't you tell me?"

"It never came up. I really wanted to but I didn't know how. I was actually gonna tell you tonight and I'm really glad we are talking about this now." Then calmly he said, "Phew! I feel a lot better."

God, he was worse than Karl, so thorough and even-tempered. I felt like the Tasmanian Devil spinning out of control next to him. Then Charlie began to cry, too. "I'm sorry for not telling you sooner. I had no idea I would like you this much. I never meant to hurt you." He wiped his nose on his arm. I noticed how golden blond and hairy his arm hair was. The snot made a silvery trail as it dried on his skin.

Click click click click click—my mind was a busy arrivals and departures sign updating its schedule again. That would explain why he never tried to kiss me, why he never walked me to my door and never even came in my house, ever. I thought, Have I filled in the empty spaces with my own explanations and deductions *again?* What did I do THIS time? I wanted to run out to my car and drive away, but even standing here arguing and being sad with him was more fun than anything else in the world, so I stared out his big bay window instead. The sun was setting now.

She's a part-time model who works with the blind repeated in my head. I thought, Part-time. Oh, she's beautiful *all* of the time, but she just models part of the time, making a fortune when it's convenient for *her.* But her *real* passion? That's donating her time *training dogs for the blind.*

I looked at Charlie now, watched him light three blue candles. His eyes were damp and shone wet in the flickering light. I thought, This guy is never going to leave her. I'd have to be modeling for Amnesty International on a full-time basis to turn his head and even make a dent. "She's coming back in two weeks and I'd really love for you two to meet. I think you'll really like each other."

"Yeah, sure, whatever." I tried to laugh it all off, but I snorted snot out of my nose and had to excuse myself.

In the safety of their bathroom, hugging my knees in close, I said her name out loud, "Arielle." That made it real. Then I rested my head on the toilet with the clear undersea themed polyurethane lid. Seeing the seaweed and tiny opalescent seashells and a sea horse trapped forever in plastic made me feel even sadder. Charlie knocked on the door.

"Everything OK in there?"

I wondered if I would ever have real love all to myself with someone as real as Charlie, forever.

"Mer, please come out here and have dinner with me."

I wanted to hate him. Instead I opened the door. "Charlie," I said.

"Yeah?"

"Does she know about me? I mean what did you tell her about *me*?"

But their phone rang.

The machine picked up and a girl's voice, soft and nervous, pleaded "Baby, are you there? It's an emergency." He ran for it. I moved outside to give him some privacy. Under a million twinkling galaxies I wondered how many other people were sitting down to awkward heartbreaking dinners this minute.

I could see him pacing from the warm yellow light of the kitchen to the dark of the den. Then I heard him say, "OK. I'll be on the next flight out." With heavy steps Charlie came outside to tell me the news: "Arielle's father had a heart attack." This hit me like a bowling ball punch in the teeth. "They don't know how serious it is, but . . ."

"Of course, yeah, my God. Is there anything I can do?" I said, gathering up the dishes.

"No, just leave it," he said before scurrying off to pack.

The air felt cool against my face. Suddenly I'm three, sitting in my father's lap in a dark room. I am holding my stillborn baby sister. I'm trying not to spill her off my lap. I like how tiny her fingers are. I think my mom is mad at me because she won't let me hold her all by myself, even though she is not heavy at all. She holds the head and says, "We are going to say good-bye now." My mom says her name over and over again. Shiva Plum Shiva Plum. My daddy is crying, I think he is mad at me, too. Then the men put her in the tiny coffin my daddy made for the baby. My mom just keeps kissing her and I get to kiss her, too. Then my daddy pulls her away gently and my mom's fingers are stiff and she is crying and won't look at us. Thinking of it now, I wonder why our capacity for grief has to grow roots, too.

With their mismatched dishes in my arms I looked up in time to see a shooting star streak across the night sky. I made a healing wish for her, for them, then wiped the blue frosting off my nose.

I came home to two messages. One was Charlie, calling me from the airport to tell me he was just thinking about me and wanted to make sure I was all right. He wondered if I wanted to have coffee on Thursday when he got back to town. "No, thank you," I said out loud.

The second, from my mother: "Mer, darling, it's Camilla calling. Listen, Larry Flynt saw the piece they ran on me in *Vanity Fair,* the one with the family photo; anyway, like I said, his office called and wanted to know if you and Grandma and I would be interested in doing a photo spread entitled 'Three Generations of Pussy' for *Hustler.* I told them I didn't think you would be interested, but just call me so I can let them know for sure. Grandma said whatever you decide is fine. It would be a free trip to Capri or the Bahamas, but I'm fine either way. Love you! *Mchwa!*"

TWENTY-SIX
RADIOACTIVATE (REPRISE)

"You are a free moth, go chase the light."
—Innocence Mission

"Jasper are you there? It's me. America. Of course you're not there: it's voice mail. I . . . I just wanted to tell you . . . I'm thinking about you . . . and that I love you. Bye."

Fuck.

TWENTY-SEVEN
CRACK BABY PETEY

"Pull me out of the aircrash."

—Radiohead

"As far as calling Jasper a year ago, six *months* ago even, you would have driven up there, so although it's a minor backslide, calling and *not* engaging is actually tremendous progress. And Charlie, well . . ." Karl said, patient as always, ". . . it's a hard lesson to learn that you can have it all and it still might not work out, that nice guys can sometimes just be boy *friends*." I looked at the stuffed animals all lined up in a row now, Elmo and Kanga and Froof-Bunny, their blank black googily eyes staring back at me from the tantrum couch. I faked a gag reflex. I disgusted myself.

"Well, I want the rest of it, goddamnit!"

"I hear your anger, but maybe Charlie can be a *friend* to you." The way he said "friend" made me think of movies about cavemen. Me friend, this fire, fire bad.

"Ha! If I'm so anxious to give love away, why don't I just adopt a little crack baby? At *least* give it away to someone who *deserves* it. It's insane—I'm healthy, educated, I can vote, I can wear whatever I like, I have no REAL money worries, my car is paid for, I have a beautiful home, I'm white . . ." I looked at Karl pleadingly. "What kind of happiness can I really expect to have?"

He coughed into his hand, adjusted his ass in his seat. "Well . . ."

"Why isn't that enough? Why do I want a boyfriend so much?" I pounded my fist into my thigh.

"Don't beat yourself up, America. I think we are doing real work here to make sure you are whole in YOU first. The true desire to reach out to others naturally arises when it stems from a real satisfaction with Self." He traced an invisible capital S in thin air.

"I'm so bored of being sad."

"How bored?"

He faced his desk, unlocked his file cabinet, pulled a piece of paper free from a tan folder and handed it to me. It was a flyer, black ink on glossy white paper; in calligraphy font next to a dark-haired woman's smiling face, it read:

> There can be no suffering in True Freedom. Join Luna Forrest at The Thistlewood Community Retreat Center conveniently located an hour from Portland for eleven days of silence in the beauty of an old growth forest for an opportunity to remember your true nature.

I looked over at Karl's smiling face. *Eleven* days of silence? The worst cases in his practice only needed nine. Was I *worse* than the worst case? Karl must have seen my panic because he said, "Mer, she's a wonderful teacher, she cuts right to the heart of things; well, actually, *you* do . . ." He trailed off, as if remembering a wonderful vacation. Outside the sun was beginning its descent. I traced a slat of light and dark across the deep-sea carpet. It cast a shadow across Karl's face and made him appear as though he were wearing an executioner's hood. Then he looked at me. "I think you're ready."

I swallowed. "Can I think about it?"

"You mean *postpone?*"

I forgot how annoying he could be. I promised myself never to come back, ever. If I only accomplished one thing in my life it would be to never return to that office.

Dr. Karl leaned in and rested his elbow on his tweed leg. "If you do decide to go, I guarantee you will be a different person." A fire truck roared by, sirens blaring. I felt like that truck.

"I want a good life."

"You have a good life now. You are just playing some old tapes that you need to unlearn." He sounded like one now. "All right now, I think we are done for today. This one's on me."

When I moved toward the open door to go, Dr. Karl held his arms out and offered me a hug, smelling of almond massage oil and tobacco. I leaned forward and stuck my butt out so our hips wouldn't touch. He patted me on my back behind my heart like he was trying to burp me. "How 'bout letting the Future You start to make some of your decisions from here on out. And remember, the treasure doesn't do the hunting. All right, now!"

I was turning left onto 26ᵗʰ, heading toward San Vicente, past hacienda-style homes with neatly clipped hedges, when Sadie called.

"There you are! He fucks like a goddamned criminal, Mer. I'm serious. I'm totally in love."

I stopped at a red light and watched a blonde woman in an all-white G-string yoga getup drop her purple rubber yoga mat, only to be helped by some dreamy yoga hunk with long flowing brown hair.

"That's great, Sadie," I said, forcing enthusiasm.

"What's the matter? You sound sad."

"I'm just a little depressed. I just came from—"

She cut me off. "Listen, come and meet me and Swane tonight down at Spaceland. Swane wants us to go see this band Rows Five Through Seven. Supposedly they do an insane version of 'Wind Beneath My Wings.'" I squinted. The light turned green.

"You mean like a chaperone?"

"OOOH!" she squealed. "No, but that is so funny . . ."

"Wait, who's Swane?"

"Swane Swanee. That guy I met at New Year's."

"Fat Spock?"

"He called me the minute he got back. He's been out of the country. Location scouting. So do you want to come?"

"Oh, I don't know, I'm just feeling . . ."

"Oh, boo, never mind then." She whispered now, "Mer, he's huge, I'm serious. Hung like a horse. I have to whisper 'cause I'm at his house and . . ." I heard a male voice now, shouting something from another room. She called out to him, "What, honey? I can't hear you. Yeah, OK, in a minute. Mer, he wants me to join him in the fucking shower. Can you fucking believe this? I totally get what you mean by 'you just know'! I gotta go. If you change your mind meet us down there at eleven!"

"Yeah, OK," I said, stopping at another red light. I hung up and thought, This is so my life. Just when I'm single and miserable, Sadie gets a boyfriend.

Suddenly the Tom Hanksy coffee guy, clad in newsprint biker paraphernalia, rapped on my car window with his gloved knuckle. I jumped. "Oh, sorry! I didn't mean to scare you!"

Horrified that he caught me looking so awful, I rolled down my window, forced a big smile, and accidentally said, "I'm doing great!" before he even asked me how I was.

He looked at me quizzically and said, "Me, too. Hey, I'd give you another flyer to see my band but I know you won't show." I wanted to apologize, or at the very least follow him home and make out, but I knew that fixation was not where my health was at, so I just nodded. I could tell that he felt my blow-off energy by the way he looked away and wiped his mouth with the back of his gloved hand. Just then, "Wind Beneath My Wings" came on on my car radio. All I could do was flap my hands as if trying to put out a campfire. "Oh no. Oh no!" I said. I was so weirded out by the synchronicity of Sadie's call and horrified at the same time that Mr. Dreamy caught me dialed into an easy listening station that I turned nine shades of beet red. The light turned green. Then the coffee guy bit the Velcro end of his black glove, tightening the strap, and half-waved good-bye.

"See ya!" I called after, then thought, This is so my life.

As I sped up the tree-lined street, past joggers on cell phones with miniature headsets in the center divider, a flock of migratory birds caught my eye. I leaned against my car door, craning to see the birds rise and fall, rise and fall, felt the cool of the glass against my skin.

"I'm coming, I'm coming!" I shouted to my ringing phone as I turned the key in the lock of my front door that I had only recently painted cranberry—to attract love. "Hello?"

"Mer, it's Camilla calling."

"Yes, Mother, I recognize your voice." I dropped my keys on the kitchen table, thumbed through mail, bills, coupons, a postcard from my dentist reminding me to come in for a cleaning, and a menu from Totally Thai!

"Listen, darling, I really need you to help me clean out the office. Those documentary people are coming and I need you to help me pull slides and . . ."

"What documentary people? When?" Tulie scratched on the back door asking to be let out.

"The people from Belgium radio." She made a crunching, chewing sound. "For the show in April to coincide with the show at the Kunstmuseum in Frankfurt." She was slurring some of the words, trying to talk and swallow at the same time. "Yunno, the one I asked Jasper to do the program cover for." Hearing Jasper's name plunged me into a frozen lake. My mother took another bite of something loud. "Now, I need you to be available to be interviewed and I need the house to look—"

"Radio, Belgium, Frankfurt, wait—what? Why did you call Jasper? When did you talk to him? And what the *fuck* are you eating?" Tulie scratched the back door again. *Please let me out.*

"Potato chips. I didn't, he called me." I was pacing now. "America, I told you all this. We are all going over there in the spring and Jasper expressed interest in doing the program guide and I don't think he can be there at the show but—"

Deep creases formed along my brow. "No, Mother, no you didn't tell me, because if you did I would have told you then what I'm telling you now, *do not fucking talk to him.* And I certainly would have told you not to ask him to do the program. When did you talk to him? WHEN?" I absentmindedly rapid-fire flexed and released the muscles in my calf.

"Oh, I don't know, right around your birthday? He said he has the time even though he's right in the middle of about seventeen things . . ." Tulie scratched at the door again.

"Please don't chew in my ear, Mother." I grabbed a clump of hair on the top of my head, began to pace again, stretching as far as the cord would allow. "I cannot fucking believe this. Jasper and I aren't even speaking and . . ."

"I can't talk to you when you're like this. Good-bye, Mer."

"He broke my fucking heart, Mother! Do you understand that?"

"He's a fine artist and I really don't see . . ."

"How come you don't see *me* as a fine artist? How come you don't think about *me?*"

She cut me off. "America Throne, I did not call you to bear witness to a psychic meltdown, so I'm going to put the phone down."

Tulie made a whimpering sound. I watched her squat then, heard the sound of liquid against wood. "NOOOOOO!" I screamed, as I watched a fine clear stream make a puddle on the floor between her legs.

"Fine. Then shall I tell them Tuesday? You and I can get the room done quickly at the weekend and . . ."

"No! No!"

"Well, what about Jasper?"

"I really have to go, Mother. I have to *go!*" I slammed the phone down so hard, I startled myself.

After I damp-mopped with lemon-scented ammonia, I smoothed the blank page of my journal with my hand and at the top of the page wrote:

THINGS I AM GOOD AT:
Being annoyed by my mother
Being single when Sadie has a man and vice versa
Choosing bad men
And, later, hating them
Looking ugly and saying stupid things when cute guys are near
Being jealous of Spoonie and Lila
Getting dumped
Getting mad
Staying mad
Not believing in God
Breaking out
Having continuous thoughts about dying or killing myself
    alternating with guilt about having those thoughts in the
    first place
Missing my dad
Hating Tulie
Hating myself for hating her
Secretly staying in love with Jasper no matter how much he
    has hurt me or how awful he is

That night I dreamed I was a long-distance runner. I am running along a sidewalk in a suburban neighborhood with neatly trimmed hedges, pacing myself in even measures, my breathing perfectly in sync with my body and the scenery I pass. I run past aspens with shimmery leaves and houses with picket fences and dogs and parked cars in clean driveways. Past Spoonie and Lila smiling and waving. Past my mother gardening. Charlie is there trying to hit *Star Wars* piñatas out of my tree with the end of a broom. I jog in place now and the sky grows suddenly dark. Then I see a woman with a large-brimmed hat drive by in a red pickup truck. In the flatbed I see Jasper in a naked back bend. He has an enormous erection. He massages it in long strokes in time to my breathing. He looks at me and smiles. Then I see that the woman driving the truck is my father. He is smiling, too.

I woke up to a ringing phone. I looked at the clock. 2:17 A.M. "Hello?" I said, clutching at the bosom of my cotton nightie. It was Sadie on her cell. I could hear a mixture of loud garbled voices and then bustling street sounds.

"I'm at Canter's. I have to walk outside so he can't hear me. I think I may have found your dream man. As I am speaking to you I can see the outline of his penis in his jeans. He was on that show *Roswell*. His last name is Rose. Chuck *Rose*nzweig."

"Bye, Sadie." Even in the dark I easily put the phone down back in its cradle. No more Roses, no more Jasper, no more therapy, no more men.

The phone rang again, but I didn't pick up.

I knew what I had to do.

PART THREE
AWAKE AT LAST

TWENTY-EIGHT
OM SWEET OM

"Hold on hold on to yourself,
this is going to hurt like hell."
—Sarah McLachlan

I arrived at Thistlewood, in a light drizzle, in the dark. At a badly constructed rickety wood and glass kiosk a heavyset bearded mountain man told me where I could park my white cigarette-smelling rental car.

I noisily made my way back to Grizzly Adams, dragging my enormous rolling luggage across the gravel parking lot, led mostly by the slender glow of a small red pocket flashlight on the end of my key ring.

The mountain man then proceeded to give me still more spaced-out directions to a certain cabin. He pointed to it on a handout and gave me a wheelbarrow for my gear. "It needs to be promptly returned for others to use." Little brown teeth appeared under the mustache now.

When I asked him the reason why there were absolutely no lights on anywhere, he said it was because they make their own energy here at The Thistlewood Community Retreat Center, using a generator and rushing river water. "It gets recharged overnight, so use electricity sparingly, if at all, man." Then he added, "But hey, isn't it fun to learn to see in the dark like our owl brothers and sisters?" I thanked him and he bade me farewell with a final "Make yourself at home!" The little brown teeth shone again in the dark.

Oh, he's *smiling,* I thought, as I felt my way along a sloping garden path.

After several minutes and zero luck in locating my thatch-roofed shelter, but finding several others, the drizzle turned to rain, then into an actual full-blown storm.

It was muddy and I was frightened to the point of temporary blindness, though I did manage to notice how good it smelled there. Wet and woodsy. Air so clean it stung my lungs to inhale.

Marching over leaf-covered terrain, I finally found cabin eight, the one with the infinity sign—the one I had been cir-cling for nearly an hour because I did not realize that they did not use numbers here, only symbols (a simple fact that I felt should have been explained right up front).

I opened the squeaky screen door and went inside, vowing to get a certain stoner's resignation by lunch. When I turned on the light, it dimmed and hummed. Still, I saw two of the three "beds" were already taken. The room looked like a kidnapper's crime scene *after* the police bust; stained mattresses and sleep-ing bags rolled tight on the floor near an old dirty sink. A faded, drooping army cot by a drafty window, the glass of which was cracked and sort of whistled when the wind whipped by.

Getting settled can be one of my favorite things about trav-eling, unpacking tiny containers from home, but here, my expensive imported creams in black and gold containers looked garishly out of place. I suddenly saw myself as a spoiled over-packed Empress of Good Taste. Then the light flickered out.

Irritated to be trapped alone, in the dark, in an abandoned garden shed, I decided to punish the entire Thistlewood com-munity by not returning the wheelbarrow.

I sat on my cot and after a few minutes of extremely shock-ing dark and quietude, decided I did not want to be alone. So, against my will, I fished through my luggage for my rain slicker, Banana Republic pink-and-blue cashmere scarf, and matching cap. Led by intuition, the smell of burning wood, and a bit of light I could make out in the distance, I headed to the main room of the big log cabin.

Once inside the main cabin, I spied a carved wooden placard above two double doors that read "Om Sweet Om." And another one that said "Namaste." I could hear my father in my head: Namastay-*away* is more like it.

In the dimly lit room I identified a desk, a darkened room beyond with tables and chairs I assumed to be our mess hall, according to the tattered rain-soaked treasure map. Beige couches. Beige chairs. Warped plank floors and several braided rugs in royal blue, rust, and Beige. Homey.

Near an old-fashioned radiator I noticed about thirty pairs of muddy shoes. Did they expect me to remove mine? Ha!

On the wall above them were candid photos of the staff at work in their various practices: Mystical Theatre, Creative Movement, River Rock Meditation, Massage (Watsu, Swedish, Deep Tissue, Thai, Reiki, *or* Esalen style), Continuum Faerie Dancing. When I saw the "e" in "Faerie," I was beginning to feel my depression turn from sadness to horror and devastation, realizing what loving Jasper Husch had amounted to.

I chewed on my pinky fingernail and entered the room where fifty or so people in mismatched mountain attire and wool socks were sitting upright, meditating cross-legged on the forest green–carpeted floor or in folding metal chairs in front of a big roaring fire. At the front of the room I recognized a radiant dark-haired woman, roughly fortyish, in a taupe sweater set and long white skirt, sitting in the lotus position. I thought, Am I as crazy as these people? Do I look like these sad women with the braided hair and these lonely balding men, all gathered together in miserable quietude? I thought not. Still, I guessed we had all been through something pretty awful to end up here.

I scanned their pathetic faces, not a cute guy in the bunch to distract me. I sighed—then took a seat in the back next to a woman swathed in a tie-dyed blanket thrown over her shoulder like a cape.

My chair made a loud squeak when I sat down but no one acknowledged it. I sat upright, crossed my stripy sock-covered feet, and folded my palms in my lap, mostly taking my cues from a large man to my right in an even larger poncho. I listened to the sound of rain beating on a tin roof, to the crackling fire, the modest coughs and blowing of noses, the rustling of fabric, the syrupy yawns and deviated septum breathing, the whistling of the wind. I was just settling into a quiet moment in my busy head when I heard the ding of a tiny bell and looked to its source; Luna clutched a little copper bowl and a small wooden wand and she let its sound resonate and dissipate completely.

She said nothing, just set the bowl back down on a small table with a burning candle, folded her hands in prayer, held them to her forehead, and turned her head to everyone, smiling, until she had blessed every last one of us.

People stood now, and either stretched or wandered out of the room toward their shoes. Some headed toward Luna's empty chair and pressed their foreheads to the floor in respect, or bowed their heads at her as she passed them. Luna smelled like sterling roses. I was so stunned by her radiance, I bowed my head, too. When I looked back up at her, she was bowing back at me. Then she leaned in close, whispered "Welcome," in a thick Scottish accent, her voice as sweet as bananas and cream. "We are now in the silent portion of the retreat but there is a handout for latecomers at the front desk which lets you know what times to gather together. Are you America?"

I wanted to speak but I made the mistake of looking directly into her eyes, which contained a certain vastness that made me feel both instantly at home and homesick.

I rested my hand on the back of a nearby chair to steady myself. I wanted to collapse at her hem and beg her never to let me return to my little pit of despair back in dumb old Hollywood, California. I thought, Oh my God, is she for real? "Are you America Throne?" she said again.

I wiggled my toes inside my socks and managed to find my way back into my body and nodded yes. She smiled at me even more radiantly than before, obliterating any of the irritation from my arrival.

In silence she guided me to the desk where the handouts were resting on a knotty wooden shelf next to a bowl of floating flowers and a small tea light glowing inside a blue jar. I read the schedule:

Namaste and Welcome to Your Self! Three bells will ring indicating the following:

6:30 A.M. rise and shine! (stick figure of a guy yawning with his arms in the air)

7:30 A.M. breakfast (stick figure holding a steaming bowl and a spoon)

9 A.M. group meditation (stick figure in the lotus position)

11 A.M. silent yoga (stick figure with his hands folded at his heart)

12 P.M. lunch (stick figure patting his stomach with his eyes closed and tongue sticking out upwards and the word YUM)

2–5 P.M. volunteer chores (sticky with a bandanna on his head hoeing)

5 P.M. river gazing (sticky in profile next to squiggly lines for water)

6 P.M. dinner (sticky with a fork and knife and a bib around his
  neck)
7:30 P.M. Satsang (sticky with an open mouth)
9:30 P.M. sky gazing (sticky with his head tilted back)
10 P.M. lights out (sticky horizontal with his eyes closed. And
  a bunch of zzzzz)

At the bottom of the page Sticky bids a farewell with a final
finger to his mouth, with Shhhh next to him and the words
"No reading no music no writing no talking. Just being."

"In the meantime, just enjoy the silence and ReeeLOXshh,"
Luna whispered, before heading off into the darkness.

I thought, In the meantime, in the meantime—What a
funny saying! What a funny concept, "the mean time." Then
my roving eye landed on a quote written on a little white
board in blue erasable marker, near the water fountain, underneath the heading FOR CONTEMPLATION:

> "The Real never dies and the unreal never lived."
> —NISARGADATTA MAHARAJ

Suddenly I did not know how long I had been standing
there. My feet were both cement and jelly with little tingles of
electricity rushing through my legs.

One of my roommates had lit a candle and was washing her
face in a little sink by my cot while the other was already in
her sleeping bag in the back of the room. I prepared my toothbrush alongside roomie number one, running icy cold water
on the chewed bristles. When I needed to spit, roomie num-

ber one was still hunched over the sink, with soap all over her face, so I flung the cabin door open and hocked it on the forest floor. The door accidentally closed with a slam, and when I turned around, I got what I perceived as an evil look from the fresh-faced roomie clutching a towel at her cheek and neck. Roomie number two only changed positions and snored into the wall.

As I wrestled myself into my nightie inside my sleeping bag I thought, Fuck her for not making eye contact. Fuck her for judging me when *she* was the one hogging the sink. If she weren't hoarding the basin I wouldn't have *had* to startle her. Fuck the snorer, too. Fuck this whole place. Why do we have to have roommates anyway? This facility is completely ill-equipped to even DEAL. I don't need a retreat, I need a fucking *vacation.* I told myself, First thing in the morning I'm outta here. I will fly home and drive down to Twentynine Palms, or stay at a spa somewhere.

Fuck this.

Then roomie one blew out the candle and the room went dark. As I lay there with my eyes open I thought, How clinically depressed was I to pay money to not speak and share a room with two strangers in the middle of hippie nowhere? No nothing even remotely vacation-like or nurturing. What on earth could Dr. Karl have been thinking? He acted like I'd be instantly healed the second I stepped foot on the premises. There and then I vowed to have Dr. Karl's license revoked. I was suddenly startled into outrage as I listened to roomie two bark through her nose.

That's when I named them. Snorey and Hoardie.

As I finally began to drift off, I could hear Hoardie shaking several pill bottles, like maracas. She probably thought she was being polite by not turning the lights back on.

She was wrong.

Day Two

Three loud gongs sounded throughout the camp and let anyone within a thirty-mile radius know we had beaten the sun by a hair.

My roomies were beginning to stir but I was unconvinced this was even happening. I tested the air with my finger. Too cold. I snuggled down a little deeper into my squishy tomb, pressed my face into the downy nylon trying to warm my cheeks and nose, and decided to remain in bed. Forever. But my bladder had different plans for me.

Heckle and Jeckle were well into their little morning rituals now. One assumed various yogic postures while still remaining horizontal, while the other covered her yellow hair with a reusable yellow shower cap and walked out the door.

Outside the window I saw several modest but scantily clad men and women trudging off toward a co-ed bathhouse.

This realization was bad, but not awful because in the light of day, it came to my attention that I happened to be in the middle of the most gorgeous old growth forest I had ever seen. Rain forest documentary, *National Geographic* gorgeous. Trees, trees everywhere. I thought, Maybe this isn't so bad. Maybe there is a God. And maybe, during the night, I died and went to heaven.

I unzipped my sleeping bag, felt the sting of cold against my arms and legs, and hurriedly slipped my feet into a waiting pair of rubber and canvas flip-flops. That's when I heard the first clap of thunder.

At breakfast, people with wet hair moved slowly, pretentiously, I thought, as they made their way toward the choice of Tofu Scramble with scallions, bell peppers, and sweet potatoes, or ass blaster special number two, oatmeal with stewed prunes. Hot licorice tea and sliced oranges all around. I thought, Sweet monkey Christ, I'll starve.

I stared at my meal with the courage of a mountain climber on a slippery rock face. Some people hung their heads in prayer, blessing their food, or perhaps, like me, wishing it would turn into sausage and eggs.

I checked the clock on the wall: only an hour until meditation. And only another ten and three-quarter days until I could leave. I thought, OK, Dr. Karl Sage, Ph.D., where's my fucking revelation?

Then I thought, At least I'm not thinking about Jasper. Maybe I can hang in there after all.

Day Three

At morning meditation I politely battled for a seat very close to the foot of Luna's chair. Even in silence people competed for a chance to be next to her. She was already meditating. I watched her eyeballs travel from left to right under a soft canopy of moisturized lids. I looked around at everyone else as they adjusted their spines and sat up too straight. They all seemed a little too anxious to go "inside," if you asked me.

Softly Luna said, "See your mind as a flowing river and let your thoughts effortlessly drift downstream." Instantly my mind became a flowing river I tried to cross, but my thoughts were slippery rocks—I leapt from one to another.

When they were at an earsplitting decibel level, I opened my eyes and came up for air, deciding instead to study the room. I noticed things like water damage along one wall or a place in the carpet where the corner turned up to reveal a carpet tack, and how I still held my stomach in even though the men there were strangers (and unattractive strangers to boot), and how five big asses could easily sit on the brick hearth comfortably. Then I thought about my mother and how if she were here, she wouldn't be able to keep her mouth shut.

Then came the demonic open-eye imagery: me dying, my dog dying, my mother dying, my grandmother dying, Spoonie dying, Charlie, Jym, and Jasper dying, everyone else dying, and me left alone to grieve their loss—and then dying myself. Then came the living horror fantasies: me homeless, my family homeless, my family rich and me homeless and they won't help, me rich and my family homeless and I won't help, me rich and my family homeless and coming to live with me, me rich and Jasper homeless coming back to live with me.

After almost an hour of fending off additional grotesque images of Charlie fucking a model, Jym fucking a model, Jasper fucking a model, and then moving in together, Luna finally rang her little bell. I was the first one out the door.

I thought, How come *they* all came out smiling? As I put on my rain slicker, I noticed the little posted quote of the day. "Marry the one who never leaves."

When Jasper answered the phone he would say Guava like I was his favorite pet. Whenever I would screen he would say it loudly and I would run to pick up the phone. It meant he was in a good mood. It meant that he missed me. It meant that he loved me. It was the best when he would say it in person because it meant that he wanted to be as close to me as possible. At least that is how I had taken it, because I always wanted to be as close to him as possible. I loved him so much that I felt I missed him even when he was deep inside of me. What makes a person mean Guava one day and then never again? I could feel my hot tears intermingled with the raindrops.

By dinner, I was a complete wreck. I piled too much food I wouldn't eat onto my plate, and took no fork. My plan was to punish everyone by eating like a savage. My internal rebellious brat was on overdrive. I wanted to ruin everyone else's peace since I wasn't having any.

In my head I shouted at Dr. Karl: What's the point of this place, you fuck? I'm here, aren't I? Where is it, huh? Where is my BIG BREAKTHROUGH?

That night I did not sleep. The rain had paused but my mind was out of control, now with thoughts of chemical warfare and the pope and Sheryl Crow. It was too late for me to make arrangements to get home tonight but I vowed to leave when the sun came up. I closed my eyes and tried to lie on my side. Snorey bulldozed away, and Hoardie snacked on the loudest granola ever created.

I was going crazy but at least I was not alone.

Day Four

Luna had posted a note saying morning meditation had been canceled as she felt there was a lot of restlessness in the air. Which was fine with me because I was going to blow it off anyway and make arrangements to leave.

But the office was closed, so I trudged over to an enclosed area where the natural lithium hot springs bubbled amidst viny flowering plants. In a fakey tropical Japan, I beheld four tiled tubs representing the four directions, and the four seasons. I checked the wooden schedule on the creaky hand-wrought gate to make sure it was the Women Only day. Mercifully, it was. Not that I was going to wash my hair or shave my legs or even shower.

I chose autumn because my birthday is in the fall and because its temperature suited me the best, but mainly because it wasn't as crowded as the other tubs. Being nude with strangers was not exactly what I had in mind, but my bathing suit seemed wildly out of place.

I lowered myself into the slippery brown-and-blue–tiled

tub. Little bubbles formed on every little hair on my legs. Boy did I need a good waxing. The hair was long and black and coarse. The water made everything super-reflective and up-close looking. I squeezed a large section of my leg underwater and thought of car hoods in hailstorms, realizing I found me even more disgusting when magnified. Especially the toes with the thick yellowing nails and the black tufts of hair.

I thought, No wonder all men leave me.

I looked over at the other women: sagging breasts, loose flesh over aging bones, cellulite, overly bushy pubic hair. Or the skinny ones with dairy-free skin, adorable freckles, boyish hips, and patchy coiffed pubes. I wondered if I was alone in my self-loathing. We were all grotesque.

Just then, two pale feet slipped past me and slunk down into the water. It was Luna. I blushed. I was suddenly embarrassed that I was sharing a naked soak with a teacher, but more than that, I felt ashamed: I had the distinct impression that Luna could read my every thought.

I went underwater, held my breath, tried to shake her loose. The humming generator sounded in my ears along with my heartbeat and bubbles as they rushed past me to escape. When I surfaced, Luna let her head drift back on the rounded cement edge of the tub, and was now gazing up at the sky, fingers barely touching the water. She seemed to be just listening to the outside sounds. To the birds, the lapping of water, the wet vacuum sound as some women exited the tub, the sound of wet feet smacking against cement as they moved toward their clothes.

She looked vulnerable and relaxed in a modest way. I envied her tranquil enjoyment of merely being human in some hot water. Mimicking her, I pressed my back against the tile, head back, feeling the pulling weight of the water in my hair, the difference between the smacking cold against my exposed flesh and the heat of my steeping skin. I smelled flowers and earth and noticed dragonflies and small shimmery leaves in nearby trees. Suddenly I felt very beautiful. Suddenly it all seemed so obvious that we were *all* very beautiful; it was only my mind that was ugly, and for a moment, everything was still.

Wending my way back to my little cabin, I realized something had loosened in me. I had softened. I felt like something had been hatched and set free. I held my arms open and pressed my chest into the sky.

Looking up past the canopy of trees and into infinite blue, I saw something that took my breath away. A bird falling toward the earth, dropping rapidly, its beak pulled toward the ground by gravity in a seemingly perilous nose dive, suddenly pulled up and out at the last possible minute.

I thought, Oh, so *this* is what retreat is about—moments of immeasurable sweetness. I decided to stick out the day and leave the next. Or maybe the day after that. I thought, Eleven days is nothing.

Day Five

What is wrong with you, Mer? One minute you're at peace and the next minute you're psychotic! It was as if the past nine months and my entire life had been crammed into eleven excruciating days. A single *moment* doled out a complete emotional roller-coaster ride. When I was on the verge of hysteria, I got up.

My plan was to go to the restroom and gather my wits, but once outside the meditation hall, I just took off running.

Up the path through the woods, past the cabins, past the parking lot, past the welcome kiosk to a nearby yert which looked more like an abandoned circus tent than a holy place. It was freezing inside and smelled like plastic and dirt. I lay flat on my belly, trying not to be absorbed into The Mother, while the sentence *I am going to die* began to repeat in my head.

Miraculously, a few minutes later, the small wooden door with the stained-glass moon opened and Luna entered. "What's the matter, Dear?"

Luna knelt down, put a consoling arm around my shoulders and rocked me. She brushed my hair with her hand. In her most musical lilt, she told me, "You are only telling yourself a story. Those are just thoughts suspended in a great peace. Try to reeeloxshh into right now. Be here right here, right now, in this moment. You're in imagination, Dear, now go to the truth."

Luna then did something that to anyone watching would appear to be wholly unremarkable; she lifted my chin in her hands and looked me directly in the eye. The only thing is, that's not at all what happened.

A mystical experience by its very definition is something that cannot be explained or understood by anyone other than the person having it. How do you put into words a momentary flash that illuminates everything it touches—a revelation that burns so bright it lights up the darkest recesses of your soul and leaves nothing for the mind to grasp, only empty space.

Luna looked at me for only a few moments but all was obliterated. Lightning-flash fast, I understood that it didn't matter if I knew what my purpose was or what I did for a living. I might be a race car driver or an astronaut—it made no difference because I understood the Great Mystery was moving through me, expressing itself as me.

In my mind's eye I saw myself as swirling colors that turned into a painting, a peacock, a frosted cupcake, a tiny painted Russian doll that just kept opening to reveal a smaller and even smaller me, until I disappeared entirely and was, therefore, everything. What I had known previously—that I was America Throne, that I was the broken dumpee of a very painful breakup, the sad daughter of a genius, the very embodiment of loneliness and despair—suddenly dissolved and was replaced by tremendous optimism, an avalanche of sweetness, leaving every cell in my being light-drenched.

I thought, Maybe I'll go back to school. Maybe even sell my car to do it. I could take cheap art classes at Santa Monica College: pottery, painting, wallpaper design, cake decorating. Everyone likes cake. I thought, It's going to be my mother's birthday soon and I want to make her a cake. In fact, I want to bake her five cakes! I want to be her own personal cupcake chef. Maybe I could even specialize in it and open up a shop. I imagined telling her I don't want to take money from her anymore and how I want to be a cupcake chef so I can pay her back for everything. She'd say, "You mean pastry chef," and I'd say, No, I really mean just cupcakes, and she'd say, "Just keep the money and use it for yourself, I don't really need it." And then I sneak and save it up and give it to her anyway because I love her more than anything in the world.

And it occurs to me that I have always been afraid to be an artist.

Afraid to ask myself, "What if I fail?" like my father, like Jasper, probably did, every time they sat down to work. Afraid I wouldn't be any good, afraid I wouldn't make any money, afraid I'd suffer the pain I'd already been through, as if you could avoid or stave off what you already are. If you at least do what you love some of the time, then you have a better chance of some happiness. Then came a rushing feeling. I *felt:* I am a river and these are just my mind-thoughts calmly rushing by.

"Accept loss forever" is what Luna said next. "Let sleeping Buddhas be."

TWENTY-NINE

FREE DUMB PART 2

"America! America! God shed His grace on thee
and crown thy good with brotherhood from sea
   to shining sea."

—Katherine Lee Bates

Luna accepted me just as I was without asking for anything in return, and because of this I saw myself; it didn't matter whether Jasper loved me because I was love itself. And my father, well, he did the best he could. Now I understood that the only thing I could count on was impermanence. This is what I'm thinking as I stared blankly at the man behind the United counter.

"Any relation?" he said.

"Pardon?" I said over the din of echoey loudspeaker announcements, crying babies, squeaky luggage carts, and rushing feet. I was still in shock, going from total silence back into worldly chaos.

"Any relation?" he said, again smiling shyly. I noticed his two front teeth overlapped and he kind of whistled when he spoke. "To Boris Throne. I mean, 'cause I noticed here on your driver's license your name is America Throne, born in 1969. You're not by any chance . . ."

"Yes," I said.

He promptly blushed, dropped his pen, picked it up again, and began typing furiously. "I loved your father! He was my total hero, screw it, still is. What was it like? Having Boris Throne as a father, I mean."

"He was an amazing man," I said, smiling from my feet.

"That's what I thought. I went to a book signing in Pittsburgh once. I stood in the back and watched. People waited for hours for him to sign his book!"

"Which one, *Letters to the Editor*? *Gift*? *A Catastrophe in Rome*?"

"No, the cubist one, *From Russia with Glove*. He was so amazing, so patient. He waited until every last freak and geek had said his peace. He was kind to every last one, do you know how rare that is?"

"My mom is probably going to put out another coffee table book of all his stuff. She runs the estate."

"I know. I'll bet she's amazing, too!"

"She's really the glue of the whole operation." Some people in line behind me began to get annoyed now.

"I'll tell you a little confession. At the show, I was so naïve . . ." the counter guy covered his eyes with his hand, ". . . I showed your dad some of my stuff—I was working with wax at the time—and he told me he thought I should do something with animals instead, so I chose the *airlines!*" He laughed at his own joke.

I slid my luggage under the metal counter, smiled.

He coyly looked up from his station. "I saw your brother's band play once, too. At the Viper Room. They played with the Butt Pirates of the Caribbean and Redeemer. What are they called again?"

"Free Dumb."

"That's right!" He dropped his pen again. "I'm sorry, I'm just really nervous. I don't know if you can tell but I'm a really big fan. Can I give you a hug? I loved your dad so much."

Without thinking, I leaned across the counter and held out my arms. I felt the sweaty airless fabric embrace of all the lonely nights my father's existence got this man through, and I understood something about myself and about the beauty and satisfaction of *total* adoration.

He pulled away and wiped his eyes with the back of a luggage tag. "I'm gonna bump you up to first class."

"Cool," I said.

THIRTY
MEAT ME IN ST. LOUIS (BALLOONS)

"Why can't we give ourselves one more chance?
Why can't we give love give love give love . . ."
—Freddie Mercury and David Bowie

"Huh?" I said when I picked up the phone at 10:19 the next morning from the warmth of my own bed. I was groggy and recovering from the fact that Sadie and Swane had had sex in my bed while I was away. That's what you get for letting love-birds baby-sit your dog.

"Mustard," said Spoonie.

"*Mustard!*" I said bolting upright, hand instinctively reaching for my heart. "Is it Mom?"

"No," he said, "no one is dead or dying, I mean except all of us every minute, heh-heh, no. I mean I don't really think it's really any big deal but . . ."

"Then why did you say Mustard?"

"Well, when I ran it past Lila she thought it counted."

"Wait, you told Lila about Mustard? That's practically Mustard in itself," I said, yawning.

"I'm here for you, America."

"Oh hi, Lila, I didn't know you were on the phone." I bit the inside of my cheek. "Uh, so what's going on?"

"On a scale of honey mustard to horseradish Dijon . . ." Spoonie mused, "I mean it's definitely not Dijon. It's more like Gulden's or French's in terms of seriousness."

"I'm not so sure, you're not a woman. It didn't happen to you."

"I don't understand. What didn't happen to who?" I said frantically.

"Well, it didn't happen to you, either," Spoonie calmly said to Lila, ignoring me entirely.

"Even so, I'm a woman and I think from this perspective I should know better. Plus, remember that stalker I had?"

"That's true."

"Um, hello! Remember me?"

Then in unison they said, "I think we should meet in person."

"For French's?"

"Yeah," they said.

"Can you meet us at Nirvanarama in half an hour?" asked Lila.

"Why can't you just . . ."

"America," said Spoonie seriously.

I flinched. "OK, OK, I'll see you both in half an hour." I thought, This is so my life.

Find peace and truth and come home to more distractions.

My mind raced. Was it Grandma? Had my mother squandered away our fortune? Did Lila need an abortion? Calmly I told myself my mind is a river and these are just thoughts gently floating downstream.

Outside, birds were chirping away. I could hear Edie Brickell singing in the distance: ". . . I know I'll be all right as soon as I let go."

Calmly I found my car keys, calmly I locked my door, and calmly I drove.

I circled the block around a hundred times before eventually settling on a spot several blocks away from Nirvanarama, a high-tech health food restaurant, complete with healing tonics, elixirs, TV monitors, and endless newsracks. I looked around the restaurant but Spoonie and Lila weren't there, so I asked to be seated at a table to wait. I was nestled in a corner between three confirmed lifelong bachelors and a mother-son combo.

The boy to my right looked like a smaller, more evil, version of Jasper. The mother kept holding food up to his mouth saying, "Do you like this?" He'd shake his head and scream "Noooooo!" "OK, how about this?" Finally she managed to get some egg in his mouth, but some of it fell onto the toast below and he began to shriek at top volume, "The eggs are tickling the bread!" He was so adorable I debated the idea of stuffing him in my purse.

Then Spoonie and Lila sat down opposite me. They both had serious expressions and outfits to match—black turtlenecks, wool caps, and jeans. They looked like chic foreign spies.

"We have something to show you." They looked at each other and then back at me. Lila reached into her purse and slid a five-by-seven card into my hand. It was an invitation to Jasper's upcoming art show. It read: "Bugs and Fishes: New Works by Jasper Husch and Maya Richter." At the bottom, under the date and time, Jasper had handwritten in perfect block caps, "I can't remember America's address, so please give this to her, but you're all invited! Loveyoumissyouhopetoseeyouthere, love J. p.s. thanks for the nice message!" I said nothing.

Spoonie punched Lila in the arm. "See? French's. Just like I told you." I could only nod and stare.

"What an asshole, right?" said Lila. I thought, Since when are Spoonie and Lila sympathetic to my feelings? They must really love me. "Turn it over," said Lila.

I did. The picture on the back was of two people sitting

across from each other in thrones divided by a great chasm. In one chair, a naked man with a giant snake-like erection sat stoic, with his back to the girl on the other side of the great divide. The girl, who had long brown hair, sat facing him, and held a glowing moon in her lap. She was naked also but her skin was a map.

"It's me," I said out loud.

"We *know!*" said Lila.

I wondered if I had killed Jasper in a previous life and now he was making it up to me in small, deadly increments. I wondered when the pain would stop and who or what would be strong enough to put an end to it. I held my breath.

"It's called *Adam and Even Now*—did you see that?" said Lila. "I'd be, like, What the fuck, right? I think that is totally horseradish Dijon, right?" I nodded again. Lila punched Spoonie in the arm. "See?"

"What do you want us to do?" asked Spoonie.

"We thought you should hear it from us," said Lila, eyes as big as pancakes. She looked at me with such concern, I claimed her as family now.

"Mer? Are you OK?" Spoonie asked.

I didn't say anything, just wiped my nose on the sleeve of my faded jeans jacket, removed an orange-and-yellow elastic band from my wrist and piled my hair on top of my head, like a wedding cake, and smiled.

I didn't call Jasper to say I was coming. He hadn't called to warn me about any of the bombs he dropped. I didn't know what I would say or do; I only had the sense that I had lost something and that I had to get it back. From him. I suddenly understood the quiet adrenaline of trip wires and sharpened stakes under leafy forest floors, the hidden aliveness of planning a kill.

As I sped along the I-5 on the gas fumes of old wounds, I

had several fantasy scenarios: (1) Dalai Lama–like I would forgive him on the spot; (2) I would see him and slap him, then turn to go, and he'd come running after me begging forgiveness; (3) I would see him and slap him, he'd cower in terror, then I'd turn to go and he'd come running after; (4) I'd see him and slap him, turn to go—he'd come running after and we'd make love and live happily ever after. There were others: I kick Jasper into infertility; Jasper spontaneously combusts at the mere sight of me; and a random one where I kick a pregnant passerby in the stomach. I sped up.

I am seven again. I hear my father having sex with a lady from my school. I know because I recognize her sneezes.

I am nine. I bring my father to show-and-tell, but he doesn't pay any attention to me, only tickles all the kids no one talks to.

I am fifteen, and twenty-one, and every age where my father ever left me and my brother and my mother inconsolable.

I'm twenty-six. I'm in the cemetery standing under a tree. I think, Is it an elm? The pretty lady I don't recognize can't get her umbrella to close. She's standing next to a man I recognize from the paint store. I think I might be sick thinking about him in that box.

Fuck artists. They should all be put down executioner-style. They are disowned fragments of God that need to fly home before they cause any more destruction. This is what I'm thinking as I rounded the corner and pulled into his street with its sickeningly perfect low trees in neat wooden boxes at 3:20 in the afternoon. My hands were sweating.

I found a parking space right out front.

I got out of the car, stood outside the Victorian house I almost didn't recognize because he had painted it. Red and green. I thought, Stop and go, story of my life.

I could hear a television on next door. Across the street a cat lazed in a window. The five big steps leading up to the little landing were cleaner looking than I remembered. The ocean air made everything sparkle more, like a lucid dream. He had new shades in the front window and he had painted "Jah Love" on the glass front door.

It infuriated me that he thought he was spiritual. I took a deep breath, climbed the stairs, and rang the bell. No one answered so I rang it again. Nothing. I peeked through the window to get some sense of whether he saw me and was hiding or when he might be coming home. I knocked on the door rather loudly. "Jasper?" I called. This made crazy Mel's parrot Gambler start to go berserk upstairs. I knocked again. Gambler squawked, "Who is it, who is it" over and over. I knocked again, this time the glass shook in its frame. Nothing. Now I was *really* mad.

I sat down on the stoop, buried my head between my legs, and dug my nail into the skin around my ankle until it stung and turned red. Then I thought of the lockbox beneath the stairs, in the alley, past the trashcans in the back, and I wondered if Jasper could be so stupid.

As I turned the key to the backdoor and went inside, my face went tingly around my ears. I was light-headed as I set foot in the kitchen.

I ran a finger over the butcher block counter past tea tins and pots with copper bottoms still on the stove, trying to place the feeling in my gut. The house felt different, lived in. I lifted a lid, mung beans in one, brown rice in the other—his usual hippie mush. I brushed away a hanging ivy strand with yellowing leaves and opened the fridge: yeast-free raisin bread, soy milk, hummus, feta cheese, Ry-Krisps, and Diet Coke. "Diet Coke! Oh my God, HE LIVES WITH SOMEONE!" I shrieked, not caring who heard me. Diet soda? Cancer-causing *diet soda* in his vegetarian-tree-hugging-nuclear-disarmament-peace-on-earth-om-shanti-people-come-together-not-to-remain-together-but-grow-and-move-on fridge? I couldn't believe my eyes. I closed the door and staggered back. His cats came over and circled my ankles. They meowed, so I put some more food in their bowls and headed for the bathroom.

As I rummaged through her things and smelled her grapefruit and honeysuckle body wash, I spotted a photo tucked in the corner of the mirror of a smiling Jasper with a smiling Debi Mazar look-alike. I moved to the bedroom now, the unmade bed with the new white duvet, the crumpled clothes on the floor, the misshapen blue-and-white swirled vibrator by the side of the bed. I felt the thick Egyptian cotton of the blanket cover, then I lay down on the bed, pulling the covers up and around me. The nub of my tennis shoes got a little stuck between the top sheet and the blanket.

I scanned the room, the bed, the gardenia smell of her on the sheets, the scented candles, the tantric sex books, the massage oils, the ceiling, the hanging lamp, the way that one speaker wire stuck out too much from behind the cabinet, the yellow walls with their solitariness, a dangling blind, and not a trace of me.

I pulled the blanket up over my nose now, studied the horizontal stripes of the stitching up close: white on white, lines that went nowhere, and I knew it was really over.

I moved to the living room now.

Toward his workspace. Past his "technology"—his TV and VCR and stereo system—and past his elaborate alphabetized CD collection. Past Nick Drake, Elliot Smith, Belle and Sebastian, The Pixies, Pavement, Frank Zappa. I thought, My God, I never realized how depressed this poor guy was. Past his *Star Wars* collection (now out of their boxes on a high homemade shelf), past his drafting table and open shelves covered with every conceivable art supply, until I found myself before twelve white plaster "balloons." They were weighted down with a metal base that had the title of the piece on a small brass plaque. On each of the balloons—small canvases of Jasper's new works were embedded in their plaster faces:

A ghoulish Technicolor clown with hollowed-out eyes and a massive erection poking pointily through the fabric of his colorful striped attire.

A nude of a woman with a smoking cigar sticking out of her vagina, dropping ashes on a caricature of Bill Gates holding a swarming beehive on a stick like a hobo.

A homeless man wearing a coonskin cap and nametag that says "Louis," holding half a map and eating a Slim Jim like a Popsicle.

Another with swans and pelicans and businessmen in a tarry swamp, struggling to get free.

One after the other, brilliantly rendered but awful to behold. Sick. Deviated. Lonely.

In the corner Jasper had painted one with a deadly traffic accident. Twisted metal and bodies strewn across a darkened highway. Once I had seen such an accident on my way to visiting Jasper. I thought now of the heavyset woman I had seen that day, facedown and lifeless in white shorts, alongside a man I presumed to be her husband. They looked like they might have been vacationing. I had cried as I passed them and prayed for those who would receive the news. Jasper depicted his crash scene inside a giant bloody vagina, lips spread apart like theater curtains.

Finally I stare at the one of me and Jasper, at the two people in uncomfortable chairs across a great divide, and I'm not angry anymore. All this time I had mistaken Jasper's attention to detail for my father's depth, the intensity of Jasper's subject matter for my father's passionate satiric look at the world he loved so well. His work had been under my nose all along, only I never saw it. His silence, my answer.

Outside I can hear the twinkling of wind chimes cling-clanging away. That's something, I think.

As the sun came up over Silicon Valley I thought, Yes, I have seen dead bodies and fires on this highway. Not to mention the slaughterhouses. Did you know the word "laughter" is smack in the middle of "slaughterhouse"?

This occurs to me on the long drive home for the very last time. And even though nothing is very funny, I have to laugh.

THIRTY-ONE
BOLIFAR CARFISH INN

"When I was young, younger than before,
I never saw the truth hanging from the door.
Now I'm older I see it face to face.
Now I'm older gotta get out and clean the place."
—Nick Drake

My mother and I sorted through various closets, drawers, and boxes in my father's office and I noticed how pretty she is. The grey in her eyebrows and at her temples makes her look vulnerable, though I am sure she would say her roots need to be redyed. I notice things like the black witch's hairs on her chin (the ones I've started to notice on myself), and how her pores run in cascading patterns, like eyelet lace. I smile at how her crow's-feet are set so deep they look like bird footprints in wet sand. Her laugh lines are there, even when she isn't smiling. My mother gets so much pleasure from being with me and Spoonie, but my father was the only one who could really make her laugh.

Digging deep into musty boxes, I come across several drawings that Spoonie and I did when we were small. Underneath them, tucked in a small red traveling sketchbook of my father's, I find a photo of my parents when they were my age. He is wearing a long plaid jacket and she is wearing a gardenia behind her ear and they are holding hands, squinting in bright sunlight in a modest sunny garden. And another, of me at age two. I am clutching a ratty little yellow blanket and I have on big plastic rings and a tiny, pink crocheted bikini. My father looks uncomfortable holding me, in his red Speedo-type bathing suit bottoms and pale, hairy, knock-knees. And still another, of him and my mother and Spoonie and me.

Then I found a little wooden toy I bought for my father in a toy store in Germany. It had come with music paper to make your own songs. You could punch out the holes on a long rectangular piece of paper by sight and then play what you made on the little crank piano. My father made drawings on all the pages, and then we played them.

I remember one was of a snot monster, for Spoonie, and when he played it for us it actually sounded scary. All of the pieces were framed afterwards and promptly sold.

In an envelope of slides of old paintings I find my favorite one. I hold it up to the light. It's called *Bolifar Carfish Inn*. It had a tiny cabin with little dancing insect innkeepers and a real wood-burning fireplace. In the little koi pond the fish were tiny people.

That's when I realized what I missed most about Jasper and my father. Time. The time they took to put into their work, the time it took to make the individual pieces, the time it took away from me. The time they *chose* their work over me. I was jealous of their paintings because they had their total attention, because time is what I did not have enough of with my own father. I would give anything to hug him again. Even to be ignored by him now would be a sweet consolation; to know he could do it from the other room or a thousand miles away.

I studied my mother's face at rest now, lost in thought, as she folded one of my father's shirts and placed it in the box, along with his enamel palette with the dried paint, the colors B. Throne loved into textured splotches, a rough sea of sanguine, eggplant, ocher, ebony, green-grey, and midnight blue.

In permanent black ink she labels the box "For Keeps."

• • •

The day my father died was sunny. I remember because I was in the gallery and he was talking to, well, flirting with, a young woman in a short cream-colored skirt. She had seen his work being hung for the show that evening and had wandered in off the street to talk to him. My father asked me to run and get him a piece of cheesecake and I didn't want to go because I knew he wanted to be alone with her. I was mad at him because my mother was in the back room. I turned. Suddenly there was commotion. My mother and I ran to the front of the gallery. He was already dead by the time we got there, slumped in the pretty woman's lap. The girl had said he touched his hand to his forehead and just collapsed. That she tried to catch him. My mother pushed her out of the way, and held my father in her arms, saying, "Don't go my baby, not yet." She just kept rocking him and stroking his hair, saying, "Come back, don't leave me behind." Then the ambulance came. Sound dropped away.

Later, the doctors would say "brain aneurysm" and I would imagine a lump of all the things my father had wished he'd said to us, traveling from his heart all the way to his head.

I'm twenty-six. Standing in the cemetery, under an elm, my brother's shoelaces come undone. My grandmother demurely raises her hand and coughs into her white glove. The pretty lady I don't recognize can't get her umbrella to close. She's standing next to the mole man from the paint store and Jamilla Tyrell, the editor of my father's book. There's the boy who stretches my father's canvases and Maxim VanPelt and the gallery owner I don't like and a cluster of my father's solemn-faced students. And Nick Glue, who looks different with pants on. My grandmother coughs again and I notice the corally lipstick smudge on the edge of her glove. Everyone stands around looking like Chaucer characters. I take my mother's hand. It is ice cold. My mother won't look at me. I give her lifeless icy fingers a squeeze and watch her lips quiver. Then she nods her head and the men in cheap grey suits lower the mahogany box with the sky blue satin interior into the ground. I think, He would have hated the color and design. Now we sprinkle dirt and white lilies on the lid and the men with shovels begin to pile the soft moist dirt back into the hole.

"How about Cups and Dishes," said Camilla, breaking my reverie.

"What?"

"Cups and Dishes. Instead of Bugs and Fishes. Spoonie and Lila came up with it. It's only for family. I told them Lila can say it, too, when Lila and Spoonie get married." She winked at me. "Are you coming to the concert tonight? Spoonie is performing with Despairagus and Suzanne Somers Thighs."

"Mother, where is the copper dragon? I only just noticed it's gone!"

"Oh, I sold it. That nice Japanese man I met at the Playboy mansion made me an offer I couldn't refuse. We're millionaires," she said, smiling quietly, then resumed rummaging, as though she had just mentioned something obscenely mundane, like, I think it might rain today. She yawned. "You're up awfully early."

I thought, This is so my life. Just when you think you can't get any happier, you can, and you do. The heart keeps bursting open wider and wider until you feel you might explode. Then I saw it.

Shining up at me from the bottom of the soft old cardboard box, there, hanging on a maroon ribbon. I slipped it over my head, held it in my hand. I noticed the weight of it against my breast, the warmth of the ribbon against the nape of my neck. The charm my father gave me. I picture him perfectly now, standing in that airport, waiting for the embossed coin to be finished so long ago. I recall his wild white hair in points like meringue, like flapping bird wings, smelling like Winstons and dandruff shampoo; his hands, the tips of his fingers curling upward like the wings of a hawk, like Buddha's fingers; and I hear his deep resonating voice—he is laughing.

I read it slowly. It says, "I love you America the Beautiful."

THIRTY-TWO
LADIES AND GENTLEMEN

"I'm gonna love you 'til the wheels come off. Oh yea."
—Tom Waits

Spoonie played an Auden poem he set to music at his show. I thought about how happy I was for him and Lila and about how much Spoonie looks like my father. Especially the way light hit his cheekbones. "*Beloved,*" he sang,

> *we are always in the wrong*
> *handling so clumsily our stupid lives,*
> *Suffering too little or too long*
> *Too careful even in our selfish love*
> *The decorative manias we obey*
> *Die in grimaces round us every day*
> *Yet through their tohu-bohu comes a voice*
> *Which utters an absurd command:*
> *Rejoice!*

As I watched him strut across the stage, I wondered if my father was proud of him, too. At that moment, Sadie and Swane looked over at me and smiled.

They had big white flowers behind their ears and were toasting each other with flaming blue drinks. It *was* their four-month anniversary, after all. "Ladies and gentlemen, may I please have everyone's attention . . ." announced Spoonie from the stage, ". . . I'd like to introduce Otto Guthrie from

293

Rows Five Through Seven." There came a handsome man I recognized from the coffee place. He was wearing a painter's smock, a dusty-looking top hat, and an embroidered Western shirt. He played stand-up bass, saw, and didgeridoo on a hillbilly/fusion cover version of "Amazing Grace."

I sat there slack-jawed.

Later, in the little club with the pretty phosphorescent insects on the wall, after the applause died down the handsome stranger sat down next to me, removed two mugs from a blue backpack, and opened up a silver thermos with the mud-flap girl. I smelled the cinnamon and ginger.

"Unleaded," he said, as he poured me a cup of homemade chai tea with milk and a little too much sugar.

"Cheers," I said.

"You seem different," he said.

"Do I?" I took another sip. "How?"

"More open, maybe? More at peace? I'm not sure yet."

"*Yet*, huh?" I had to smile about that one.

"Does that mean you'll have coffee with me?"

I blushed, grateful that it was so dark in there, then watched as he took out a red plastic cylinder with a yellow top, unscrewed it, and blew bubbles in my direction. Then he dipped the wand back into the clear soapy liquid, slid the container toward me, gathered up his things, and started to walk away.

"Wait," I said, "that is so sweet."

"Yeah, well, I'm rot-your-teeth sweet."

At home, I lit several tea lights, poured myself a cup of Earl Grey, placed a small canvas on my father's easel, squeezed the creamy colors onto a piece of cardboard, reached for a slender brush in the jelly jar, and began. As I looked around my house for some inspiration, I thought, Home, *my* home.

I thought, Nine months. All this time spent in labor giving birth to myself.

While Tulie snored, the tip of my brush filled in the spaces between narrow lines, the stalk of a flower, the branches of a winter tree, in time to her rhythmic breathing. I painted sky and stars and fluffy cotton candy creatures, and, though it didn't turn out quite like I wanted, I didn't edit a single longing.

That night, safely back in my bed, I dream that I am a long distance runner pacing myself perfectly, breathing, feeling perfectly in sync with my body and the scenery I pass. Past aspens with shimmery leaves and parked cars and dogs and people. I run past picket fences and Jym watching TV, past Charlie licking stamps, past Spoonie and Lila dressed like penguins in top hats and tails. Past my mother talking on the telephone while feeding birds dried crusts of bread. Past Sadie and Tulie rolling around on green green grass. Past Jasper fast asleep in a hammock.

And past my father who stands on an endless green lawn, watering that great yard, in a pink dress, with his white hair in pigtails, waving good-bye.

THIRTY-THREE
WELCOME POINTLESSNESS

"You will find me down by the river
getting high on my mortality.
I'll be holding hands with my nameless beauty
or whoever wants to stand next to me."

—Sinead Lohan

The next day I visited Otto at the coffee place downtown and, so, that is how it came to pass that I am scrunched in my seat, watching a guy show up an hour early for our date, wondering whether I should get out of my car and go through with all of this.

I finally get that the trick to life is getting out of your own way and letting life go on as it does. Because it will anyway. So I unscrunch a little, in spite of myself. Yeah, but why get out of the car? Why bother if I'm whole and lit from within and all? Because, just as I'm thinking all this, I see Tom Hanks drive by with his wife Rita.

They are in a beat-up black '82 Bronco and I realize I've graduated. I'm no longer Meg Ryan, living out the fantasy onscreen romance; I'm Tom's real-life wife Rita, and she smiles and waves at me for no reason at all.

That's why I get out of my car.

That's why I go to the crosswalk and push the cold metal button with the little dancing man. And that's why, when it says Walk, I do. In my own time, in my own way, clutching the little good luck coin at my heart.

Everything is in slow motion now. To my left and right, cars wait for the light to turn green. Beside me, cars pass, full of people coming from or going to somewhere. People with cell phones making business deals, people heading into town or toward the water or the hills. To love their spouses or murder their mothers or take their dogs to the park. Smiling people. Frowning people. People with bouffant hair and eyeglasses and fear and regret and loneliness and buried dreams and desires and gardening abilities and a knack for making money or losing car keys.

Fear of Intimacy zips by in a red Porsche.

I feel the heat of the engines as I walk past, and I feel like I'm on a runway. I'm a model. A model citizen. Gandhi carrying a message of peace, benevolent Mary with shining eyes and open palms, the Buddha watching spears turn into flowers when they meet skin. So soft. Chrissie Hynde doesn't let anyone shake her hand—I read that. What a lovely thought, that only those close to her get to know how tender her skin is.

Once I saw a deer stand perfectly still in the middle of the road. Right in the middle of the city.

Otto sees me now and my face goes all sweaty. I read somewhere that in certain Indian cultures you are allowed to be a part of the festivities as soon as you show your first smile, that based on the smile you are given a career, a home, a mate. He smiled like *that*.

Otto stands up to greet me and as he does he hits his knee on the underside of the table. I lurch forward trying to catch the rose as it tumbles off. My little good luck charm taps my breastbone. A gust of wind comes up. The orangy pink petals scatter. I lean in to help. He hands me the stem and kneels down to collect the fallen petals. People in the café stare or move their chairs back, some try to help.

Otto keeps scooping, chasing the soft flowers as they scatter for cover under nearby tables or customers' shoes or into the sunlight on the sparkly grey sidewalk. Otto walks back with careful steps. He opens his palms and reveals a small handful. Then he holds his cupped hands close to my nose so I can smell the luminous rose.

"It's from my garden," he says as soft as Tulie's ears.

I feel the weight in my legs like little roots digging their fine threads deep into the earth.

I lean in a little more, smelling the musk of his skin mixed with the heavy fragrance of the bloom. When I lift my head up I see he has tears in his eyes. He blinks once and lets his hands fall to his sides. The rest of the petals drop to the ground and blow away on the wind, dancing along the side-walk as they go.

For a moment we both stand absolutely still and look into each other's eyes. His are blue. He smiles. I smile, too. I think about storybooks and fairy tales and epic movies about epic love. "Hi," he says finally, his voice cracking.

Once there was a girl who lived ever after, sometimes happily, is what I'm thinking, but what I say back is "Hello."

PERMISSIONS

ABOUT THE AUTHOR

Moon Unit Zappa is the daughter of legendary composer Frank Zappa. An actress, musician, and stand-up comic, she lives in Los Angeles with her rockstar fella and dog Olive. This is her first novel.